THE PIERCING

THE PIERCING

John Coyne

G.P. Putnam's Sons
New York

Published simultaneously in Canada by
Longman Canada Limited, Toronto.

SBN: 399-12172-2

Library of Congress Cataloging in Publication Data

Coyne, John.
The piercing.

I. Title.
PZ4.C8813Pas   1978   [PS3553.096]   813'.5'4   78-7337

PRINTED IN THE UNITED STATES OF AMERICA

ACKNOWLEDGMENTS

A number of people were very helpful in my researching and writing of this novel and I would like to thank them: Father Eugene Geinzer, S. J., of Georgetown University, who was kind enough to read early drafts and offer valuable information about the Catholic Church and stigmata. Doctor Blaise Scavullo of Richmond, Virginia, who also read the manuscript and discussed with me the psychological behavior of hysterical neurotics.

My thanks to Sharon Thorn, Hilda Lynch, John Ware, Gerald Allan Schwinn, Tom Hebert, and Stu Frisch, all of whom read this novel and made helpful suggestions. And my special thanks to Essie Jacobs who read the novel page by page as it came from the typewriter.

To Judy Wederholt, my editor.

THE PIERCING

February, 1973

Prologue

The land was called The Hand of God for it seemed as if God himself had grabbed that remote corner of the southern state and crushed the terrain in his palm and fingers, shaping the valleys, the hollows, and the far mountains with his Almighty strength. The capital was squeezed into the heel of the hand and a new highway left the city, cut across the dry flat palm, and then switchbacked up the ridges to the town of Mossy Creek at the top of the rift.

The town hugged the ridge at the second finger of The Hand. It was only a single street wide and just a few miles long and curved around the ridge, stopping at the edges of the rift. Beyond the town a thin road, bending like an arthritic finger, poked into the thick woods and disappeared in these Appalachian mountains.

The road was called Rabbit Hop and late on a wet Friday afternoon in February, the town's yellow school bus raced along it, carrying the last children to the end of the line.

It had been raining all day in the mountains. Fog had moved into the hollows, closing off the sky and clouding the trees that grew thick on both sides of the curving tarmac. The driver hurried. He didn't want to be caught on Rabbit Hop road, trapped by fog or a late winter ice storm. The land here was owned by the Wadkins family and their kin; they weren't people to ask if one needed help. The driver could see their wood and tarpaper shacks on the hillsides, built at the corners of clearings or close to cold mountain streams. The five schoolchildren left on his bus were all Wadkinses of one kind or another.

He glanced in his rear-view mirror. Four of them sat together at the front of the bus. They were squirrelly looking kids with thin brown faces, hard like hazel nuts. Only Betty Sue Wadkins, sitting in the back, was different. She was tall and slim, standoffish, a beautiful child with skin the color of churned milk.

Watching her, the driver accidentally hit the brake pedal and the bus skidded on the slick road. Two of the girls screamed and when he glanced again in the mirror, he could see that Betty Sue had turned her face toward him. She was frowning, as if his clumsiness had upset her. He began to sweat. And she was only twelve, he thought, realizing the craziness of his notion.

The Wadkins women were all tough and hawkfaced, with high cheekbones and coarse blond hair. But Betty Sue was different. She had a creamy doll face, a large mouth, and wet brown eyes. Her breasts were just developing and the tiny globes filled the bodice of her cotton dress. Watching her, the driver skidded the bus a second time. He hit the brakes and eased the bus to a stop at the end of Rabbit Hop road.

The kids in front scrambled off and he turned to watch

Betty Sue as she collected her books. If she had been another mountain kid, he would have yelled at her to get her ass moving, but instead he pulled out a metal comb, slicked back his hair, and eyed her as she came forward.

She was buttoning her raincoat as she walked, but her brown eyes regarded him coolly and he started to think of what it would be like to take her down in the back seat. He had done it before with mountain kids. Every few years one came along who liked to fuck and they'd do it on the bus after he finished the run. He pulled the cigar from his mouth and said, "Hey, Betty Sue, how you-all doin'?"

She paused at the door to finish buttoning her coat and he reached out for her, but she skipped out the door and jumped to the ground. When she glanced back, her face had lost its creamy sweetness.

"If you try to touch me again, Mr. Willis, I'm gonna tell my Pa, hear that! And he'll come get you with his shotgun." Then she spun around and ran toward the Pit.

"Bitch!" The bus driver slammed the door and hit the clutch.

Betty Sue Wadkins lived a mile above Rabbit Hop road and back in the woods. A dirt logging road went up the mountainside and passed her place, but she took the short cut, going through a deep hollow called the Pit. Old cars had been dumped there and lay abandoned among the weeds, piled together like a massive auto wreck.

The mountain children were told to keep out of the Pit, for rattlers nested under the cars and sunned themselves on the warm upholstered seats. Betty Sue was afraid of snakes; afraid, too, of her Pa catching her crossing the hollow, but she didn't want to stay on Rabbit Hop road and have Mr. Willis follow her, so she darted down the slippery slope and into the underbrush.

There were still patches of snow beneath the wrecks, but

the path was hard and Betty Sue raced by the wrecked cars. She was watching the ground for rattlers and did not see the hired hand sitting on the hood of the '57 Plymouth until he called out. Her heart jumped and she stumbled forward, scattering her schoolbooks in the snow.

"You scared me, Rufus!" she cried, and her voice echoed on the Pit's walls. The way it sounded silenced her and she wiped the tears off her face and said again, softer this time, "You frightened me, Rufus!"

He slid off the hood and quickly fetched her books for her. Then he climbed onto the car hood. She had never seen anyone move so fast.

"Whatcha doin'?" she demanded. She stood tall, holding her books in one arm and positioning her other hand against her hip. She was trembling.

"Nothin'." He smiled at her and then tossed back his head, clearing his thin face of his blond hair. He was wearing bib overalls and a red flannel shirt with the sleeves rolled up to his elbows. His arms were hairless.

"You ain't supposed to be here in the Pit, Rufus," she declared and stepped closer to where he was perched on the Plymouth. "I'm gonna tell Pa."

"You do that, Betty Sue," he answered offhandedly. Reaching inside the bib of his overalls he pulled out four bright red balls.

"Where ya get those balls, Rufus?" Her voice softened, seeing them.

"In town." His voice was gentler than hers.

"I ain't seen no balls like them in town. You get 'em at Mussler's?"

He shook his head and began to juggle, talking to her as he flipped the balls swiftly in the air. "I've been wantin' to talk to you, Betty Sue."

"Ma says I ain't supposed to talk to you, Rufus. She says

I ain't to go out into the fields unless Pa's with me. Why don't she like you, Rufus?"

Rufus shrugged. "Watch this, Betty Sue." He pulled his legs out from under him and stood on the hood. Now he began to toss the four balls higher. They sailed up ten, twenty, then thirty feet into the sky. The sky was filled with them. They flew out of his hands and into the mist and her head was spinning from looking up. Then, abruptly, the sky was empty. She glanced at him straddling the hood. He was grinning and holding out his empty palms.

"How did you do that?" she demanded. She was both angry that he had tricked her and delighted by his magic. Her brown eyes sparkled. She stepped closer to the car and asked, "Where are those red balls?" She was embarrassed not knowing where the balls had gone.

"Turn 'round," he said, still smiling.

She watched him closely, thinking that this was another trick, but he was nice to her. She moved away a few feet.

"Go ahead," he encouraged.

"You ain't gonna hurt me?"

He shook his head and said, smiling, "Look up and close your eyes."

Slowly she turned and looked up. The mist filled the trees and she could not see the rim of the Pit. She was thinking that she better get home before it got dark, when he told her again to close her eyes. She did for an instant, until she heard him snap his fingers, and then she opened them and saw the red balls fall out of the sky, dropping on her like hail. She ducked her head and squealed. The balls bounced on the path and rolled away, into the underbrush and beneath the wrecked cars.

"How did you do that?" she demanded again, excited now. She bent over and picked up one of the red balls; it felt like a stuffed toy in her hand. She tossed the ball to him on the hood and he grabbed it from the air and in the same motion snapped his fingers. The ball disappeared. He opened his hand and showed her his empty palm. Three more times she threw him a ball; three times he made them disappear. Betty Sue's eyes widened.

She ran to the car shouting, "Show me, Rufus!"

"I'll show you another one," he said. Crouching down on the hood, he plucked a half-dollar from behind her ear and gave it to her. Her brown eyes sparkled and she squeezed the coin in her hand and kept watching him. She had never noticed that Rufus was so pretty. His skin was soft and fair and his blond hair silky like a girl's, but it was his eyes that captivated her. They were the blue of the early morning sky. It seemed to Betty Sue that she could see through them and into the distance.

Rufus took two short pieces of rope and tied them together. He jerked the rope taut, turning it into a black cane with a gold knob. He spun the cane in his fingers and tapped it rapidly on the hood, making the car sound like a metal drum.

Betty Sue held out her hand for the cane. "Please?" She looked coyly at him. The cane would be something to keep, she thought, something to take to school; but he only shook his head and when she reached to grab it, he shoved both ends together, changing the cane back into pieces of rope. "But I wanted it!" She screwed up her face and looked hurt.

Rufus pulled the balls from inside his overalls and began to juggle them again. She watched a moment and then climbed up on the front bumper and tried to catch one in mid-flight, but each time she tried, he changed the direction and her tiny hand just grabbed air.

"I want one, Rufus," she laughed, liking the game.

"I need them," he answered, smiling.

She watched as he kept tossing the red balls, doing it so swiftly that it did not seem like a trick at all.

"I'll give you money," she offered, holding out her hand and opening her sweaty palm.

"But I found that for you!" he laughed, enjoying her persistence.

"Please." She touched his knee. She wanted to climb into his lap, as she would with her father when she wanted something, but she still was afraid of him.

Rufus shook his head and, catching all the balls, slipped them inside his overalls.

"Teach me how to throw balls like that," she asked, kneeling before him and smiling. Her bare legs were cold on the metal hood.

"Well, I don't know." He scratched his chin. "It isn't easy, learning. . . ."

"Please! Please!" She leaned forward, her pretty face just inches from his. She blinked her eyes and looked worried.

"Whatcha gonna do for me?" He kept grinning.

She dropped the coin on the hood. "It's yours!"

"I don't want no coin. I can find coins anywhere. Look here!" He reached out and slipped his fingers between the buttons on the front of her cotton dress. She could feel his cold fingers touching her breast and when he pulled his hand away he was holding another shiny half dollar. He tossed it on the hood. "Nope, I can find money anywhere, Betty Sue." Then he stretched out on his back and slipped his arms behind his head, staring up at the sky.

"I'll show you my bottom!" She stood quickly and held the edges of her dress, waiting for him to say yes. "I ain't got no underpants."

Rufus turned on his side and braced his head with his right hand. "Betty Sue, if I'm gonna teach you to juggle those red balls, you've got to do more than let me see your little bare ass."

"You can touch me—once!"

"I don't want to touch your ass, Betty Sue." He sat up.

"The boys in school do. They're always chasing after me and Cindy and Mary Lou. We told Mrs. Ramsey about them." She grinned, pleased with herself.

Rufus shook his head. "Betty Sue, are you going to tell Mrs. Ramsey about me?"

She was shaking her head before he finished talking. "Not if you teach me to throw them balls."

He laughed and jumped off the hood, landing lightly on the ground.

"Where ya goin'?" She was afraid now that he'd leave without showing her the trick. She watched as. he went around the old Plymouth and opened the back door. The metal was bent and rusty and scraped when he jerked it.

"Watch out for them rattlers," she told him. "They hide in those seats. My Pa told me——"

"I ain't afraid of rattlers, Betty Sue."

She liked the way he said her name, making it sound so pretty. She climbed off the hood and went around to the back door of the wreck and peered inside. He sat in the middle of the seat, his long legs filling up the space.

"There ain't no room for me," she whined.

"Why, sure there is, Betty Sue." He reached for her and his fingers engulfed her tiny hand as he gently pulled her into the car.

She let him settle her on his lap and then she buried her head against his neck. He smelled like candy, and she thought maybe he did have candy with him and tried to decide how she could ask for it.

"You're a nice little girl, Betty Sue," he said, stroking her hair.

She pulled back and asked quickly, "Are you gonna give me them balls?"

"Maybe, and maybe something else." He kept smiling.

"What?"

"Well, what would you like?"

She was going to say candy, but the way he watched her, and the way his breathing had altered when she climbed upon him, changed her mind, and she blurted out, "A kiss!"

"How 'bout five kisses for five pieces of candy?"

She grinned and wrapped her arms around his neck, hugging him. She liked him because he made everything a game. "Okay," she answered.

"First the kisses," he said and pulled her arms from his neck and took her small hands and held them up before his face. "Your palms," he whispered. The smile had slipped away.

"You ain't gonna hurt me?" She was suddenly frightened.

"No, Betty Sue, I won't hurt you." He kissed her palms but his lips were dry and hot and stung her hands.

"Ouch! You're hurtin' me, Rufus." She pulled her hands away and rubbed them against her legs. The palms itched.

"Just one more minute." He was encouraging like a doctor, as he reached over and unbuckled her shoes.

"My feet? You ain't gonna kiss my feet! That's silly!" She jerked her legs away.

"But you want your candy, don't you?" He held her right foot in his hand and leaning over, kissed the high arch.

"Ouch! Rufus, please don't hurt me no more." Tears came to her eyes.

"Shhhh. Only one more." He bent and quickly kissed her other foot.

She tried to get away, but he had one arm wrapped around her and with his free hand, he unbuttoned her dress and exposed her breasts. They were white and soft and he licked the pink buds and then, just below her left breast, he sucked her skin. She screamed.

"It's all right," he whispered, "everything is all right. See! No marks."

She carefully touched herself. The skin was raw, but the pain had passed.

"My candy!" she demanded.

Rufus reached inside his overalls and pulled out five chocolate bars. "There's more candy for later," he added.

She unwrapped one bar and bit off the end. "My red balls?" she asked.

"Another favor."

Betty Sue shook her head. "You ain't kissing me, that hurts." She tried to climb off him, but he held her at the wrists and said, "No more kisses."

"What, then?" She watched him carefully.

"You said I could touch your bottom. . . ."

"Just once. . . ."

"Once and you can have the red balls."

She bit off another inch of chocolate and sighed, "All right, but only once!"

"Turn around," he ordered, and she could tell by his voice that he wanted her to hurry.

She slid around without getting off his lap and leaned against the front seat, staring out the broken windshield at the other cars. She could look down the empty path and see the rim of the Pit and she was thinking that she better get home soon or she'd be in trouble for not doing the evening chores when she felt the pain driving up inside her. She screamed and tried to get away, but he had her by her thin shoulders and pulled her back against him. His breath burned her cheek.

She gasped, but she couldn't cry out. It was as if a wedge of wood had been driven into her buttocks. Her head spun and she began to faint when he grabbed her beneath the arms and lifted her free of him, pulling her from the pain.

She lay against the front seat and sobbed into the dirty upholstery. He pulled down her thin dress and stroked her hair and kept saying that everything was okay, but she hurt so much she couldn't sit. Then he let her go and she pulled away and stumbled out of the wreck.

"I'm tellin' Pa," she cried, but he only grinned and kept buttoning his fly.

"Oh, come on, Betty Sue. You ain't gonna tell your Pa. And if you do, I'll tell them how you show your bottom to the boys at school."

"I do not!" she cried, but she knew he didn't believe her, and she turned and ran down the path.

She had forgotten her books and didn't remember them until she reached the rim of the Pit, but then she was too afraid to go back. The pain in her rear had stopped and she was able to run through the woods and across the fields to her house at the edge of the clearing.

The shack was low and built against the hillside. Its tin roof sloped over the wide porch that ran the length of the house. The porch sagged and was crowded with old furniture that had been left outside in the weather.

An old pickup was off to one side of the shack and raised up on blocks. The tires had been removed and the driver's door thrown open and left to hang. A clothesline stretched between the open car door and the corner of the porch.

Betty Sue could see her parents behind the house, working in the backyard. Her mother stood to wipe her brow and waved for Betty Sue to join them, but the young girl kept running across the yard and into the empty house.

She ran straight to the bathroom and slamming the door behind her fell exhausted against it. She was trembling and out of breath, and when she held out her hands, she could see blood dripping from her palms. There was blood, too, on her feet, oozing from the arches. And blood soaked the front of her cotton dress. It gushed out as if her heart had been lanced, and flowered from where his lips had kissed her.

1

Five Years Later

Ash Wednesday, February 8

Father Matt Driscoll reached over and pulled the small white envelope from the church's collection basket. It stood out like a marker among the brown Saint John of the Cross tidings. The white envelope was sealed and across the front the word PRIEST had been printed in crude lettering, as if scribbled by an illiterate.

It was late in the evening and the pastor had just sat down at the kitchen table of the rectory to count the collection from Ash Wednesday's masses. Usually his young assistant did it, but Father Kinsella had gone off to visit a sick parishioner and left him the job.

Father Driscoll finished his scotch and turned the white envelope over in his thick fingers. For some inexplicable reason the letter made him apprehensive.

He tapped the envelope against the kitchen table thoughtfully. He'd open the envelope, then pour himself another drink. As he tore open the sealed flap, a sudden, violent electric bolt ripped through his fingers and up his arm. He cried out and dropped the letter.

For a moment he sat stunned, massaging his forearm and studying the envelope, wondering if it might be a practical joke put into the collection basket by one of the elementary school kids.

Cautiously he touched the envelope again. This time there was no shock and he sighed and slid out the letter. It was a single sheet of paper with the crudely written message:

FOR CHRIST'S SAKE
BETTY SUE WADKINS

And under the lettering a dark stain the size of a dime.

The priest lifted the slip of paper and sniffed the dark stain. It smelled like perfume, but looked to him like blood. He'd been in the war; he didn't need anyone to tell him what blood looked like. Father Driscoll leaned back in the kitchen chair and stared at the message.

He knew the Wadkins' name. There was a large clan of them outside of town, up in the hills near Blue Haze Ridge. Over the years he had heard stories about them, rumors of people disappearing while hunting near their land, but they were just mountain stories and he hadn't paid much attention to them. Besides, the Wadkins were Baptists; they didn't belong to his parish. Very few people in the area did.

Father Driscoll decided to disregard the note. Slipping the letter and envelope into his shirt pocket, he went back to counting the collection, but he was at it for just a few minutes when he began to feel hot and feverish. He stood up, and taking his glass to the kitchen, reached up to the top of the cabinets and took down the scotch bottle from where it was hidden behind the detergent boxes.

Perhaps he was getting the flu, he thought as he poured

himself another drink. The Swine Flu, he hoped. He wouldn't mind dying from the flu. It would be an honorable way to go; better than some of his suicide schemes. Then again, it might only be the whiskey. Another drink and he'd feel fine. He'd lie down for a while and get some rest, then finish the collection.

The pastor left the kitchen, shutting off lights as he walked, and went along the dark hallway to his room. There were only the two of them living in the rectory and he could have had any of the bedrooms on the second floor, but he rather liked the privacy and closeness of this small room. He had crowded all his possessions into it and used the space as both his office and bedroom.

He tried to sleep, but it was too hot in the house. Father Kinsella, he decided, must have turned up the heat. The young priest's bedroom was at the back of the rectory and he was always complaining about the cold. The boy had thin blood, the pastor thought.

Father Driscoll sat up on the edge of the bed and wiped the perspiration off his forehead. Maybe it was a heart attack. Well, if it was one, he thought, then let it be quick; he didn't want to spend his life crippled up in some nursing home, being cared for by the nuns.

That winter he had begun to feel his age. They had had endless days of snow and freezing cold, and his right leg, stiffened with arthritis, had made it difficult for him to walk. Still he knew he didn't appear sixty years old. He had a square, blunt face that looked as if it had been chiseled from granite and would last forever. And though his hair was white and clipped short, his eyebrows were thick and dark and took a decade off his years. Only when he was drunk did he seem old.

His shirt began to itch and he stood to take off his clothes. He was unbuttoning his shirt when he felt the blood. The shirt pocket was wet and he touched himself carefully, his hand shaking at the discovery. There was no pain in his chest, but the fresh blood continued to spread, soaking the shirt and staining the white cotton.

He jerked the shirt loose from his trousers and off his shoulders. The front was completely stained and dripping with blood. He reached into the pocket and pulled out the envelope. It was hot in his fingers and soaking wet. The blood pumped through the open flap and gushed into the priest's hand.

Father Driscoll was not afraid. He held the bleeding envelope and watched as the blood blistered the soft flesh of his palm. That there could be no natural explanation for what he saw did not disturb him. The old priest had spent his whole life preaching about miracles, and now in his fingers was the proof. He began to pray.

Then, holding the envelope before him like the Holy Eucharist, he moved toward the door. Blood seeped through his fingers and dripped to the hardwood floor. He would have to wipe it up later with holy water, but first he had to place the bleeding envelope in the chapel, near the Blessed Sacrament.

He cupped his hands and let the drops fill his palms. The skin sizzled as the blood touched him and he staggered from the pain, but he held on to the envelope and went down the dark hallway into the chapel of the rectory.

When he entered the room a soft glow haloed the envelope and he did not need a light to find his way. He carried the bleeding note to the front, genuflected before the altar, and placed the note in the paten, a small, shallow silver dish. The thin envelope floated free in the blood. Then, slowly, the dripping stopped and the soft glow dimmed. Father Driscoll touched his fingers. The blood had dried and the blisters had shriveled up. The pain was gone.

He knelt before the altar and tried to pray. It had been a long time since he had. He said mass every morning of his priesthood, and he seldom missed the hour of meditation required by his vows, but of late the prayers he uttered were without meaning, and often he fell into a drunken sleep before finishing the breviary. Now, in the silent chapel, he prayed as he had as a young seminarian, full of hope and a belief in God.

He stayed on his knees for over an hour and only when he heard Father Kinsella's car did he bless himself, genuflect, and rush out of the chapel to tell his young assistant.

Father Kinsella was in the dark kitchen, peering into the open refrigerator. He had a carton of milk in one hand and was reaching for the bologna. In the frame of the light, he looked like a young thief.

"Oh, Father, something wonderful has happened to us!" the pastor exclaimed as he burst into the room and flipped on the overhead light.

"What's that, Father?" The young priest smiled at the old man, then took out the bologna and shut the refrigerator door with his elbow.

"I found this letter in the collection basket," the pastor went on. "A small white envelope addressed to PRIEST, and when I opened it there was a slip of paper and a message. An obscure message, really, just a few awkwardly printed words. It said, 'For Christ's Sake,' and was signed by a girl named Betty Sue Wadkins. I think she might be one of that clan up on Blue Haze Ridge, those Baptists."

Father Driscoll was breathing fast and he grabbed the back of a kitchen chair for support, then rushed on with his story, telling how he had found blood on his undershirt.

Father Kinsella had only been half listening, and when the pastor stopped, waiting for a reaction, he realized he had lost the point of the story. "What blood?" he asked.

"The envelope!" The old priest leaned across the kitchen table, shouting at him. "The envelope was bleeding, for Christ's sake!"

Father Kinsella tried to stay calm. When he had come up to the mountain parish and met Matt Driscoll he had known it would come to this: that someday he'd have to arrange for the old man to leave the parish. The Bishop had hinted as much: Father Driscoll had a drinking problem. But it had happened so soon, and Father Kinsella hadn't seen it coming. Also, he was aware of the differences between them and did not want to offend the pastor.

Father Kinsella would turn thirty that spring, but he still looked like a college student with his long dark hair and thin face. When he was with the campus ministry at the university he had tried to grow a beard to make himself look older, but it had come out shaggy and he had shaved it off within weeks.

Also it had covered his best features: a square, blunt chin and a wide mouth that slipped naturally into a quick smile, making him appear boyish, like a seminarian, or a young man who had not yet suffered in love.

On campus the college girls—Catholic and non-Catholic— had crowded into the chapel for his morning masses, and when he stepped to the pulpit and swept the pews with his eyes the soft gray color of dusk he had sent thrills through them. In his first year as the campus chaplain, six women converted to Catholicism.

"I'm telling you, son, that envelope bled in these fingers." Father Driscoll raised his hands as if they were proof. "Look in the chapel if you don't believe me. It's a miracle!"

Father Kinsella sipped the glass of milk and kept watching the pastor, wondering what he should do next. He hadn't moved from where he stood, leaning against the kitchen sink.

Father Driscoll shot him a glance. "You don't believe, I suppose, in miracles?"

"Not in Mossy Creek." He kept smiling, trying to keep it light.

"Maybe if you believed a little more in the simple teachings of the Church and the power of Jesus Christ, you wouldn't have gotten yourself into such a fix at the university." Father Driscoll did not look at the young man as he spoke, and for a moment there was silence between them.

"You know, Father, that I asked for this assignment," the young priest finally answered.

"Under pressure," the pastor retorted. "I know what you were up to at that university."

"I had my options."

"Like what? Leaving the priesthood?"

"Yes, like leaving the order," he answered softly.

They never discussed why Father Kinsella had been transferred. When the young priest had come to the mountain parish, Father Driscoll accepted him without a protest. He knew he had no clout at the Chancery and couldn't have stopped the assignment even if he had wanted to. They were both exiles in this remote corner of the diocese.

The old priest slowly pulled his aching body from the chair. He was stiff from the kneeling. "I'm going into the chapel," he announced, as if defying Father Kinsella with his own conviction.

"Okay, Father." The young priest grinned. "Let's have a look." He shook his head and finished off the glass of milk.

"Suit yourself." Father Driscoll no longer cared. The boy either believed or he didn't. Father Driscoll knew that once someone lost the faith it wasn't easily gained again.

"Show me, Father, and then let's get some sleep. It's late enough." Father Kinsella followed the pastor down the hallway and into the chapel, flipping on the light as he entered.

"There's no need for lights," Father Driscoll whispered and moved forward, supporting himself by grabbing the pews as he went toward the altar. At the front of the chapel he genuflected and the pain in his leg made him gasp.

"Easy, Father!" The young priest grabbed the arm of the pastor.

Father Driscoll motioned toward the sacristy. "Look for yourself. On the altar."

Father Kinsella stepped onto the altar platform and saw the white envelope in the silver dish before the tabernacle. The flap was open and the envelope was spotless. He reached out, touched it, and was thrown back against the front pew as if hit by a bolt of electricity. He slipped dazed to the floor.

"Are you all right, son?" Father Driscoll put his arm under the priest to help him up.

"What was that?" The priest shook his head, a little dazed.

"The envelope! I felt a shock myself when I first touched it, but nothing like that! Are you all right?"

"There must be a short in the wiring . . ."

"No, it's the envelope. I told you! It's the power of God."

Father Kinsella pulled himself up. "More likely it's the Duke Power Company, Father."

Father Driscoll left him and went to the altar. "Look for yourself! See what I told you!" His face beamed.

Father Kinsella stepped onto the altar, being careful where he walked, and looked again. Now the silver paten was filled with blood and the envelope was soaked red. He reached into the dish and plucked out the envelope. There was no shock this time, but blood pumped out of the open flap and ran through his fingers.

He pulled the slip of paper from the envelope and saw where the blood gushed from the dime-size mark. Then, pressing the heel of his hand against the flowing blood, he squeezed the spot as if applying a tourniquet. His fingers blistered and pus ran from the sores, but slowly he cut off the flow of sweet-smelling blood. He dropped the slip of paper and the bloody envelope into the silver paten. He could hear Father Driscoll whisper that he would be all right, that the blisters would heal. But it was not the blisters that terrified the young priest: it was the slip of paper that bled like an open heart in his hands.

2

Thursday, February 9

Father Driscoll stopped the station wagon at the end of Rabbit Hop road and, looking up toward the top of Blue Haze Ridge said, "We'll walk from here."

On the other side of the road and halfway up the ridge, a patch of woods had been cut away, exposing the land. At the edge of the clearing a tarpaper shack hugged the hillside, looking like a huge rock that had been unearthed and tumbled into the sun to dry.

The house was tin roofed, but the tin was rusty and had been patched over the years and now had to be held in place with cement blocks. A stovepipe stuck out one window and was wired up the side of the house. Black, oily smoke poured from it. The other windows were sealed with thick plastic to keep out the cold.

Father Kinsella could see a red sofa on the wooden front porch. It, too, was covered with plastic. In the yard a bathtub was turned over and abandoned, and farther away an old Chevy pickup truck was propped on blocks, the windows smashed as if they had been hit from the road with buckshot. A clothesline stretched from the truck to the house and on this cold winter day a wash of sheets snapped in the wind. The sheets were white, but discolored with huge rust-colored stains.

"I spoke to a cousin of theirs, Billy Wadkins. He said the family keeps her at home," Father Driscoll said, mentioning the girl for the first time that morning. "Most of the mountain people think she's retarded. No one sees her much."

"Did you tell Billy about the bleeding envelope?" Father Kinsella asked.

"No, it's none of his business."

"What about the Chancery?"

"Not a word, and don't you go mentioning it!" Father Driscoll shot a glance at his young assistant. "They'll be up here taking over if they find out!"

Father Kinsella sighed, relieved that no one yet knew. He could just imagine what they'd have thought at the Chancery if they had gotten a call from their whiskey priest, telling them about a bleeding envelope in the collection basket.

Father Kinsella did not know what to believe. He had seen the blood pumping from the envelope. Or at least he thought he had. Later, when the blisters disappeared and the blood dried, he wasn't so sure, but he was too ashamed to ask to see the envelope again, to see if it would bleed a second time.

"Did you bring her letter with you, Father?"

The pastor nodded and tapped his chest.

Then Father Kinsella asked, surprised he hadn't thought of it before, "Did you bring the Blessed Sacrament with you too?"

Father Driscoll nodded.

"She isn't Catholic, Father." The young assistant spoke

carefully, anxious not to upset the pastor. "We know at least that much about her."

"I didn't bring it for her." Father Driscoll glanced at his assistant, annoyed at his questioning. "I brought the Blessed Sacrament to protect us."

"Oh, Christ!" The young priest pushed open the car door and stepped into the cold afternoon. Now he was worried. Whatever else might happen in the hills, Father Kinsella knew that wafers of the Holy Eucharist wouldn't protect them from the Wadkins clan.

They were downwind from the house and the dogs did not notice them until they reached the clearing. Then the two hounds ran out from beneath the porch and stood tense before the tarpaper shack, howling as the priests approached through the fresh snow.

Father Driscoll grabbed his assistant's arm and stopped him, but it wasn't because of the dogs. The steady climb to the ridge had exhausted him and he leaned against Father Kinsella to catch his breath. Looking down, they could see the station wagon parked on the road. It looked small and far away.

They turned at the sound of the front door opening and slamming shut. Several men had come onto the porch of the shack. They looked like relatives, their faces thin and gaunt with lantern jaws and black eyes. They wore farm clothes and heavy boots that thumped on the wooden planks as they fanned out on the porch, keeping in the shadows of the tarpaper house. Only one man stepped forward.

He was older than the others, but had the solid build of a man who did hard labor. He had not shaved for several days and white stubble covered his face in rough patches. His hair was thick, but cut short above his ears, as if done at home. He wore a long-sleeved blue work shirt, buttoned to his throat, and dark wool trousers held up with suspenders. In his arms he cradled a shotgun.

"I'll handle this," Father Driscoll said, and letting go of his assistant's arm, he strode forward, calling out, "Mr. Wadkins? My name's Matt Driscoll—Father Driscoll from Saint John's parish in——"

The dogs went for him then, springing at the old man and snapping at his black-trousered legs. The priest stumbled and Father Kinsella jumped forward to catch him. He looked up in time to see the man swing his shotgun around, aim, and fire a double load of buckshot over their heads. The hound dogs yelped at the noise and, cowering, ran off to hide under the wooden porch.

"Whatcha want?" the man asked. He broke open the chamber of the shotgun and the empty shells popped out and flew across the porch. From inside his shirt pocket he fished out more shells and dropped them into the double-barrel.

"I'm Father Driscoll—from Saint John of the Cross." The pastor moved toward the porch, but when the man casually shifted the shotgun in his arms and leveled it at him, he stopped and shouted out his explanation. He told the man about the letter in the collection basket, and then pulled it out, holding it up like evidence. "Does Betty Sue Wadkins live here?" He glanced at the other men standing silently on the porch.

The man in front was in no hurry to reply. He stood with his feet apart and his head tilted back, watching the priest with eyes the color and size of pennies.

"We just stopped by to see if we could be of any help," Father Driscoll went on, moving slowly forward and propping his foot against the bottom step of the porch. "Billy Wadkins told us the child was ill."

"Billy ain't got no right talkin'," the man answered. "The girl's sick, been sick for five years; you ain't gonna help her none."

"She asked for our help," Father Kinsella pointed out, and held up the white envelope.

The man shook his head. "The girl can't write much."

"Perhaps someone wrote it for her," Father Driscoll suggested.

"Nope." He shook his head and looked past the two priests, dismissing them.

Father Kinsella shifted his position and gazed over the fields. He was thinking how cold he was with the wind whipping through his jeans and chilling his face and he noticed Father Driscoll glancing at him and then at the man on the porch. He wanted Father Kinsella to do something.

The young priest pointed toward the cleared fields.

"You plant tobacco here?"

The man nodded slowly. "Here and out back."

"How's this land for tobacco? Seems too high, doesn't it?"

"Land's fine, but the season's a mite short."

They talked then about the winter weather and the damage to crops and the rising cost of bottled gas. The conversation worked aimlessly among the three men: questions by the priests and short replies by the old man.

No one was in a hurry, but by now both of the priests were freezing cold, and Father Driscoll's leg had stiffened up. He knew he wouldn't be able to walk down the hill by himself; still, he couldn't force the conversation back to the girl. He understood what Father Kinsella was doing and he let the young priest negotiate.

It was when they began to talk about the county schools closing because of the bad weather that Father Kinsella quietly asked, "Is Betty Sue your daughter, sir?"

The old man nodded slowly, as if he still didn't want to talk about her, but he explained, "She's my young one. The others are gone off. I lost a couple. I lost one boy in the army whilst back."

"Have you ever taken her to the doctor?"

"The doc ain't no good for her." The old man shook his head. It was as if he had struggled with this question himself.

"Has Reverend Hoppes seen her?" Father Kinsella asked, referring to the pastor of the Baptist church.

The old man set his shotgun against the porch rail and stuck his big farmer's hands into his trousers before answering. "He took a look at her when she first got sick. She wasn't as bad then, y'know, as now. He wanted us to take her over to the county hospital in New Lenox, but ain't no good reason for that. They can't help the girl. Them snakes got her, that's all." He looked at the young priest and nodded emphatically.

"The snakes—?"

"In the Pit." He pointed towards the hollow below the clearing. "She was comin' home from school one day and cut through them wrecked cars. She ain't s'ppose to go into the Pit, y'know, and she said them rattlers set upon her. Bit the poor girl near to death. She ain't been right since. Fittibied, y'know, in the head. And she bleeds."

The priests glanced at each other and Father Kinsella asked quickly, "Mr. Wadkins, would you mind if we just said hello to her?" He found himself holding his breath waiting for the old man to answer.

Wadkins looked shocked, then angry. "We ain't never had no Catholics in our house," he said. "People here 'bout get upset with foreigners. Lots of them comin', y'know, nowadays." He picked up the shotgun again and held it cradled. "My people don't like Catholics much, to be fair with y'all. We got our reasons, I guess, but maybe you folks think likewise 'bout us. Don't know for sure.

"Now my little girl," he went on, standing firm and staring at both priests, "she ain't right in the head and I'm her pa and it's my place to see nothin' more happens to her.

You're not gonna do anything to her, hear?" It was both a plea and a statement of fact.

Father Kinsella saw the fear in the man's face now. Perhaps he was just afraid of Catholics, of what they might do to his daughter, but the young priest thought it was something else: the man was afraid of whatever had happened to his child. "Mr. Wadkins, we want to help your daughter if we can. We won't hurt her. Betty Sue's been hurt enough."

The old man watched them a moment longer, as if deciding finally whether he could trust them. Then he nodded and motioned the priests to follow him into the house.

It was dark inside and it took the priests a few moments for their eyes to adjust. Slowly they realized they were in a room crowded with women and children. The chairs and sofas were filled with people. They sat in silence, children clinging to their mothers, and watched the two priests with the same blank, black eyes of the men. No one offered a greeting or a reason for why they were there.

In one corner of the crowded room a television set was turned on. A ghostly picture glowed without sound. The only noise in the house came from the kitchen where, through the open doorway, the priests could see several women working; they were bent over the sink washing sheets and towels.

Mr. Wadkins crossed the room and then stopped at a rear doorway. He was smaller than the two priests and now, inside the house, he seemed less threatening.

"On Thursday she starts gettin' real bad," he whispered. "Sometimes, Lord, I don't figure she's gonna make it. Course she does. . . . "

"What happens to her?" the pastor asked impatiently, anxious now for answers.

Her father shook his head. "Ain't right, y'know; I

wouldn't believe it myself unless I seen it with my own eyes." He pulled himself together and stated, "Now I'm tellin' you once more, don't go sayin' no Catholic prayer over that girl." He held up the shotgun to make his point and walked into the back room of the house.

The bedroom was small and square with a low flat ceiling and two windows sealed with more plastic. Father Kinsella guessed that it must have been added on after the house was built, perhaps when the girl first became ill. It was dark as well, with only one lamp lit in the corner, away from the double bed where the young girl lay under white sheets and homemade quilts.

There was an older woman by the head of the bed holding a towel on the girl's brow. She looked up nervously when they came into the room, but the girl's father only motioned the priests to the foot of the bed and out of the woman's way.

When Father Kinsella looked down at the bed he saw that Betty Sue Wadkins was not an adolescent at all, but a lovely young woman in her teens. She was fair with delicate features, a thin straight nose, a large mouth, and deep-set eyes. Her eyelashes were dark and her hair long cornsilk.

And she was ill. Her cheeks were flushed and beads of perspiration formed on her upper lip and beneath her dark eyes.

He was thinking how lost she seemed, so young and helpless in the wide bed, when he noticed the pastor take out the small silver container holding the Holy Eucharist. He reached to stop the older priest, but Father Driscoll brushed his hand aside. As he approached the head of the bed, he made the sign of the cross, intoning, "In the name of the Father, and of the Son, and of the Holy Spirit." Halfway through his blessing, the young woman bolted upright in the wide bed and screamed.

"Pa, get 'em out of here!" the older woman shouted. She grabbed the young woman by the shoulders and tried to pull her down, but the girl twisted from her grasp.

"I told you none of them Catholic prayers!" The father stepped back and pointed his shotgun at the priests. "Now both of ya; get off my land!"

Father Kinsella backed off immediately, starting for the bedroom door, but the pastor did not move. Staring transfixed at the girl, he exclaimed, almost as if it were a prayer, "Jesus, Mary, and Joseph!"

Father Kinsella turned back to Betty Sue. She was sitting up with her hands out as if to receive an offering, and her face captivated him immediately. He had seen such expressions on children at their first Holy Communion and among nuns receiving the veil. Her face was dazzlingly bright, glistening in the dark room as if lit by a mysterious interior light.

"I see him," she whispered. "I see Jesus." She spoke slowly. "He's in a garden. I see . . . flowers . . . and trees . . ." Her voice faltered and fear, like a fast-moving cloud, crossed her face. The corners of her mouth quivered and she began to tremble. "I see men with spears! Oh, run Jesus! Run quickly! No, don't hurt him!" She fell back on the mattress and curled up, as if to shield herself from invisible blows. Her thin body was wet with sweat.

Then she stopped thrashing and sat up, holding out her arms again. "Judas," she whispered, "have you come to help Jesus? See how he loves Jesus. He kisses Jesus." She smiled sweetly and slipped peacefully into the bed. Her lips were slightly parted and looked like the first petals of a spring rose. She was very beautiful, Father Kinsella realized.

As he watched, her mouth began to quiver. "Don't," she pleaded. "Please don't hurt Jesus." Her body went rigid on the bed. She was delirious, Father Kinsella decided, when unexplainably, she flew off the bed several inches, then slammed down against the mattress. The bed shook from the impact and struck the wall of the room. Now she was kneeling on the mattress, her arms outstretched. There was fear in her eyes as she stared across the room.

"Put away that sword, Peter!" she ordered. "No, Peter, don't," she screamed. The scream was fierce and Father Kinsella backed a few feet away from the bed.

"See! See!" She pointed her finger into the dark bedroom. Her voice was scolding. "See what Jesus must do because of you." She shook her head reproachfully. "Obey Jesus, Peter, and no more of that." Then, as if exhausted from her vision, she slipped back into bed and for the moment lay quietly.

"It's the Bible," her father said. "She sees things from the Bible." He put his finger to his lips and nodded at his daughter. Her eyes were closed, her face serene. She raised her arms and for the first time Father Kinsella noticed the small reddish nodules on her palms.

"Give her your hands," her father said. "She gets to know strangers that way."

Tentatively the priests gave her their hands and she held them gently in her fingers, as if weighing the worth of each man. Her pondering made Father Kinsella uneasy and he was about to pull away when she spoke, her voice strong and certain.

"One of you will die a sinner and suffer much in purgatory. And one will live as a saint and suffer much on earth."

She let go of their hands then, apparently drained of strength by the effort of speaking to them. Her breathing frightened Father Kinsella; she looked and sounded like many of the people at whose deathbeds he had prayed.

Desperately he looked around the room. No one was moving to help her. Then he remembered the white envelope and its miraculous bleeding.

"The envelope!" he said to the pastor urgently.

Father Driscoll frowned, not understanding.

"The letter that came to Saint John's; it might help."

The old priest drew the letter from his suit pocket. Father Kinsella leaned over the young woman and softly touched her lips with the note. Her eyes opened slowly. She blinked and smiled directly at the young priest.

"Stephen, you've come for me," she whispered.

Father Kinsella froze, his eyes held by hers.

"I was afraid you wouldn't come, but Rufus said you would."

"Who?"

She turned her head toward the dark corner of the room, and Father Kinsella looked around to see a young man watching him. He sat straight in a hardwood chair, a young man with the same golden hair as hers, the same fine features. His eyes were fixed on the priest and held him for a moment like a lover's embrace. Then Father Kinsella looked away.

"Stephen?" she whispered. "Help me, Stephen."

The priest saw then that her hands were bleeding, pumping blood into her palms and through her fingers, and spreading a dark stain on her nightgown beneath her heart. He reached down and lifted the quilt off her feet. She was bleeding as well from both her arches.

Her father was talking, telling them about the snake bites, but Father Kinsella was not listening. For he was witnessing a phenomenon he had only read about in his religious studies. She was actually bleeding. Bleeding from the five sacred wounds, the wounds of Jesus Christ's passion and death, and the mystical blood filled the room with its sweet scent, touching them all like a perfume.

3

Saturday, February 11

Feast of Our Lady of Lourdes

Father Kinsella opened the back door of Saint John of the Cross and walked into the sacristy. The two elementary school boys were already there, dressed in their cassocks and surplices. They looked up and grinned when they saw it was Father Kinsella and not the pastor who would be saying the eight o'clock mass, but their smiles faded when Father Kinsella said curtly, "Tim, light the candles for a low mass."

"Yes, Father." The boy jumped to comply.

"And, Michael, take the cruets onto the altar and see that they're filled with water and wine."

The second altar boy was moving before the priest finished his order.

The two boys glanced nervously at each other as they went through the curtained doorway and out into the sanctuary. Father Kinsella was always friendly and happy before mass, joking and kidding with them, but this morning he was acting like the pastor himself.

Alone in the sacristy, Stephen tried to calm himself. He paced the small room and took deep breaths, but it was no good; he could not relax. He had not slept well for two nights and his nerves were on edge. He knew he shouldn't have been short with the altar boys. They had no idea of what was bothering him.

He went to the sacrarium and turned on the warm water, letting the steady flow wash over his hands. His fingers were trembling. He could not shake the memory of the girl on Blue Haze Ridge, of her strange agony and affliction, of her knowing him by name. The Catholics in Mossy Creek kept to themselves, as did mountain people like the Wadkins. Some of the Baptist storekeepers in town certainly knew him by sight or name, but not a seventeen-year-old girl who had probably never been off Blue Haze Ridge.

But now he had a mass to say and he forced himself to concentrate on the ritual of dressing, beginning with the century-old prayer as he symbolically washed his hands, *"Give virtue, O Lord, unto my hands, that every stain may be wiped away: that I may be enabled to serve thee without defilement of mind or body."*

Then he went to the wooden cabinet and took down the white linen amice and slipped it over his head, saying, *"Place, O Lord, the helmet of salvation upon my head, that I may overcome the assaults of the Devil."*

Dressing for the celebration of the mass, he did begin to relax. Of all the aspects of his priesthood, he loved most the beauty and solemnity of the mass. Once adorned by the richly brocaded vestments, he felt the power and majesty of the long history of the Catholic Church. It was then that he most felt like an ordained priest, like a true disciple of Jesus Christ.

He took the white linen alb from the cabinet and slipped it on. The tunic reached to his ankles. *"Cleanse me, O Lord,"* he whispered, *"and purify my heart."*

He gathered the material together with the cincture. Knotting the white cord, he said, *"Gird me, O Lord, with the girdle of purity and extinguish in my loins the desire of lust: so that the virtue of continence and chastity may ever abide in me."*

Then he took the long, narrow stole, the distinctive sign of his priesthood, placed it on his shoulders and crossed it over his chest as he whispered the prayer that had come down from the Middle Ages.

Finally he picked the matching chasuble, purple for Lent, and standing before the full-length mirror, dropped the heavy silk outer vestment over his shoulders, straightening the panels on his front and back as he prayed, *"O Lord, who hast said: My yoke is easy and my burden is light: make me so able to bear that I may obtain thy favor. Amen."*

The altar boys had returned from the sanctuary and he turned to them and smiled. He felt immensely better. "Are we ready, men?" he asked.

They nodded and grinned back.

He glanced a final time in the mirror to check his vestments and caught his eyes in the reflection, those gray eyes that he knew women found so appealing. And he knew why: it was the sadness. They thought they could make him happy. If only they knew why his eyes were so sad, he thought, what would they think of him then? He shook his head and said to the two boys, "Let's go."

Tim pulled the cord and the bell rang through the church, announcing the beginning of mass. Father Kinsella picked up his silver chalice, an ordination gift from his parents, and moved through the sacristy curtain.

He could hear the early-morning congregation shuffle slowly to their feet as he walked onto the altar. Out of the corner of his eyes he saw them scattered throughout the big church.

He bent to kiss the altar cloth, then walked back to the celebrant's chair, turned and faced the congregation. One of the altar boys stood nearby, holding the large missal open before him, and Stephen raised both his hands and said out loud, "In the Name of the Father, and of the Son, and of the Holy Spirit ..." He paused and for the first time that morning looked straight out at the congregation.

She was alone in the back pew, sitting in the shadows, and he would not have noticed her except for the green suede coat. He had gone with her that August when she bought it. On her head she wore a white silk scarf. He would have to tell her that most Catholic women didn't cover their heads in church anymore, he thought irrelevantly.

He felt the congregation shift nervously at his delay and he focused on the missal and continued, conscious now of his voice and actions, for she had never seen him saying Mass, practicing his profession, performing, as she liked to kid him, like a charlatan.

He waited for the church to clear out after mass before he went to her, walking down a side aisle toward her pew. As he approached, she stood up and preceded him and they met in the vestibule.

"That was a good homily," she said, as if determined to say something nice.

"I didn't expect you so early," he whispered, though no one else was around.

"I left the city at five o'clock and there wasn't any traffic on the interstate." She paused and studied his face for a moment. "What's the matter, Stephen? Why did you telephone? I thought we had an agreement."

Her green eyes had darkened a shade, and he realized again how vulnerable she was: a slender woman with a small delicate face dwarfed by enormous tortoiseshell glasses. Why was he involving her? he wondered. It would only make everything more difficult between them.

"I needed to talk to you," he explained, speaking softly. "Something has happened."

She nodded hesitantly, still not understanding, but accepting his answer. "All right. But where can we talk?" She glanced around the church, looking for somewhere comfortable to sit, but the church—enormous and wide open with a high dome ceiling—was very draughty. It looked, she thought, like the interior of an old train station, except for a huge wooden crucifix that hung, as if suspended in midair, over the center altar.

"In the rectory," Stephen answered. He had thought it all out already. "The pastor is out of town this morning; we have the house to ourselves."

"Isn't there anywhere else?"

"It's okay, Deborah. No one will see you." He spoke quickly, as if trying to convince her.

"I just don't want to get you in trouble," she explained.

"It's all right," he said again and sighed, suddenly realizing how happy he was to see her again. "Come on, let's go."

"Let me look at you a moment," he said when she had taken off her coat. They were in the front parlor of the old Victorian house, a room that the two priests seldom used, but the antique furniture was kept well waxed by the housekeeper. The smell of lemon polish hung in the air.

Stephen had her at arm's length, holding her by the shoulders and she looked up at him and smiled, her green eyes flashing with pleasure.

Her eyes were her best feature. They were what he had first noticed when they met, and what he remembered most now that they were separated. Her eyes, he had once told her, summed up her whole personality the way grass and leaves signal spring.

They had met in the spring, a year before, walking from

the campus Newman Club to the Hillel Center where he was to give a talk on "Jesus Christ as a Romantic Hero." She had arranged the lecture, and would introduce him to the group.

"You have wonderful eyes," he had said. "They're the color of fresh mint. But I guess your boyfriends have already told you that."

She shook her head, shifting the pile of textbooks she was carrying in her arms, but didn't flirt back at him.

"Well, they are," he added, momentarily unsure of what to say. He decided to change the subject. "I thought that approaching Christ as a romantic figure might be more ecumenical for the Jewish Center." Still no answer. "Listen," he said, "shall I help you carry those books?"

"You're something of a romantic figure yourself, Father," she said, and handed him the books with a curious look of triumph.

"It's this outfit." He laughed, gesturing at his black suit and white collar.

"No," she answered, for this was something she had thought about and decided. "It's your eyes and that little-boy expression you have. It makes all the girls want to mother you." She had watched him as she said this, her eyes full of play, as if she enjoyed making the Catholic priest uncomfortable with her remarks. It was a habit of hers that she never got over.

Now she was staring back at him, surveying him as he was surveying her. "I see they have you in basic black again," she commented, pulling from his grasp and walking away. She did not sit down immediately, but toured the room, noting the formal furniture. "Is this where you play bingo?" she asked, but he did not smile.

"It's just a house," he said defensively. "Don't be such a smartass, Deborah. I wish you'd settle down; I really want to talk to you."

Obligingly, she sat on the stiff upholstered sofa across the room from him and gave him her full attention.

He started to pace the small parlor and it was a moment before he began. "Something very strange happened to me this Thursday. That's one of the reasons I asked you to come up. I had to talk to someone rational!"

"What is it, Stephen?" she said quickly, seeing that he was clearly worried.

"Have you ever heard of stigmata, Deborah?"

She shook her head, but then hesitated and said, "Oh, wait—yes, it's when—the crucifixion wounds of Christ appear on a person. Religious crazies, aren't they?"

"Not always." He stopped and sat down in a chair, leaning forward and speaking softly as if there were other people in the rectory. "They are usually nuns or priests; mystics, very religious people who receive the wounds from Christ Himself as a sign of their holiness.

"You don't have to be a nun or a priest, though. Some stigmatics are just exceptionally holy lay people. The most famous example is probably Theresa Neumann, a woman who lived in Germany and died in 1962."

"What are they, some sort of supernatural joke?"

"Deborah, this is important," he snapped. "I need your help."

Deborah watched him. She had come a long way to see him, and it hurt to find out that he had called after all this time because he wanted to discuss some fine point of Catholicism. This was nothing new: his religion had always been between them.

When they had first met, she had tried to explain away his religion as just an intellectual fascination with myths. But then they had become lovers and she saw for the first time that the Catholic Church had a stranglehold on him. "It's faith," he once explained. "It has no link with common sense or logic. It's what I believe and it's been part of me since I was a child. I was raised believing in God and his supernatural powers."

"Well," she had laughed, "I was raised in New York City and God never made it to the West Side. I think he got mugged somewhere in Central Park." But her humor could not dissolve their problem, and from the beginning his vows were part of the love affair, affecting their passion like a cold wind from the Middle Ages.

"All right," she answered slowly, "I'm sorry. What is it? What's the matter?"

"Let me give you some background," he began. "The Church doesn't have a firm position about stigmata. In fact, the Holy See has always been slow to recognize cases. Sometimes a local bishop will appoint what's called an Ecclesiastical Commission to investigate. But usually they try to ignore the situation, hoping the furor will die down.

"One of the first stigmatics, and one of the few whom everyone accepts as legitimate, was Saint Francis of Assisi, who died in 1226. You've seen pictures of him standing in a garden and surrounded by animals. There's usually divine light radiating from his hands and heart."

"I don't understand," said Deborah impatiently. "I mean, how do you get it in the first place? Do you just wake up with it one morning like your period?"

She hoped her irreverence would irritate him, perhaps enough to make him change the subject, but instead he said, "I did some research on Theresa Neumann when I was at the seminary. Would you like to hear her story?" He spoke calmly, determined to keep his temper until Deborah gave up and really listened.

Deborah turned in the chair to make herself comfortable and sighed. "Okay, so tell me."

"Well, she was just a farm girl, and very religious. When she was about twenty she hurt herself fighting a fire and was paralyzed for a short time. The doctor couldn't find any-thing wrong, but for several years after that, odd, unex-plained sicknesses began to plague her. Once, while she was milking the cows, she had a convulsive seizure. Next, for no apparent reason, she lost her sight temporarily. Things like that.

"And she also began to assume other people's illnesses. There was a young theology student, for example, who was suffering from a throat ailment and was going to be dismissed from the seminary because of it. Theresa heard about this and prayed that God would cure him and let her suffer instead.

"Shortly after that she began to cough and spit up blood. An abscess had formed in her throat and from then on it became difficult for her even to swallow water. The semi-narian, however, was immediately cured and later became a priest."

"That's spooky," Deborah said. "You're giving me the chills."

"There's more. In 1926, during Lent, Theresa was ill again. She could hardly pray and kept repeating the same simple thought: 'Our Divine Saviour has suffered much more for us.'

"Then, on the first Thursday night of Lent, she saw a vision of Jesus Christ. It was the night before the crucifixion, and he was alone in the Garden of Olives, kneeling among the trees and rocks. She realized he was undergoing his agony in the garden and began to experience the same suffering and share his agony when she suddenly felt a deep pain in her left side. It was so penetrating that she thought she was going to die and when she felt her side she found warm blood trickling down her body. It oozed from her left side until noon the next day."

"Come on, this is ridiculous," Deborah interrupted.

"Wait." The priest raised his hand for her to be quiet. "All during Lent she witnessed various scenes of Christ's passion. She saw the agony in the garden. She saw the Roman soldiers scourge Jesus with whips after his trial before Pilate. She also saw the soldiers make a crown of thorn branches and put it on Christ's head, mocking him for his claim that he was King of the Jews. In the fourth week of Lent, she accompanied Jesus as he carried the cross on his back all the way from the city out to Golgotha, the hill outside Jerusalem where the Romans held their executions. On each of these occasions she bled from her side as she watched Christ's passion.

"Then, on Good Friday—between noon and three o'clock, when Christ was crucified—she was transfixed and seemed to be experiencing all of Christ's suffering on the cross. She bled from her hands and feet, as well as her left side, and there were seven bloody scars on her head, as if caused by the crown of thorns. From then until she died she was permanently marked with all the wounds of Christ's crucifixion."

Deborah was holding her breath, listening intently, and when he stopped she asked immediately, "Okay, why did she bleed?"

Father Kinsella shook his head. "No one knows. There's no theological or medical explanation, beyond saying that what happened to her is a miracle."

"Then why this long story?" She frowned. "What's your point?"

Stephen began to pace again and she could see then that he was frightened. "What is it, Stephen?" she whispered, frightened now herself.

"Thursday afternoon up in the mountains, the pastor and I found a young woman who bleeds from the same wounds."

Deborah's eyes widened as he kept talking, his voice a

whisper. The only thing he held back was the bleeding envelope. Deborah was skeptical enough as it was. He told her only that they had gotten an illiterately written note at the church, and left it at that.

"What doesn't fit, of course, is that the girl isn't a Catholic. Her family is Baptist and they don't even know what stigmata are."

"Why don't you have the Bishop appoint one of those Ecclesiastical Commissions?"

"Father Driscoll doesn't want to tell anyone. He's afraid the Chancery will come up and take away all his action."

"You mean that's all that's worrying you?"

"No, I'm very happy we're keeping the Bishop out of this."

"Well, then, what?" she demanded. "Why are you so worried?"

He stopped pacing and looked down at her, speaking slowly as he answered, "Because when we went up there Thursday, the girl came out of her ecstasy and spoke to me by name. She called me Stephen."

"What did she say to your pastor?" Deborah asked. "Maybe she'd heard about both of you."

"She didn't even care that he was there. I was the one she recognized, and it was frightening having her know my name. It was as if she'd been waiting for me." He ran his hand nervously through his dark hair. "I don't know what it means."

She reached up for his hand and when his fingers touched her, she pulled him down to sit next to her on the small sofa.

It was the first time they had been together since he had left the university that fall, and his sudden proximity excited her. She had forgotten how wonderful he smelled. She had never known a man to be so obviously sensual. She could feel herself becoming tense and she kept her hands off him, afraid of how she might behave if she touched his body again.

"I've missed you, Deborah," he said, his face now only inches from hers. She let her eyes sweep over him, then looked away without answering, happy that he had forgotten about the mountain girl and was thinking only of her.

He tilted his head sideways and gently kissed her lips. She didn't respond, but when he tried to kiss her a second time, she turned her face away and he halted.

"We're just going to get ourselves in trouble," she said.

"I want to get in trouble."

She looked up and caught his gray eyes. "But where?" She smiled. "Here on this horsehair sofa?"

"Upstairs. My room."

"Stephen," she said, shocked. "This is a rectory!"

"It's my home, my bedroom. The housekeeper has the day off and Father Driscoll won't be back until this afternoon. Come on." He stood and taking her hand tried to pull her off the sofa.

She was shaking her head. "I didn't come here to sleep with you. You said you wanted to talk to me." She looked betrayed.

He slid down next to her and took her forcefully into his arms. Her head was buried against his chest, in the folds of his black cassock. He could smell her hair, her body. It was true that he had wanted to talk to her about the mountain girl, to explain his strange fear of what he had seen on Blue Haze Ridge, but when he saw her he only wanted to make love to her. It was always that way when they met. He couldn't stop himself.

He could feel her body softening in his arms; he knew she wanted him too, but he did not rush her, and for a few more moments he let her snuggle against him, enjoying the warmth and security of his arms. Then he took both her

hands and stood. She came quietly, leaving behind her purse
and coat as she followed him silently upstairs to his bedroom
at the back of the rectory.

"It's so tiny," she said, stepping into the room.

He looked at the bedroom and saw it as she was seeing it,
for the first time. There was the single bed, a small desk,
and one old easy chair. She probably attributed its bareness
to his vow of poverty, but it was really more a lack of
interest on his part. He hadn't bothered putting up pictures
or prints, and the crucifix over the bed, with a frond of year-
old yellowed palm tucked behind it, had been there when he
moved into the rectory last September.

Her seeing the bedroom embarrassed him, and he quickly
explained it away, saying, "I won't be here long," and took
her into his arms.

She resisted again and stepped clear of him, moving
across the room to sit on the edge of the bed. "Would you
get out of that outfit? It makes me feel funny. When did you
start wearing skirts again? I've only seen you in a black suit
before."

He slipped the black cassock off and stood there in the
clothes he was wearing underneath, a white shirt and blue
denim jeans.

"Driscoll likes to have me dress the part up here," he said,
unbuttoning his shirt as he spoke and tossing it on the easy
chair. "He doesn't think I'm a serious enough priest."

She looked him up and down slowly as he stood before
her, her green eyes touching on his smooth, broad shoulders,
the muscles of his arms, the fine line of dark hair that ran
down from his navel and disappeared into his low-cut jeans.

"What a silly old man," she said lightly. "Anyone can see
that you're a model priest."

He stood there a moment, enduring her sarcasm, her
unhappiness at their situation.

"Deborah, I'm in love with you," he said. "I'd make love

to you here in the rectory, or in the parish stationwagon, or in the church itself; I don't care. I've put you before my vows, which means I've put you before God himself, and that's a terrifying sin—for a priest or anyone—but I can't help it. I love you."

That silenced her. She nodded slowly, stunned by the admission of his feelings. There were tears in her eyes. "Stephen, why do you do this to me?"

He shook his head, bewildered himself by the course of his actions, and then he embraced her silently and they fell backward together in the bed. He pulled her turtleneck sweater up and over her head, and then bent and gently kissed her small breasts. She shivered and moaned as he licked the soft flesh and the startled nipples.

Now she began to undress him, moving her lips hungrily across the lean muscles of his abdomen until she reached his belt buckle. She reached for it, but he stopped her.

He wanted to undress her first and he pulled away to unzip her slacks and pull them off her hips and down her legs. She started to slip out of her panties and he shook his head, tucked his thumbs into the elastic himself and rolled down the silky material. He tossed the panties aside and they sailed across the room like a white flag.

She always seemed so much smaller without clothes. He had forgotten that and it startled him, seeing her so tiny in the bed. She kept her legs braced together and slid her arms up and under the pillow, watching him enjoy the sight of her. He bent and kissed her dark tuft and she shuddered and then, sitting up, pulled again at the buckle of his jeans. "Hurry," she said and her voice was tight.

He stepped away to sit on the chair and unlace his heavy boots. It still made him uncomfortable to have her undress him, for they had only made love half a dozen times and everything about it was new and strange to him.

Then he was naked and he slipped in beside her. She came to him immediately, holding him beneath her as she began to kiss him fiercely, as if he were a great pleasure that had been denied to her.

She moved down his body and kneeling between his legs gently took his penis and engulfed the head. Her lips tightened and she raked her teeth softly over the skin. When he thought he couldn't bear the rhythm any longer, she reached up and pushed her forefinger into him. He grabbed her long hair and exclaimed, "Deborah! I'm going to come." But she wouldn't stop. She didn't want to stop. And he poured himself into her open mouth.

Deborah pulled away and stretched out across his wet body. "And how did you like that?" She smiled, pleased with herself.

He kissed her. "But I wanted to come inside you."

"You will." She touched his cheek and nestled close. "We have time."

He slept while she lay in his arms watching him. She needed to go to the bathroom, but she held off, afraid to wake him and spoil her own pleasure in studying him. There was no tension now in his face. His lips were full, his cheeks smooth and relaxed and there were no lines across his high forehead. He looked innocent.

He had not appeared that way when they had first talked, standing together near the lectern while the auditorium of the Hillel Center filled up. She saw how he recognized and smiled at most of the women students as they filed into the room. It was a smile that lingered on his lips as if it meant something secret.

"Are they your groupies?" she had laughed.

He smiled down at her with that same intense concentration and she felt her knees weaken.

"Oh, you know how undergraduates like to fall in love with their professors. It's the same with priests—all very romantic and safe." He kept hold of her with his gray eyes.

"Not that safe!" she answered, wanting to shock him for being so sure of himself. "Some of my worst lovers have been professors." It was not true, but she felt like being outrageous, and she kept it up, fabricating stories of academic liaisons while his eyes widened and lost their confidence.

"Then there was the affair I had a couple of years ago with a history professor at NYU—a full professor—and we had to do it, you know, in his office because I couldn't very well take him back to my dorm and he was married. So we'd lock ourselves into his office, but every time we did the phone would start ringing. I think his wife knew. She was in the Psych Department and I think she had some kind of extrasensory perception and knew when her husband was getting it on with . . . ."

He raised his hand and signaled her to stop. She did, in midsentence, looking up at him with her mouth open and her eyes shiny.

"What's your name again?" he asked.

"Deborah. Deborah Laste."

"Deborah, why are you giving me all this bullshit? Because I'm the Catholic priest?"

She shook her head. He had seen through her game and she felt young and foolish.

"Why then?" He leaned closer to her.

"Because I like you," she whispered.

"And I like you, Deborah. You're very attractive. Now how about having coffee with me after this lecture? Or won't your rabbi let you go out with Catholics?" He was smiling, teasing her back.

She smiled too, recovering her poise. "We won't tell him."

"Good! And we'll keep it quiet from the Bishop."

And for a while, they had.

When he woke, coming suddenly out of his brief nap, her face was only inches from his and she kissed him softly.

"What time is it?" he asked quickly.

"You've only been asleep a few minutes," she answered. "We have plenty of time."

He slid out from under her weight and began again to make love to her. He always moved too quickly for her, rushed her towards her climax, as if there wasn't enough time and they had to make love before they were caught. She knew also that he couldn't control his passion for her, and that, too, excited her and made her afraid of him.

She lay back, enjoying the sheer pleasure of his lips on her as he moved slowly down her body. Then he was kissing the smooth, cushiony web of pubic hair and she trembled as he touched her clitoris, once, quickly, with the tip of his tongue. Then he settled himself between her legs and began the steady rhythm he knew she loved and she lost herself in the pleasure until she shuddered and ran her fingers through his hair, seizing him.

At that, he sat back, pulled her buttocks onto his knees and she guided him into her. He handled her with such ease, supporting her weight easily. Gradually, slowly, he entered her, moving through the tight rings of her vagina. They began to move together, slowly at first, then he pushed harder and faster and her breath quickened and she wrapped her arms around his neck and squeezed.

Now she was telling him to hurry, begging him to come, and he was afraid that he wouldn't. It had happened before, when he began to think of what he was doing with Deborah and guilt swept over him.

But this time it was the brown eyes of Betty Sue Wadkins

that filled his mind. She was calling to him, calling him Stephen, and he closed his eyes and took her nipple in his mouth and she moaned as they both slid over the edge together. The semen pouring into her body had a life of its own.

Saturday afternoon confessions at Saint John of the Cross were two hours of schoolchildren with their venial sins and women with their worries about birth control. Stephen had decided years before that the pill wouldn't send his penitents to hell and he told them so. Now he noticed that whenever he heard confessions the line outside of his box was filled with women.

Still, by five o'clock on the wintry day the line had dwindled and the church was empty. He would wait a few more minutes for stragglers, he thought, and turned on the light in the small cubicle to read his breviary, but he couldn't concentrate. He kept thinking of Deborah. It had been a mistake calling her, for they had agreed not to see each other until he had decided about staying in the priesthood. Betty Sue Wadkins had frightened him, but he wondered whether he had just used that as an excuse.

He bowed his head and whispered, "Lord, have mercy; Lord, have mercy; Christ, have mercy on me." He kept praying, saying over and over the simple prayer, calming himself down.

Still, it was not easy for him to turn to God. He had not kept his vow of chastity and, worse, had flaunted his disobedience. Yet now he felt remorseful. Whatever people thought out in the world, even a young priest like him felt the sacredness of his vows, and the scandal of a priest who had a woman. If he left the Church he could marry Deborah. He had only to make the choice. It was not his love that shamed him, but his double life.

Yet he stalled off the final decision, for the truth was he

could not live without his faith any better than he could live without Deborah. Would God hear the tainted prayers of such a priest?

Father Kinsella heard the heavy front doors of the church open and slam shut, then footsteps echoing through the huge building. One more parishioner, he thought, coming for a last-minute absolution before Sunday mass and Holy Communion.

And what gave him the right to forgive anyone? He knew the church's theological position, that as a priest he was just Christ's representative and it was God, not him, who absolved. Still. He gave the penance, the Hail Marys and the Our Fathers. He held the power to forgive, to make the judgment and resolve the guilt.

But who could forgive *him?* His was an unforgivable sin growing on his soul like cancer. He flipped off the light and waited in the dark for the penitent.

The door opened and closed in the confessional box next to him and he heard the person kneel in the dark enclosure. He knew by the walk and the movement that it was a young man and he prepared himself for a list of sins against purity: wet dreams and masturbation; teenage girls in the back seats of cars. Stephen leaned forward and placed his ear against the grate and waited for the words of guilt.

"Bless me, Father, for I have sinned." The young man's voice was hesitant.

"Yes, son," Father Kinsella spoke up, encouraging.

"This is my first confession in a few years . . ." The voice trailed off.

He was not, the priest realized now, someone from the parish. Stephen understood the situation: the young man was afraid to confess to his parish priest and had driven into the mountains to find a church where he could be anonymous.

"Would you like me to help you go through the commandments?" the priest asked. "There's no need to number how many times; I can give you a general absolution."

"There's only one, Father." The young man paused.

"Yes?"

"I've had sex, y'know, with . . ."

"A young girl?" the priest asked, trying to help the boy. He always hated these prying questions, but if he was to give absolution, he needed to know the severity of the sin.

"No, it wasn't like that," the boy whispered.

"Oh!" The priest hesitated. "Was she married, son?"

"Father, it was a guy."

The priest tensed and he asked carefully, "And how often?"

"Whenever we could. In his house or mine, at school, y'know, in the locker room." He answered matter-of-factly.

"Is this over, son? Have you made a firm resolution?" He was having trouble talking to the boy and he slipped into the Church terminology.

"A resolution about what, Father?" The boy sounded curious.

"Your relationship with this other young man. Is it over?"

"I love him," the boy whispered through the grate.

"It's against God's law, son. A close friendship between two men is fine and wonderful, but when it involves the sex act . . . it becomes unnatural."

"We aren't hurting anyone," the boy argued. "He's my best friend, and, well, we both want to."

"Do you have any female friends?"

"You mean girl friends? Sure, but I don't sleep with them or anything. I'm gay, Father. I know that and it doesn't bother me. If they'd just leave us alone, that's all."

"Who, son?"

"People! Everyone! We aren't some goddam freaks." He began to cry.

"Easy, son, take your time." Father Kinsella leaned back

in his chair to wait. He wanted the young man to cry and calm himself with tears. Besides, he had nothing to tell him, no advice. In the eyes of the Church, the boy had committed an unnatural act.

In the dark cubicle, Father Kinsella closed his eyes and whispered the Lord's Prayer, saying the words so he'd be forced to concentrate, but one memory kept coming to mind, slipping through his conscience like a nightmare, always part of him and threatening his life.

"Can't you tell me what to do?" the young man asked. "I won't stop seeing him," he added quickly.

"I know this friendship is important to you, but in time, I think, you'll see that the relationship is destructive. Any real happiness you can hope for in this life or the hereafter comes from living within God's natural order."

"Bullshit!" the young man snapped. "If God made me this way, it's his fault, not mine."

"You have a choice." Father Kinsella kept speaking, reasoning, "We all have a choice. You're not alone. Homosexual tendencies are part of us all. It's our decision what we do about it, how we act."

"How do you know?" the young man challenged.

"We all have the same emotions, son. Every day I face the desires of the flesh, just like you." He had a brief flash of Deborah lying naked in the small room. "Sometimes the flesh is weak and we fall from grace, but we have to remember that God will forgive us. The forgiveness of God is what the Catholic Church is all about."

He was whispering fast and leaning forward, his head braced against the grate. "We can't despair, son. We have to believe in God and his mercy. He understands our failings and weaknesses. He'll help us." The priest spoke with conviction, for in his heart it was what he tried to believe.

"Father, are you okay?"

"Yes, yes, I'm fine." The priest sat up and took a deep

breath. Now he just felt cold throughout his body. A door must have been left open at the back of the church. "It's up to you, son," he said. "You have to decide. It's like that in all our lives. It's our choices; we choose the lives we live."

"Father?" the young man whispered into the grate. "Am I absolved? Can I receive Holy Communion?"

"Yes, son, you're absolved." Father Kinsella made the sign of the cross in the dark. He mumbled the words of absolution, saying, "Go with God."

"But you didn't give me my penance. What prayers do I say?"

"You've suffered enough," answered the priest, his mind elsewhere. "What you have to live with is penance enough."

"Like you, huh, Father?"

"What?" The priest turned his head and leaned closer to the wooden grate. It was then that he smelled the young man's stench, and it was as if someone had pulled the lid off a garbage can, exposing the rancid odors of gamy fish and dank sewage.

"You know what I mean." The boy's voice was low. "You like having your cock sucked, don't you, Father?"

"Who the hell is this?" The priest pushed open the door of his confessional and bolted into the aisle. The empty building was dark, lit only by the red flickering sanctuary candles, and the twin spotlights that pinpointed the massive crucifix over the center altar.

Father Kinsella could see the young man's shadow racing down the aisle and he cut across the middle of the church to stop him at the vestibule. But the boy was unbelievably fast. As Stephen pulled open the heavy door to the vestibule, he felt the cold wind blow into the church and swirl around him. The boy was already out the front door, and by the time Stephen dashed down the steps the street was deserted.

Slowly he climbed the steps again, locking the church's heavy front doors behind him. Confessions were over. He

walked up the aisle to the altar, hoping the boy hadn't
stolen anything before entering the confessional.

The red flickering vigil lights made the gold tabernacle
glow in their soft light and the heavy wooden crucifix
hanging fifty feet over the center altar seemed to float
unsupported in the darkness.

The crucifix had been handmade by one of the parishioners, a mountain craftsman who had suspended it from the
domed ceiling by a single thick cord of rope. When Father
Kinsella had arrived at Saint John's, the pastor had pointed
it out with pride. Father Kinsella thought it looked gro-
tesque with its distorted Christ figure, the blood dripping
from the five wounds and the crown of thorns so realistically
carved that the tips of the thorns could draw blood. The
figure looked too real, like a victim of an automobile wreck.

"It makes the parishioners recall the suffering of Christ,"
Father Driscoll had explained, looking up.

"And it keeps them in line, right, Father?" the young
priest said. To him it depicted a vengeful religion, and he
told the pastor what he thought of that kind of Catholicism.

"And you'd do away with sin, I suppose." The pastor
raised his eyebrows.

"I don't see any value in keeping people in perpetual fear.
I don't see why we have to fill the church for mass with a
quivering congregation, and have people afraid to enjoy
life."

"Life isn't here to be enjoyed," the old priest answered.
"It's our penance for obtaining Heaven—or have you forgotten your Baltimore catechism?"

"I'm trying, Father; I'm trying."

The pastor had not been amused.

Father Kinsella stepped onto the altar platform. From the
corner of his eye he caught a light flash on the hanging
crucifix and he glanced up and saw that the massive Christ
figure, ten feet high, had begun to swing wildly back and
forth across the vaulted ceiling, gaining speed, arching high,

then dropping through space like a high-wire artist. And before he could even realize what might be creating the bizarre pendulum, the heavy rope snapped and the carved figure of suffering crashed down like a sledgehammer.

The crucifix hit the marble altar stone with its enormous weight and sent the gold tabernacle careening to the floor. Then the cross tumbled toward the young priest, the huge figure of Christ, taller than he was himself, falling forward out of the darkness as if to embrace him.

Backing away, terrified, Stephen tripped on the altar platform, landing against the altar rail. At that moment the wooden crucifix hit the floor and broke apart and the head of Jesus Christ, crowned with thorns, bounced off the hardwood and rolled across the platform, slamming against his body. The sharp thorns pierced his skin, drawing blood, and he cried out in the empty church as if impaled.

"It doesn't look like it's been cut." The pastor fingered the heavy rope. "There are no knife marks."

"We'd better call the police," Stephen said.

"No, wait, let's think a minute."

"Father, I told you what happened today. Obviously that kid and his friends are responsible. He kept me busy with that crazy confession of his while the others did this. The young priest was impatient.

"We don't know if they did anything to the crucifix," answered the pastor. "For sure, no one has tampered with this rope," he added firmly. "I'll have another crucifix made. Maybe it's even possible to glue this figure together. What I want you to do is clean up this mess so by tomorrow's masses no one in the parish will know we've had trouble here."

"But they *should* know," Father Kinsella said, bewildered by the pastor's response. "Shouldn't we warn the parishioners that Saint John's is in trouble?"

"No! No!" The pastor kept shaking his head. "Saint John's isn't under attack." He stared angrily at his assistant. "It's you, young man. You're the one under attack."

"What do you mean, Father?"

From his back pocket, Father Driscoll pulled out a piece of paper. "I found this on the window of the parish station wagon just before I came over." He unfolded the paper and handed it to Father Kinsella. It was a short message, written in the same awkward printing as the first note in the collection basket.

GET OUT OF TOWN
JEW LOVER

4

Thursday, February 16

Father Kinsella had just turned the heat on under the meat stew that the housekeeper had left them for supper when the telephone rang. He picked up the extension in the kitchen.

"Saint John's. Father Kinsella speaking."

"Hello?" The man's voice was hesitant and confused.

"Yes? This is Saint John's rectory. Father Kinsella speaking. May I help you?" He tried to sound friendly.

"You the fella that come see my daughter?" The voice was high-pitched and unsure.

"Oh, yes ... Mr. Wadkins? This is Stephen Kinsella. May I help you? Is there anything wrong, sir?"

"Betty Sue ... She's real bad today. ..."

"Betty Sue?" He glanced at the parish calendar on the wall over the phone and remembered it was Thursday, the beginning of Christ's passion.

"Ain't never seen her so bad like this." The father seemed dazed.

"Mr. Wadkins," Stephen answered quickly, "is there anything we can do for you?"

"Don't know, really, but if you fellas want to come and have yourselves a look. I tell you, Ma and me, we're plumb lost these last weeks. She's gettin' worse and worse." Behind the slow, steady mountain drawl, the man sounded desperate.

"Mr. Wadkins, I'll tell Father Driscoll and we'll be out to your place as soon as we can."

"Well, thank you thar. I'll be waitin' on you." He hung up without a good-bye.

Rufus opened the door and let them into the Wadkins' house. The front room was again filled with men and women who watched silently as the two priests entered.

At the bedroom door, Stephen stopped Rufus and asked, "Who are these people?"

"Family mainly," he answered without looking up. "Close kin from around here on Blue Haze. They've been coming over lately, since Betty Sue started getting worse." He did not sound like the others, Father Kinsella noticed, listening to the young man's voice. He had none of their mountain drawl.

"And how is she?" the pastor asked, not bothering to lower his voice.

Rufus shook his head. "Bad. I've never seen her so bad." He glanced at Father Kinsella, then added insolently as he pushed open the door, "But you'll save her, won't you, Father?"

Betty Sue was kneeling in her bed, praying. She was tilted forward at an awkward angle, as if leaning against something. Her hands were folded and her face lifted in rapture,

eyes closed in meditation. The priests moved slowly forward
and the parents stepped aside, giving them room near the
bed.

As they moved closer they could hear her soft whisper,
*"Behold, the hour is coming, and has already come, for you to be
scattered, each one to his own house, and to leave me alone. But I am
not alone, because the Father is with me."*

The priests glanced at each other. Her words were those
of Jesus, praying in the Garden of Gethsemane the night
before he was crucified.

She turned her face toward them. Now she was no longer
seized with rapture. Her brown eyes were sad and tearful as
she continued, speaking directly to the two priests, *"Amen, I
say to you, one of you will betray me."*

Rufus slid up next to the priests and whispered quickly,
"She thinks she's Christ at the Last Supper. She doesn't just
see Christ anymore, the way she used to. Now she thinks she
is him."

Father Kinsella inched his way closer. "Betty Sue, can you
hear me?" he asked tentatively.

She turned immediately towards him, her brown eyes
filled with love. *"Stephen, Stephen,"* she said softly. *"Behold—
Satan has desired to have you, that he may sift you as wheat. But I
have prayed for thee, that thy faith may not fail."*

Father Kinsella jerked back. Again it was Christ's words,
only she was talking to him, not Simon Peter.

Betty Sue was still kneeling, leaning forward with her
arms crossed and her face consumed in sorrow. How could
she stay so rigidly immobile? the priest wondered.

"My soul is sad, even unto death," she declared. *"Wait here and
watch with me."*

Father Kinsella recognized the words from the gospel of
Saint Matthew. But how could this uneducated girl know
them, and by heart?

Now she was crying silently and he could see the strain of Christ's passion on her face. The tears streamed down her cheeks and she cried out, as if pulling the words from deep inside her. *"Father, if it is possible, let this cup pass away from me. Yet not as I will, but as thou willest."*

Father Driscoll dropped to his knees beside the bed and took out his rosary beads. "Our Father, who art in heaven, hallowed be thy name," he began, bowing his head as he said The Lord's Prayer.

Stephen slipped silently to his knees next to the pastor, but he did not join in the rosary. He could not take his eyes from the young woman: she was radiant looking in Christ's passion, transported by his agony in the garden. It was all incomprehensible to Stephen.

Betty Sue was finishing Christ's prayer to his father. *"My Father, if this cup cannot pass away unless I drink it, thy will be done."* She bowed her head as if in contemplation and unexpectedly collapsed, falling forward on the wide bed.

Stepping quickly between the two priests, Rufus slipped his arms under her slender body and picked Betty Sue up with more ease than Father Kinsella would have imagined possible, placing her gently on the white sheets. Her mother also stepped forward and the two waited expectantly.

Betty Sue was still praying, muttering words from the gospel, when she began to gasp. Her whole body started to tremble, then shake, and Stephen thought she was suffering a seizure, and then he saw it and he began to tremble too.

She was sweating blood, tiny drops of it breaking out on her forehead and running down her cheeks, leaving a bloody trail.

The bloody perspiration broke in tiny drops on her flushed cheeks. He thought of the words of Saint Luke, describing Christ's agony in the garden, "and his sweat became as drops of blood running down upon the ground."

Her cheeks and forehead were crimson now. It was the same aromatic blood that the week before had oozed from her five wounds—the same scent that had gushed from the mark on the letter. The smell filled his nostrils, choked him with its relentless fragrance, and he stood to get away from the scent when Rufus turned quickly to him and ordered, "Hold her feet!"

Betty Sue was tossing on the bed, swinging her body wildly from side to side. Her arms and legs had broken out in the same terrifying sweat; the blood ran down her neck as well, and her nightgown was suffused with the blood that was pouring from her breasts, her stomach, from every inch of her flesh. It glistened on her skin, and as she shook in her agony, it flew off her body in drops, staining Stephen's white collar as he looked down at her.

Rufus seized one arm, her mother the other, and Stephen rushed to the bottom of the bed and grabbed Betty Sue's ankles. They were slender in his hands, but he had to strain to hold her down. The wounds in her palms and arches broke open and the thick blood spilled onto his hands, making her skin slippery, and he was afraid that he couldn't hold her, that she would tear out of his grip and somehow do damage to herself.

Slowly her struggling subsided. He could feel the strength leave her legs as she calmed down, weary from her effort. The thin cotton material of her nightgown was bloodsoaked and it clung to her, outlining her breasts and thighs. Father Kinsella could see the impression of her nipples on the cloth and the dark triangle of her sex. He glanced away and let go of her ankles. He was exhausted as well, and his fingers ached.

She lay still, but her body kept heaving as she gasped for breath. The bloody sweat was drying on her body and he watched as her mother tenderly cleaned her face and arms.

He leaned against the wall gaining back his own strength and Betty Sue turned her haggard face to him and uttered Christ's last words in the garden of Gethsemane, *"Sleep on now, and take your rest! It is enough; the hour has come. Behold, the Son of Man is betrayed into the hands of sinners."*

5

February 18

Saturday

"If you wouldn't mind, I'd like to examine Betty Sue."
Dr. Lear paused. Stephen had told him that the parents
were suspicious of doctors, and he had been careful when
asking questions about the child's medical history. From
what Stephen had told him when he telephoned the university Medical Center, the girl was an interesting case, and he
didn't want to ruin his opportunity to examine her.

"You won't hurt her or anything?" asked the father.

Jim Lear smiled. "No, sir, and I'd like Mrs. Wadkins with
me in the bedroom."

The father glanced at his wife and reluctantly nodded.
"Okay, then, but she ain't used to strangers, especially no
doctor."

"I understand, sir." He picked up his bag and waited to
be led into the girl's bedroom.

"We'll wait here, Jim," said Stephen. It had been his idea
to have his friend come up to Blue Haze Ridge.

"The girl is not physically sick, Stephen," Father Driscoll had replied, when Stephen had told him about Dr. Lear. "Don't forget the bleeding envelope. There's more here than just illness."

"You mean a miracle? The presence of God."

The pastor had nodded yes. Stephen knew that Driscoll wanted to believe that Betty Sue was a true stigmatic saint, but so far he had avoided discussing that with the pastor. There were other, much likelier explanations, and, with Jim Lear's help, he would find them.

Dr. Lear ducked his head and walked into the bedroom. In the far corner he saw Betty Sue sitting up in bed under heavy quilts. She was being entertained by a young man who sat on a footstool juggling red balls.

Mrs. Wadkins brushed by and spoke sharply to the young man. "Rufus, you leave Betty Sue, hear! This man's a doctor and he wants to look on her."

Rufus put the balls away and glanced furtively at Jim Lear as he hurried from the room.

The girl watched the doctor with wide brown eyes. Jim Lear had seen that look on other young patients' faces, that mixture of fear and anticipation.

"Hello, Betty Sue," he said smiling. She was a beautiful young woman; Steve had not told him that.

"My name is Dr. Lear. I'm from the university, from the medical school."

"Do you know Stephen?" she asked immediately.

"Stephen?" He paused. "You mean Father Kinsella?"

"Yeah, y'know, Stephen!" She kept smiling.

"Yes, I know Stephen; he asked me to come see you."

"Is he here?" She looked first at the doctor and then at her mother.

She didn't look sick, the young doctor thought, watching her. Her complexion was good—beautiful, in fact—and she was alert and responsive.

"He's with Pa, Betty Sue," her mother answered. "You can see him later. First let this doctor look at your sores. Do like he says."

Betty Sue shook her head, "This man ain't gonna touch me, Ma, unless Stephen's right here." Her lips curved into a pout.

Doctor Lear set his bag on the stool and sat carefully on the edge of the bed. The young woman shifted to give him room, moving, he noticed, without pain. Her hands were above the quilt and he spotted the small dark sores on the back of each one. "You'd like Stephen in the room, Betty Sue?" he asked softly.

She nodded firmly, watching for his reaction, her brown eyes still showing an edge of fear.

Doctor Lear turned to the mother and said, "Would you ask Father Kinsella to step inside?" He reached over and opened his bag while waiting for the priest.

"Hello, Stephen," she whispered as he came in.

"Betty Sue would like you here, Father," Lear explained, speaking formally. Then he turned back to the girl.

"Betty Sue, how old are you?" he asked.

"Seventeen. I'll be eighteen come fall." She smiled, eager now to be helpful.

"Steve—Father Kinsella says your hands and feet have been bleeding."

"And my side." She touched herself.

"Do you know why, Betty Sue?"

The young woman shook her head.

"When do you bleed?" He spoke softly so as not to upset her.

"On Fridays mostly."

"Every Friday?"

She nodded.

"And for how long?"

"I think all afternoon. ..."

"You're not sure?"

"She ain't right then, Doc." Her mother came forward and Jim Lear turned toward her.

"When she gets like that she don't know where she is," the mother continued, speaking rapidly, as if she had a lot to tell him. "Her mind, y'know, goes crazy like and she sees things, you understand—things from the Bible. She don't make no sense a'tall." The woman sighed and swept her hand across the crown of her head, as if to put her hair in place. She was a thin woman, with high cheekbones and the tough skin that comes from years in the sun. He could see the worry on her face. Over the years it had become a part of her.

"When does she bleed from the sores?" he asked.

"On Friday, like she says. Hit starts at twelve thereabouts and ends around three, but she gets sick before that. She's sick, y'know, not feelin' good, gettin' pains in her joints and like, by Thursday night. She bleeds sometimes all night Thursday. Last week she was real bad." The mother shook her head. "I'm tellin' you, it's hard carin' for her and Pa, and doin' the chores 'bout the place. I got me a big wash every Saturday morning because of the bleeding and I ain't getting no younger. Course Rufus helps some with her, but I gotta change the girl and keep her clean."

"Oh, Ma, quiet! Hush now!" The young woman glanced at the doctor and Father Kinsella and then looked away, embarrassed.

"What about the pain?" Lear looked from the mother to Betty Sue. "When do you have pain?"

"I'm always havin' pain at first," she whispered, "but when I see things I don't feel nothin'. Everything is wonderful, and I'm happy." She smiled, looking past the doctor toward Father Kinsella.

"Betty Sue?" The doctor pulled her attention back. "How many years have you had these bleedings?"

"It started first when I was twelve, I think, but it wasn't so bad. Then this fall it got real bad."

"Lordy," said her mother, "sometimes I think she's gonna bleed herself to death."

"And do you know why it started?"

Betty Sue shook her head, but the doctor noticed a slight hesitation and he asked again, pressing her to talk.

"Maybe it was the snakes," she answered softly.

"The snakes?"

"I got bitten by snakes when I was twelve."

"Do you remember how?"

She shook her head. "I got bitten by snakes in the Pit. I don't recall nothin'." She looked away, obviously unwilling to say more.

Jim Lear did not press her. "Betty Sue," he said gently, "I'd like to examine you and see if we can find out why you have these bleedings."

She nodded and smiled, cheerful again. "If Stephen wants you to examine me, it's okay." She glanced at the young priest, her brown eyes bright. She sat up in bed and reached to pull her wool nightgown over her head.

"No, that's not necessary," the doctor said. He was used to having young women at the university flirt outrageously while he examined them, but the girl's behavior toward the priest surprised him.

"But ain't you gonna look at me?"

"Yes, but it's not necessary to undress. Let me see your hands." She was just childlike, he decided, not immodest.

He took both her hands in his and looked at the sores on the backs and in her palms. The sores were in the middle of the palms and went through her hands, as if she had been jabbed with spikes. They were round, the size of dimes, but not inflamed or bleeding. A thin, transparent, jellylike shield covered them. He pressed his finger across one of the sores to see if there was blood under the transparent mark. The redness didn't disappear. It wasn't just a blood vessel exposed to the skin.

He placed his fingers on her wrist and checked the second hand of his watch. She was silent as he counted. Her pulse was fast and her hands were sweaty. Behind her calm talk, the girl was afraid.

"We'll take your blood pressure," he explained as he reached into his bag and took out the blood pressure cuff. He kept talking as he wrapped the Velcro sleeve around her left forearm and pumped up the cuff. Her blood pressure was 130 over 90. Normal. "No problem," he said smiling.

Then he stood up. "Betty Sue, could you sit up and swing your legs over the side of the bed?" He stepped away and watched to see if she had difficulty, but she tossed off the quilt and sat up quickly.

Her nightgown was pulled up, exposing long and slender legs. She had looked small in the bed, but now he could see she was tall, over five-seven. He checked her legs for bruises. It was possible, he thought, that her parents beat her, but her legs were white and unblemished. He crouched down and took hold of her bare feet. They had the same dime-sized sores on her arches and the soles. He pressed his hand against the bottom of her right foot, asking, "Does this hurt?"

"No. It hurts some when I walk, that's all."

He reached into his bag and took out the ophthalmoscope. "I'm just going to look into your eyes with this," he explained. "A light will shine, but it won't hurt you."

"There ain't nothin' wrong with my eyes. I can see fine," she giggled.

"I know, but this instrument tells us about you."

"Like what?"

The doctor straddled her legs and directed the pinpoint beam into her eyes. "Well," he answered slowly as he

worked, "it shows us if there is any bleeding at the back of
your eyes, you know, like you have in your hands and feet."

"My side, too," she added.

"Yes, your side; well, we'll get around to looking at your
side." He moved away and placed the ophthalmoscope back
in his bag. There had been no visible bleeding in the veins
at the back of the retina.

He picked up the otoscope and bending over looked into
her ears and nose for signs of blood. "Okay, Betty Sue, stick
out your tongue." There were no red spots on her tongue or
bleeding at the back of her mouth or on her gums. Then
with the tips of his fingers, he carefully palpated her neck,
searching for enlarged lymph nodes, and moved his fingers
down the clavicular chain searching for a hard mass of
matted nodes which could mean a tumor in the lungs or
even leukemia. But her glands were fine.

"Let's look at that sore on your chest. Untie the top of
your nightgown, please." Betty Sue quickly loosened the
bow and slipped the gown off her shoulders, pulling it down
off her full breasts. As she did, she glanced over at the priest
and smiled. Doctor Lear moved to the right, blocking her
view of Father Kinsella.

"Lie down now, Betty Sue," he said, "and get comfortable." He watched her as she stretched herself out. She was
well developed, all right, with fine long limbs and firm
breasts. Except for her strange sores, he couldn't see anything wrong.

"Here's my sore," she said, arching her left shoulder to
display the long, thin gash on her side. She cupped her hand
under the left breast and lifted it, as if to give the doctor
more room to see, but he knew without looking that her eyes
were on the priest.

Doctor Lear touched the sore experimentally. It was six
inches long and covered with the same transparent skin as

the others. He moved his hand down her body and felt her abdomen.

"Ouch, that tickles." She squirmed under his fingers.

"Inhale, Betty Sue," he said as he slowly pressed her right side, feeling for her liver's edge to flip by his fingers as he pressed down. The liver wasn't enlarged.

"Now turn on your right side," he directed. He pressed his hand against her left side, saying, "Relax and take a deep breath." He could feel her spleen coming up at his fingers like an iceberg. No problem. "Okay, Betty Sue, pull up your nightgown and sit on the edge of the bed."

He took the neurological hammer from his bag and checked the reflexes on her biceps and softly hit her Achilles tendon and her knees. Her reflexes were all right. He took a pin and jabbed her lightly on the flank of her left leg and at the same spot on her right leg. "Close your eyes and tell me where I'm touching," he said, and ran smoothly through a series of pin pricks. Again, all okay.

"Can you walk for me?" he asked.

"Well, it hurts, y'know." She smiled gamely. "But if you want me to, I'll try . . ." She slid off the bed and on tiptoe moved slowly, holding out the edges of her nightgown. She was fine until she went by Father Kinsella, and then she stumbled. The priest caught her in his arms.

"Betty Sue, are you all right?" Father Kinsella asked gently, holding her by the shoulders as she leaned against him. Her head was pressed against his shoulder and she smelled strongly of woman, startling him.

"Yes—thank you," she answered and walked back to her bed.

Doctor Lear stood and sighed, "Well, I can't seem to find anything that might suggest why you have these sores, but I'll take some blood and a urine sample for the university lab to check."

"Are you gonna take it all?" she asked, watching the

syringe he had inserted in her vein fill up with blood.

"Oh, no, thirty cc's isn't much at all." He slipped out the needle and placed a cotton swatch on the vein. "Hold this position for a moment, Betty Sue," he said, bending her arm up.

"Now I want you to go into the bathroom and see if you can produce some urine for me, okay?" He handed her a small laboratory jar.

"Urine?" She frowned.

"Yes. When you go to the bathroom—you pass liquid."

"I'll get her, Doc." The mother took the jar. "Come on, Betty Sue." She took her daughter by the elbow and helped her off the bed.

"Well, what do you think, Jim?" Stephen asked when the two women had left the room.

The doctor shook his head, speaking softly as he repacked his bag. "It's intriguing, and I'm baffled. She shows nothing wrong on the physical exam. There's no bleeding in her body except in those spots and if she had some leukemia or blood dyserasia she would almost certainly be bleeding from her gums or nose. Her difficulty in walking seems only because of the sores on her feet; there's no muscle weakness or neurological disorder.

"I might think she was a hysteric, but she's willing to talk to me and let me examine her; and she doesn't appear crazy, just sexually provocative. But that's not at all unusual for a girl her age." He shook his head. "Let's see what a hematologist can do with these blood samples. I'll get back to you later this week." He snapped his bag closed and added, smiling, "There's one thing I'm positive about. She's nuts about you. I think you've got yourself another convert, Steve."

Stephen knocked on the front door of the Wadkins house and stepped back so anyone looking out a window could see who it was. He knew the family wouldn't be expecting him, especially since he had just been to the house that morning.

He hadn't told Father Driscoll he was driving out to Blue Haze Ridge for the pastor, he knew, would have forbidden it, or worse, come with him. Father Kinsella wasn't sure why, but he sensed that, flirtatiousness aside, Betty Sue wanted to talk to him.

The front door opened a few inches and the priest saw Rufus standing in the dark, a thin shadow behind the screen.

"Hello, Rufus. Is Mr. Wadkins around?"

"They've gone over to the Phelpses' 'bout an hour ago. You come to see Betty Sue?" His voice was friendly.

"Yes, but now I'm not sure—not if her parents aren't here."

"Oh, it's all right." He pushed open the screen door.

Father Kinsella moved hesitantly into the living room, then stopped abruptly, thinking it would be better if he didn't see Betty Sue without at least one of her parents present. He turned around and caught the hired hand watching him.

It was only a moment, but for an instant Stephen thought he saw Rufus's eyes flare up like egg whites blistering on a skillet, glaring at the priest without focus and consumed in their own intense heat. Father Kinsella blinked. Then Rufus was smiling again and his eyes were sky blue.

"This way, please," he said invitingly, as. if he were the host.

Betty Sue was in bed playing cards. The deck was spread across the quilt and she had her legs tucked under her. She was wearing the same dark blue nightgown and her long blond hair had been combed out.

Seeing her looking so clean and lovely, the priest realized what good care she was receiving from her parents. It was not common among mountain children. Often on the back roads, he'd pass tarpaper shacks and spot scrawny kids hanging from the porch rails, shoeless and in rags. But this young woman looked like a captive princess, immaculately dressed and cared for. Perhaps, he thought, her parents did realize in a primitive way that something special had happened to their daughter.

"Oh, Stephen!" Betty Sue's eyes widened at seeing the priest. "I was hoping you'd come back; Rufus said you might." She leaned forward to clear away the playing cards and Father Kinsella glanced around at Rufus, but the hired hand hadn't followed him into the room. The bedroom door was closed and the priest was alone with the young woman.

"Betty Sue, you're looking fine." Father Kinsella moved toward the straight back chair near her bed. He had not done much visiting of the sick and he was still unsure of the role.

"Sit here, Stephen!" She patted the edge of the mattress.

Father Kinsella paused. The afternoon sun had reached the back of the house and it lit the room with a pale yellow winter light that enveloped Betty Sue in its soft glow. She looked startlingly beautiful. For a moment, he forgot her affliction and just enjoyed the pleasure of looking at her.

She was sitting up in the bed, inviting him with her smile to come closer, and he could feel her adolescent sexuality permeating the room like steam heat, leaving him breathless. He grabbed the straight back chair and moved it nearer, but kept his distance from the bed.

"You're looking fine," he said again, his voice slipping into the cheery tone he always found himself using in hospitals.

Betty Sue nodded. Her smile was infectious and he smiled back. She had not let the long misery of her affliction dishearten her. She had, he could tell, a good-naturedness that drew people to her.

"I'm always fine when the bleeding stops. See!" She

turned her palms so he could see the marks, the thin shield of transparent scar tissue that covered the wounds protecting, but leaving them exposed. They were like windows to her strange mystery, he thought.

"And what have you been doing?" Father Kinsella leaned forward in the chair, smiling, but still not relaxed.

"Rufus has been showing me card tricks. He can do all kinds. It helps pass the time." She picked up the cards, shuffled them, and set them aside.

"But you're able to get out of bed, aren't you?"

She nodded. "Rufus made me some shoes. I can walk without any pain." She looked towards the windows. "I like to walk in the woods, especially come spring, but Ma won't let me go out much." She sighed and Father Kinsella caught a moment of sadness beneath her sunny disposition.

"Betty Sue, do you think it was snakebites that did this?" The priest asked the question gently, afraid of upsetting her, but she replied quickly, matter-of-factly, "That's what Pa says."

"But you don't remember?"

She shook her head. "Rufus, he says I've been blessed."

"Blessed?" Father Kinsella frowned. "Why did he say that?"

She shrugged and looked away. "I don't want to talk about it." She glanced at Father Kinsella, pleading with her brown eyes.

She was so vulnerable, he realized, a victim of whatever had happened to her. He had to resist a desire to go and shelter her in his arms.

"Betty Sue," he whispered, "I'll try and help you if you want me to."

Her smile brightened and the threat of tears passed. "Can you find out what's wrong with me?" She slid down into the pillows and curled up, but her eyes never left the priest.

"Well, first I have to ask you some questions." The priest spoke quickly, eager for the chance, and she nodded submissively.

"Betty Sue," he began, "do you believe in God?"

"Of course I do!"

"And that Jesus Christ is our Saviour?"

She nodded and he continued, working his way through a catechism of simple beliefs shared by all Christians. He wasn't trying to convert her, but to discover how much she knew about God and the passion of Jesus Christ.

"How did Christ die?" he asked.

"He was crucified."

"Where?"

She paused, lowering her eyes as she pondered, and the priest took in the lovely line of her cheekbones and the thick brush of her eyelashes. Then she burst out, smiling and pleased with herself, "In the Holy Land."

"Where's the Holy Land?"

"Jerusalem. He was crucified on a cross in Jerusalem." She nodded smugly.

Father Kinsella smiled at her pleasure and said, flattering her, "You know your Bible history, Betty Sue."

"I have a book," she explained. "Do you want to see it?"

"Yes, I'd like to very much."

While he was still answering, she ducked down over the the side of the bed, and came up with a wooden stick that she struck sharply against the wall. A small thump sounded through the thin walls and Rufus opened the bedroom door. It was as if he had been waiting outside.

"Rufus, get me my Bible book." She was the captive princess again, issuing orders. Her self-possession was amusing, the priest thought; he liked her style.

Rufus returned in a moment with the book. He moved so silently that Father Kinsella did not know he had returned until he spoke up in his young, almost girlish voice. "Anything else, Betty Sue?" he asked.

"No, Rufus, thanks." She was immediately engrossed in the large book, carefully turning the illustrated pages. There was something special she wanted to show the priest. "I haven't looked at this in a while," she explained, "but when I was first sick it helped pass the time." She glanced at Father Kinsella and her eyes held his for a moment longer than necessary, then she added, "Rufus would explain the pictures—y'know, tell me who everyone was. He's a mighty fine story teller and he made the whole Bible seem as if it actually happened."

"It *did* actually happen," Father Kinsella pointed out.

"Oh, yeah, but, y'know, that was a long time ago. Here!" She found what she was looking for and turned the huge book towards him.

It was the scene of Calvary, a two-page color spread of the Crucifixion. The three crosses were staged against a turbulent sky. Christ was looking toward the heavens, toward a bright shaft of sunlight in a darkened sky. The apostles were kneeling at the foot of the cross and the Blessed Virgin Mary, dressed in blue and surrounded by weeping women, was staring lovingly at her son.

In the background were horses and Roman soldiers and crowds of people. A few of the Roman soldiers were down on their knees shooting dice for Christ's garments, and low on the horizon was the city of Jerusalem. A dusty road led down from Calvary to the walled city.

"Isn't it a lovely picture!" exclaimed Betty Sue. "It's my favorite in the whole book. So much is happening! I use to look at that picture by the hour."

Father Kinsella thumbed through the glossy color pages. There were more full-page paintings depicting biblical history: The Last Supper, Palm Sunday, Christ walking on

water, Saint John the Baptist. He turned to the front pages
and saw the book was printed in Chicago, and written by
the Franciscans. The book had a Nihil Obstat and an
Imprimatur. How had it turned up in this Papist-fearing
corner of Appalachia? he wondered.

"Betty Sue, this book is beautiful. Where did you get it?"
he tried to ask offhandedly, as if the question had no
purpose.

"From Rufus. Rufus gave it to me right after I first got
sick. He said I was like Jesus."

"What did he mean?" Father Kinsella murmured. It was
his confessional tone: hushed and confidential.

She reached over for the book and flipped through the
pages until she found what she wanted. The priest got up
and stood beside the bed so he could see where she was
pointing. It was the scene of Christ being taken down from
the Cross. He lay in the Blessed Virgin Mary's arms.

"There!" She pointed to the wounds on Christ's hands
and feet and to the mark of the lance on his left side. "I
have the wounds of Jesus."

They were only inches apart as the priest leaned over the
bed, bracing himself against the headboard; he shifted his
gaze from the picture to her eyes. What he saw he had seen
in the eyes of many undergraduates at the university.
Overcome by the idea of being in love with a priest, they
would worship faithfully at the campus chapel on Sunday
mornings, memorizing his every gesture.

Until he had met Deborah Laste, he had found all this
teenage affection amusing. These young women, he knew,
were playing with their emotions, trying them out on
someone safe like a priest. They'd flirt, secure in an established code of conduct between them.

Deborah was different. She did not respect the prohibi-
tions about involvement with a priest and was not stopped

by what she called the mythology of the Catholic Church. Her love for him was simple and direct and it was the first sexual emotion that had ever really touched him. Afterward, nothing was the same. Ever since, he had been vulnerable to the world.

Father Kinsella moved abruptly away from the bed and sat down, at a safe distance from the girl, but when he looked again at her, his gray eyes flashed with excitement. "Betty Sue," he said, still whispering, intense in what he wanted to tell her, "the doctor who examined you this morning doesn't think there is anything medically wrong with you. It's possible, though, that there's a psychological explanation." Father Kinsella saw her puzzled frown and he tried again, "It's possible, Betty Sue, that you were bitten by snakes and while the snakes didn't cause your sores, that experience did disturb your mind so much it resulted in these strange afflictions. Or"—he paused, not even sure if he believed this himself—"or you might in some way be, as Rufus says, *blessed.* I just don't know, but if you'd let me, I'd like to find out." He stopped and waited for her to answer, but she only smiled knowingly, lowered her eyelashes, and was silent.

6

Monday, February 20

Father Kinsella watched the tall, effeminate university librarian walk back through the stacks toward him. The priest knew he should be more understanding, but he just didn't like the man. Now the librarian was shaking his head. Father Kinsella understood what that meant. There was a problem.

"We don't have much on the subject, Father Kinsella, but when you called this morning I did a quick look-see and it seems all the books we have—that's about eight or nine—have been checked out." He smiled regretfully across the library counter.

"All? But who would be doing work on stigmata?"

"Well, it is sort of the occult, and there's always a demand for those kinds of books, even among our students." He winced, as if appalled by the idea.

Father Kinsella leaned over the counter and asked confidentially, "Is there any way we can find out who might have those books?"

"Well, we're really not supposed to, but because it's you ..." The librarian rolled his eyes around to see who was within earshot and whispered, "We could get a readout on the computer and see." He smiled and motioned the priest to follow him.

Father Kinsella walked around the counter to the computer terminal and stood behind the librarian as he typed in the call numbers from the card catalog.

"These books on stigmata are all catalogued together," the librarian explained. "Therefore, the call numbers are close. See?" He pointed to the green numbers on the screen.

"What's that number next to them?"

"The student's I.D. Actually, it's his social security number; we use it as the I.D. number here at the university. Look, I thought so! It's the same I.D. for all the stigmata books. And it's a grad student. That tenth digit indicates the status of the borrower."

He jotted down the number and turned off the terminal. "Now we check this I.D. against a master list of names and addresses." Going back to his desk, he pulled out a bulky black ledger. "This is a printout of all the university I.D.s."

He paused to look at the number again and then flipped through the pages with long, fine fingers. "Here it is!" He sounded pleased. "It's a grad student—a Deborah Laste." The librarian frowned. "Would you like her address, Father?"

He hadn't planned on seeing Deborah. Father Driscoll had only given him permission to drive down to the city and pick up any books he could on stigmata. "But stay away from the Chancery," the pastor had said. "I don't want those boys to find out what we've got here. I'll tell them

when I'm good and ready." So he had just gone to the
university to check their library. That was all. It would do
neither Deborah nor him any good to see each other. He
knew what would happen if they met.

He left his car in the library parking lot and walked
across campus to her apartment. As he walked down the
block, he could see that she was home. The MGB was
parked in front and he could see a dim light in the upstairs
bedroom of the old Victorian house. He hadn't thought he
missed her until he'd realized she might not be home, and
now he skidded up the stairs in a rush to see her.

"Yes?" she asked, calling through the locked door when
he knocked.

"It's me," he answered. He was nervous standing outside
her door, afraid he'd be seen by other students in the
rooming house; still, it was outside her door that he had first
awkwardly kissed her.

When he had kissed her that first time she hadn't said
anything, just touched his cheek with the tips of her fingers
and disappeared into the dark apartment, leaving him
breathless in the hallway.

The next day he couldn't find her on campus and when
she didn't meet him for lunch at the Student Union, he
went to her place.

"Are you okay?" he had asked when she opened the door.

She was wearing a blue work shirt and cutoffs. Her feet
were bare and she had her hair braided. She didn't answer,
or look at him. She was carrying her cat, Percy, and she
only walked back inside, leaving him to follow and close the
door.

Her apartment was one large room with a high ceiling, a
fireplace, and windows facing north. Her bed was against

the rear wall, just springs and a mattress on the floor. She had been sitting on the bed: blankets were tossed aside and the pillows had been stacked to support her, but she did not go back there. Instead she let go of Percy, sat at her desk, and watched him survey the room.

The apartment was warm and inviting and stamped with her personality, filled with paintings and posters. Books were everywhere, on her desk—an unfinished door laid across yellow filing cabinets—and stacked on side tables and chairs. But it was not a dingy graduate student room. The apartment was tidy and snug and he immediately felt safe there, away from the world.

"You have a sexy apartment," he said to please her.

She reacted at once. "Come on, Stephen, what is this, 'You have a sexy apartment'?"

The force of her reply surprised him and left him unsure. "Well, it is," he said lamely.

She reached for her cigarettes, but kept her eyes on him. She looked annoyed and he went on,

"When you didn't meet me for lunch, I thought you might be sick or something, so I thought I'd stop by." He talked fast, as if he were telling lies.

"What do you want from me, Stephen?" she interrupted.

He knew what she meant but he answered innocently, "I just wanted to see if you were okay."

"You can't play your little game with me, Stephen. I won't let you."

"What little game?"

She sighed and went to the bed, dropping down gracefully. She arranged the pillows around her, and once comfortable, looked up. "Have you decided yet whether you want to sleep with me?" she asked.

"No." He tried to sound casual.

She smiled, a quick spreading grin that covered her face and lit it up. He couldn't help smiling back.

"Now what do you mean?" she asked. "I'm not another
little Catholic undergraduate infatuated with you, Stephen.
You're not going to get by with your innocent flirtation. I
don't get a big thrill from your meaningful looks and that 'I
can't be touched' attitude. It doesn't cut any ice with me.
I'm not interested in innocent good-night kisses in the
hallway and fast getaways." She stared at him, her green
eyes steady.

"Is that why you didn't show up for lunch?"

"We could go on forever having nice flirtatious lunches.
That might be your idea of a relationship, but it's not
mine."

"You forget I'm a priest, Deborah; I've taken vows."

"No. On the contrary, when I think about you—which I
must admit is quite often—I think about those vows of yours
and what a sexual relationship with me would mean to you.
Stephen, I'm not out to mess up your life."

He began to pace in the small room. "I'm attracted to
you, sure; I wouldn't be normal if I wasn't, but that doesn't
mean I need to sleep with you."

"Fine! I accept that. We have a relationship, then, which
is strictly Platonic. I would like to have you as a friend; I
enjoy being with you and we don't have to get involved."
She nodded her head as if summing up.

"Really, that's what I had in mind. You know, us being
just good friends." He kept talking, explaining his intentions
and motives, but now he really *was* lying, to her and to
himself: he did want to make love to her. As if she knew, she
lifted her head off the pillows and caught his eye. She
motioned him to her, patting the bed beside her, and he sat
down, keeping himself from touching her. His palms were
sweating.

"Stephen," she whispered, "I'm not asking you to make
love to me. I'm not going to seduce you, though it's crossed
my mind. That would be unfair, and besides"—she reached

out and touched his cheek, the palm of her hand briefly caressing him—"it would be too easy."

"I'm amusing to you, aren't I?"

"No, but I think you've found yourself in a situation where all your Latin can't help you. They don't prepare you very well, do they, to handle your emotions?"

"I can take care of myself," he answered defensively.

"I'm sure you can," she said slowly, withdrawing herself.

"Do I have to prove myself to you in some way by making love to you?" he asked.

"Stephen, you don't have to prove anything. I just wanted you to know that you weren't going to turn me into one of those vestal virgins who follow you around campus, go to all your Catholic services and look goggle-eyed when you sweep onto the altar in your flowing robes."

He stopped her with his lips. Reaching out, he pulled her into his arms. His sudden movement surprised her and she gasped and raised her arms and wrapped them tightly around his back.

He had never undressed a woman and his fingers were trembling as he slid his hands beneath her work shirt and pulled it up. He touched her breasts, filling his hands with the smoothness of her. He leaned over and touched the flushed pink nipples experimentally with his tongue, then took one in his mouth and she hugged him closer, then ran her hands lightly over his hips and down the back of his thighs.

For a moment he paused, almost dizzy at her touch, shocked at the force of his response. Then he reached for her cutoffs and unbuttoned them, sliding his hands inside. Her shorts and panties came off with one pull and he stopped again, this time to gaze at her. It was amazing to see her naked, to be that close to any woman.

He moved his hand slowly across her body, his fingers

trembling as he touched her soft skin. He ran his hand down the length of her thigh, feeling all the smooth sloping muscles. She was a marvel to him, like discovering a secret land. She took his hand and moved it between her legs. He thought his fingers would burn where he touched her.

He stood suddenly and walked away from the bed, running his hand through his hair and straightening his clothes as he paced. When he glanced back, she had gotten under the covers.

"I'm sorry," he said. "I shouldn't have gotten myself into this situation unless I planned on going all the way."

"That's right," she answered, her voice flat and unresponsive.

"It wouldn't be right, you know, if I did make love to you." He kept pacing.

"I understand."

"It wouldn't lead to anything. I can't marry you. I don't want to give up the priesthood."

"Stephen, I'm not asking you to marry me. I'm not asking you to sleep with me." He couldn't read her.

"It would be nice to fuck you, but I'm not sure it's worth the price."

"What price?" he asked curiously.

"All your guilt. I don't want you taking it out on me once we've had sex. I couldn't stand that."

"I've never slept with anyone," he said. He would admit his failings. She couldn't make fun of his honesty, his lack of experience.

"I know that," she answered softly. "That's one of the reasons I find you so appealing. I've never slept with a handsome twenty-eight-year-old virgin." She was smiling again.

He came back and sat down on the mattress. She did not move to touch him, but now that he was down on the floor again, he didn't think he would be able to get away. "I think you're very beautiful, Deborah."

She reached out and touched his hand but did not say anything.

"It's so much easier for you to sleep with someone," he went on.

"Now wait a minute!" She sat up, braced herself with her elbow. "Just because I'd like to sleep with you doesn't mean I make it with everyone who comes along. You're special."

"Yeah—I'm a priest and you've never slept with a priest."

"It's because of what you are that I'm thinking twice about all this. It's because you *are* a priest that I'm not making a big play for you. I'm not taking advantage of you. You're the one who came looking for me. Why should I get myself into a relationship which I know already will only hurt me? Just because I think you're irresistible doesn't mean we have to make love."

He pulled her into his arms, hurting her and making her gasp. He kissed her again and this time he wasn't hesitant. Then he got up and took off his own clothes, doing it quickly, not thinking of anything but making love to her, and she sat up on her knees to help him undress and then guided him inside her. It was over in minutes, as if it hadn't happened, but it had.

He listened to her unbolt the apartment door. She had three locks and they weren't all necessary. He had told her that, but she had been raised in New York City and never felt safe unless she was locked up inside.

She opened the door, smiling, happy to see him. Her pleasure made him feel wonderful, and he stepped inside, shut the door with one hand and pulled her into his arms. She was wearing jeans and the same faded work shirt that she had worn the afternoon they had first made love. Her hair was loose. She had just finished washing it and he could smell the shampoo when he kissed her.

"You've come to see me," she whispered happily.

"Yes." He kept hold of her.

"But why?" She pulled away to look at him, suspicious of his intentions.

"Because I want to make love to you." He answered as he kissed her and realized that yes, that was what he wanted; that was why he had come.

She turned over in the bed and raised herself up on her elbows. He could not see her face; only her eyes caught the late afternoon light and flashed in the darkness.

"Do you have to leave?" she asked. They had not spoken for a while and now her voice seemed like a threat, as if it was pulling them back toward responsibilities.

"In a little while," he whispered and touched her face in the dark, caressing her cheek. She turned her face into his hand and kissed the palm.

"Can you stay the night?" she asked, saying it with more wistfulness than expectation. His eyes told her no, but she kept that from disappointing her. She had accustomed herself to having him with her for only bits and pieces of time. It was like being involved with a married man. She saw her time with him only as a gift.

"Why are you in the city today?" she asked. She hadn't thought of it till now, but his being in town was unusual. He had not been down to the city all winter.

"I had a few things to do for the parish," he answered vaguely. If he mentioned the books now she would misunderstand, would think he had only come because of them. Then she saved him from the problem by saying, "Guess what I've been reading?"

"What?" He smiled, knowing what she would tell him.

"About your Catholic stigmata. I needed a topic for a paper in psych development and I thought I'd do some research on this Theresa Neumann." She slipped out of bed and crossed the room to her desk. He turned to watch her. It was still a thrill to see her naked.

She carried one of the library books back to bed and settled down, her slight body barely disturbing the mattress as she placed the book on a pillow and flipped quickly through the pages. Now she was interested in the book and what she had to tell him, and she reached for her glasses and put them on. They made her look efficient.

"I've been reading a book by a German archbishop who accepted all of Neumann's ecstasies and suffering as God given, when it is obvious that the poor woman was a simple hysteric.

"She had all the characteristics of a hysteric: the paralysis, loss of vision, skin disorder—that's your stigmata—the hallucinations, those strange biblical visions of hers.

"And the pain! This woman really suffered all those years. She shouldn't have been cared for by parish priests. What she needed was psychoanalysis."

She took off her glasses and pushing the book aside, stretched out, lying close to him but above the blankets. "God," she sighed, "people are so gullible. They'll believe anything as long as it's got a little magic and hocus-pocus about it."

He knew what she was doing: trying to hurt him by attacking his religion. He couldn't blame her. Theirs was a lousy situation and she was only getting even. Still, a thin wave of resentment ran along the edge of his nerves. It wasn't fair.

"Your point, I assume, is that Betty Sue Wadkins is also a hysteric."

"Yes," she said flatly, not even opening her eyes as she spoke.

"Jim Lear isn't as sure about that as you are."

She opened her eyes and sat up on her elbows.

"Jim? He examined her?"

"He even took blood samples and checked them out with a hematologist at the Medical Center. There's nothing wrong with Betty Sue's blood. She's healthy, according to Jim."

"Well," she answered, now defensive, "female hysterics have a way of seducing their doctors. It's a common behavior pattern. She must have gone wild, coming on to him. I mean, he's terrific looking. Did he mention that to you? Was she trying to seduce him?"

"She came on to both of us."

"You were in the room while he examined her?"

"She insisted I be there. She said she wouldn't let him look at her unless I was there to protect her."

"Well, what did she do? How did she act?"

"Pretty much like you said. She was very seductive and at one point she voluntarily stripped when there was no reason. . . ."

"See! I told you!" Deborah sat up, excited. "How can Lear not think she's a hysteric when everything she does is so classic!"

"Then how do you explain her bleeding every Friday?"

"Hysterics would do that," Deborah answered quickly. "She's just overidentifying with this whole passion thing."

Stephen hadn't wanted to worry her, but then he told her about the boy in confession, the falling crucifix, and the scribbled note on the parish station wagon. He could see her eyes widen in the dark bedroom, for what he was saying now brought everything very close to her.

"Okay." She sighed and tried to concentrate, tried in her practical way to sort it all out. "But what happened in the church doesn't really have anything to do with this girl's hysteria." She wasn't going to let go of her logical explanation for the stigmata.

"Except it's the same kind of note, the same illiterate printing we got at the rectory." Father Kinsella swung his feet around and got out of bed. It was late and he had to leave. The pastor would be worried, and worse, he'd begin to wonder why it had taken so long just to check out a few library books.

"Well, what do you think it is? Some mountain uprising to get rid of all the Catholics? Is Jim Lear sure this kid isn't faking? Maybe you're all being duped."

"She isn't exactly a kid, Deborah; she's seventeen years old, and beautiful."

"How beautiful?" she asked. "Is she as pretty as me?"

"No," he answered, reaching over to touch her face. He slipped his arm around her neck and pulled her to him. "She isn't faking it and she's not as beautiful as you."

"How do you know?" She smiled, happy to be held.

"Because of the bleeding envelope." He had kept back that information like a last bit of evidence, afraid really of what she would think of him, of what she liked to call his hocus-pocus beliefs. Now he told her, and watched the disbelief spread across her face and gather into a frown and finally a look of fear. He was speaking softly, but his voice filled the silent bedroom. And when he finished she was trembling.

"Are you okay?" he asked.

"I don't know. I just got very cold—suddenly." He reached and pulled a blanket up and around them. "Thank you. That feels better." She shrugged and hugged him tightly, then pulled away and wrapped the blanket tighter around her. She was not looking at him when she said, "Stephen, I just don't believe that story. How can you accept all that cock-and-bull stuff? It's clear Betty Sue Wadkins is a hysterical child—or young woman, or whatever she is—that she is suffering from conversion hysteria, a well-documented psychological phenomenon. You're talking about the occult—magical envelopes and bleeding palms. But we both know there is no way in the world a handwritten note on a simple slip of white paper can bleed sweet-smelling blood. If I didn't know better, I'd think you had turned into a dipsomaniac like that old whiskey pastor of yours."

He got up and began to dress. When he spoke he was almost a different person, as if the clothes had put time and space between them.

"This is not the occult," he said, and his voice was like bits of brick tossed back at her. "You know that medicine and psychology are not enough when you're talking about a mystical experience. Mysticism reaches beyond what we rationally know. The microscope cannot examine the relationship of the spirit with God. Besides, you have your own Jewish mystics, Deborah, who are still waiting for their Messiah."

"But I'm not waiting for a Messiah, Stephen, and you know that very well." She sat up in the rumpled bed, angry now and set to fight. "All that Judaism has meant to me is funny old men with long curls and black hats and a lifetime of discrimination from Catholics like you."

The lines were drawn now, and they stared coldly at each other from opposite sides of the room. Then, suddenly, she flopped down on the bed as if overwhelmingly discouraged, and buried her face in the pillows.

He went back to the bed, sat down and tried to take her in his arms, but she resisted. He stopped trying and instead began to massage her back, working his fingers slowly across her narrow tight shoulders, down her spine. Her back was taut and the muscles coiled. His fingers plied them gently and she began to relax and breathe deeply, her body softening under his probing.

Now he knew she'd be reasonable, loving. She could not resist this simplest of all manipulations. He leaned over and kissed her back and she turned in the bed, her wet eyes like slick slabs of jade.

"I can prove it to you," she challenged.

"What?" he asked, staring at her breasts. They were still a rare wonderment to him, the delicate, soft, transparent skin, the sky-blue network of veins, her nipples, flushed and excited. He was leaning forward to kiss them, to bury his head in their softness, when she braced him away from her with her arm, saying, "I can show you that even your Catholic scholars thought Theresa Neumann was a phony, that her stigmata weren't miraculous."

"I don't care about Theresa Neumann!" He had a hard-on and was calculating how much time he had before he had to leave the city and drive to Mossy Creek. He reached for her and again she stopped him.

"You may not believe me, but these books have that *Imprimi* thing, your Catholic Good Housekeeping seal of approval." Her anger had surfaced again. It was always there, just hidden by her accommodation, like hard ground beneath a white blanket of snow.

"Look," he said quickly, "I never said Theresa Neumann was a candidate for sainthood."

"But she was a bona fide stigmatic and an archbishop wrote her life story."

"The Church hasn't canonized her."

"Nor will they! I've read a half dozen books about her, and these two"—she held up the books—"make the same point I've been making, that there is nothing supernatural about her marks."

"I don't want to hear anything more." He knew her work habits, her scholarly industry. There would be notes on a yellow pad of paper and somewhere on her desk a set of file cards, a beginning bibliography on stigmata. In a week or two she'd be an authority. He stood up and started putting on his parka.

He looked so young in his jacket, she always thought. She just wanted to hold him now, care for him, keep him close and hidden away in her apartment. They could forget about his religion and her degree and just make love morning, noon and night. It made her dizzy, thinking about it.

But not now, because he was angry. She knew his ways. His irrationality, his withdrawal when he was offended, the way he'd never look at her. And now he was collecting his things, speedily and precisely. His deliberate efficiency affected her like chalk scraping across a blackboard, sending her into a rage. But before she could speak, to shout him down and tell him how babyish he was, he spoke slowly, his tone parental and the words hitting her like slaps to her face.

"I know why you're doing all this work on Theresa Neumann, Deborah. It has nothing to do with a graduate paper. It has nothing to do with stigmata, or sainthood, or even Betty Sue Wadkins." He paused, standing in the middle of the room bundled up in his bulky parka. He looked, she thought, like a man in a life jacket.

"It's just to get at me," he went on in that same calm, careful voice. His absolution voice, she called it. "You want to prove once more that my religion, my whole life, is just a lot of silliness. That anyone above the age of reason can see that Catholicism is just superstition, occultism, a lot of Middle Ages madness."

She was shaking her head, denying him, but still he kept talking, his voice as hard as the printed word.

"But you can't get to me through a Theresa Neumann."

"I'm not trying to get at you, Stephen."

"You may be right," he went on, not listening to her.

"Maybe Betty Sue Wadkins is nothing more than a hysterical adolescent. That doesn't matter. We'll find out, but Betty Sue Wadkins has nothing to do with us.

"Do you think I like myself, Deborah, for what I'm doing, sneaking up here in the middle of the day, making love to you, committing one sin after another? Do you have any comprehension in that chic, rational, New York mind of yours what my behavior is doing to me? How rotten I feel when I step up onto the altar to celebrate the mass?

"Deborah, I'm the worst possible sinner; I'm a bad priest. I am a scandal to myself, my family, the Catholic Church, an unerasable blot on all the centuries of goodness and charity of the Church. My life is worthless, Deborah. I'm worthless!

"And I don't need you to pick away at me, to keep knifing me with all your academic smugness. I don't give a goddamn about Theresa Neumann. I can't even save my own soul. How can I possibly save someone else's?"

For a moment neither of them said anything. Then Deborah answered, her voice steady and unemotional, but not submissive.

"You're being unfair, Stephen. I'm not after you, not in that way at least. And you're unfair when you say I don't comprehend the turmoil our relationship is causing you. I've understood that from the very first, from the guilty look that comes into your eyes just before you touch me. I know," she whispered, "but I love you." She shrugged. "And I can't deny that. It's a clear, certain emotion. One I understand and something I have to deal with. It's not easy, getting over you." She reached across the bed, felt around on the dark nightstand for her cigarettes and matches and sat up, leaned back against the wall and lit a cigarette. She set the pack and matches aside and brought the ashtray over, crossing her legs under the blanket to support the tray in the hollow between her legs. She did it all in a deliberate way, as if she were being filmed.

"I see you're smoking again," he commented.

"Yes," she said, silencing him.

Then she went on in her soft voice. It was as if they were in bed, whispering to each other. "When you first went away, I couldn't sleep. The only way I could get any rest at all was to masturbate while I fantasized that you were in bed with me." She stopped, embarrassed.

"We're not much good for each other, are we?"

She shook her head. Her dark hair was tangled and she kept toying with strands of it, twisting the ends and combing the knots out with her slender fingers. She was pale and exhausted and, he thought, very beautiful. One glance of her eyes, that secretive look, and he was always overwhelmed, as if she had actually hit him physically, low in the stomach.

He came back to the bed and sat down. He would never get away, he thought. She was irresistible, her every move made him want her more. He would stay the night, he decided. He would telephone Driscoll; tell him the car had broken down; tell him anything. What difference did it make, Driscoll wouldn't believe him, and she said, "I don't want to see you again, Stephen." She spoke very slowly, as if the words were in a foreign language, and he thought for an instant he'd be sick. "I just can't go on in this crazy way. We see each other and we fight. It's no good, and it's only going to get worse. You're not going to leave the order, certainly not to marry some Jewish princess from New York." Her voice was more disappointed than anything else. All her anger had washed through her.

"I thought we were going to wait until spring and then decide?" he asked meekly.

"And what good would that do?" she snapped, leveling

him with her green eyes. "What would a couple of months prove—or was your heart set on a June wedding?" She finished one cigarette, snubbed it out and lit another, striking the match with such force it was itself a small act of defiance.

"You want it all," she said. "You've got the security of the Church, those girls worshiping you, and all that supreme authority. The spokesman of Jesus Christ! It's a nice life, Stephen, but you also want"—and her eyes flashed, she was mad again, resentful of how she had been used—"you also want your pussy on the side."

"Deborah, will you stop!" It was her language more than anything that shocked him.

"Sure you do. A quick fuck now and then to keep you from getting horny. And it's even better now that you're out of the city. We can meet in motels or you can drive down here. It's terrific this way: no one is going to find out in Mossy Creek. Just tell them you're out visiting the sick and come get your piece of ass.

"You better go," she said. She felt cheap and dirty and he made her feel that way with his sneaking around, his religion. She would find someone else. He wasn't worth it. She began to weep again.

All right, she thought, one last cry. A catharsis. She would even let him hold her. It was the least he could do for causing all her pain. It really didn't matter whose shoulder it was; anyone's, just so for a few minutes she could be held, comforted, and feel, even in such a tenuous way, secure.

But he wouldn't stop. He kept trying to kiss her. He moved her head to kiss her eyes, her cheeks, her mouth. Not saying anything. He was stronger than she. She felt when she was with him that she lived in the shadow of his body.

His fingers tugged away the blankets and his hand engulfed her small breasts. A shock ran down her body and exploded in her womb. She gasped and clung to him, her long nails scraping his back. She would have liked to scar him and make him bleed. It would be a reminder of what he had done to her. But his fingers kept prodding and pushing, sliding up and into her, and she let herself be taken by his hands, arched her body to his mouth. He was touching her. His tongue licked her clitoris and another quick electric shock ripped up her spine and hit the base of her neck. She was breathless with her hunger for him.

He was still dressed and in the dark she saw him fumble with his belt and jeans. He was taking too long. Her wave was ebbing and she wanted him in her. Then he stooped and wrapped her into his arms, and she felt the pain of his entry. He never took enough time, never got her ready, but the pain passed and she got caught up in the steady rhythm of him working back and forth. It was simply wonderful how he could do that to her. She wished he would go on endlessly.

He was moaning now and they tumbled down, lying crosswise on the bed, her feet over the side. She could feel herself begin to come, the sensations warmly centered in her vagina, leaving her limbs weak. She hoped she would come before him. She loved to be on her wave when he exploded.

She concentrated on her sex, on what he was doing to her, and tried to force herself over the edge. She imagined him beating her, grabbing one of her thick blue bath towels off the rack and whipping her across her thighs. She wanted him to make her obey, submit to his demands, and to fuck her and fuck her and fuck . . .

She cried out and grabbed his hair. He was coming. She was coming. They were all right. For a few moments everything was all right. She obeyed her orgasm as if it were God.

Neither one spoke. They were both perspiring but when

the sweat dried she was cold. She could feel his breath, a hot patch below her ear, steady and even, like time ticking. His right leg was hooked over both of hers, holding them in place, and her legs still dangled over the side, as if she had been murdered.

"I've got to leave," he said in her ear, and this time she knew it was really over.

"All right," she answered. If nothing else, she would hurt him with her indifference.

Still he did not move. She knew his game. He waited for her permission, some cheery word to send him on his way. She lay still, staring blankly at the ceiling, not seeing the water marks, the peeling paint and cracks.

"The old man will think I've totaled the wagon. He doesn't like the way I drive."

Nothing. She didn't stir. The words bounced off her like tennis balls from a wall.

He moved his leg. Detached himself from her and waited another moment for her to at least touch him, give him a signal, a smile. She kept staring at the ceiling and he rolled over and off the bed. He pulled on his jeans and began to button his shirt.

She slipped into the spot he had vacated, cherishing his warmth on the sheets. She had nothing to remember him by, not even a photograph. He wouldn't let her take his picture. No letters, photos, keepsakes, except for one scribbled note he had slid into her textbook in the first frantic days of their affair. She had opened her book in the library and the note was there: *I love you,* he had written. She had slammed the book closed immediately, her hands shaking.

Now he was ready again, his down jacket zippered up. She forced herself to speak.

"I meant what I said before, Stephen. I don't want to see you again."

"I know." By his tone she knew he wouldn't telephone. His sense of fair play had returned. He wouldn't beg her to acquiesce. He would leave as if their love had never happened.

He moved slowly to the door and without turning her head, she followed him with her eyes. He would not even kiss her good-bye. He had to show her that she had hurt him. It was the adolescent in him. Once she had thought it endearing, like his initial awkwardness when they first kissed, but if she didn't stop him now, he would go out of her life. Priests were taught to live alone, to be emotionally self-sufficient, to be tiny islands in society; she knew all that, and she also knew it had left him an emotional cripple.

"Let me know sometime what happens, okay?" she finally said.

"About what?"

"The girl—Betty Sue Wadkins. I'd like to know. . . ." She could not move. His leaving was paralyzing.

"Then I can telephone you at least?" He let some of his own frustration come into his voice.

"Yes, but not for a while. Let me get you out of my system."

"It's going to be that easy?" Now he was just snide.

"No. It's not going to be easy," she answered. "But I'll get over you; you're not irreplaceable."

"No, I imagine not." He had a sudden image of her in bed with someone else, moaning with pleasure, gasping as she did when he made her come. He turned the doorknob violently and the sound broke the silence between them.

"Stephen!" She sat up, sweeping her hair off her face. "Stephen, you must realize I don't want it this way——"

"Yes, I know."

"But it's hopeless, darling . . ." She would cry again: God, she thought, hadn't she cried enough?

"Who knows, maybe I'll come to my senses yet."

"Maybe." She was smiling, a small, sad smile.

"Deborah, I do, in my own crazy way, love——"

"And I love you, Stephen. That won't stop. I'll always love you."

"Well, see you in church sometime." It was once a funny line between them, but this time it didn't work. There was no way for them to say good-bye. He opened the door and left, glancing back as he closed it. Her face was lost, hidden by the lack of light. Only her outline: the slim body and sloping shoulders; her long dark hair. She was gone.

Father Kinsella walked back across the campus to the station wagon parked behind the library. It had begun to rain, a cold rain that whipped across his face, numbed his nose and ears. Still he did not hurry. The cold and rain were good for him; he concentrated on the discomfort they caused.

The campus was empty except for small knots of students moving from the Student Union toward their dormitories and single women flanked by men, escorts seeing that they got home safely. He was the only one walking alone. The campus was dangerous after dark, he knew. Faculty members had been robbed, coeds raped.

He decided not to cut across the center of the campus and go past the lagoon. It was shorter that way but there was no need to press his luck. Enough had happened to him already, he didn't need to be mugged. Staying up on the campus ridge, he circled the university and went by the Newman Chapel.

He still had a set of keys to the chapel and his old office and he thought he'd better telephone Mossy Creek and tell the pastor he was on his way back to the mountains. It

would make things easier when he arrived home, for he had
been gone all day and half the night, and still he had no
books on stigmata.

Deborah was right: Theresa Neumann had been just a
hysterical woman. It was obvious when he thought about it
logically, all that sickness and piety, the overzealous parish
priest. He had seen Catholics who were almost as bad,
fanatical about their religion. They'd spend every day in
church, praying and tormenting themselves about sins:
victims of scruples.

And Betty Sue Wadkins would turn out to be the same. A
sick young woman obsessed with Bible stories. The young
hired hand was probably the cause, letting the girl get a
fixation on the Crucifixion. Maybe Jim Lear could convince
Father Driscoll it wasn't a saint that he had up on Blue
Haze Ridge.

Stephen unlocked the front door of the small chapel and
went inside, locking it behind him. When he had come to
the university he had wanted to keep the chapel open
twenty-four hours a day, a place where any student might
go to meditate and be alone, but the campus police said no.
They couldn't keep it secure, they told him, and students
would rip off the silver chalices and candlesticks. So Stephen
had locked it up when he wasn't saying mass.

He didn't bother with lights. That would just bring the
police racing across campus, and besides, he knew his way.
He walked up the center aisle toward the altar.

This church he liked. It was simple and homey and he
always felt at ease, saying mass and preaching. And he had
been good at it, standing at the pulpit, weaving the life of
Christ or points of the faith with the students' own lives. He
could make them laugh and think and feel good about
themselves. Often when he finished a sermon the congregation would be breathless. He'd have them hanging on his

every word and he'd hear them sigh, caught up in his language. It wouldn't have surprised him if they had applauded. It was the only time he had felt like a priest, spreading the word of God.

He paused at the front pew of the chapel and slipped to his knees, kneeling on the soft spongy rubber of the pew. Still he didn't pray. He knelt, arms braced against the seat before him, and looked at the altar, then beyond the altar to the crucifix hanging against the sanctuary wall. Christ hung in the semidarkness, lit only by vigil lights, a carved figure not as large as the wooden crucifix of Saint John's, or as gothic. This Christ figure was peaceful: the agony was over.

But not my agony, the young priest thought. He was weary of always being on his guard and he dropped his face into his open hands and tried to cry. It would have made him feel better, but the tears wouldn't come. He had suffered so much his body could no longer register emotions.

And then he heard her call his name. He jerked up his head and saw her before him.

She had been crucified. Her young body hung twisted and anguished on the cross, her bleeding hands and feet spiked to the wood. She hung suspended behind the altar, replacing the Christ figure.

She was naked except for a loincloth. Her breasts were bare and her left side lanced. Blood mixed with water flowed from her body. A crown of thorns pierced her forehead and blood dripped into her brown eyes.

Slowly, with excruciating pain, she raised her head and cried out in the silent chapel, "Oh, Stephen, Stephen, why have you forsaken me?"

He stumbled from the pew and fell away from the altar. She kept calling his name, begging him to come and take her down from the cross, but in his terror he ran from the chapel, ran wildly across the deserted campus until he reached the station wagon and then he raced out of the city, not toward the mountains and Mossy Creek, but to the only man he knew who could save his life.

7

Tuesday, February 21

The Feast of Saint Peter Damian

"Bless me, Father, for I have sinned." Stephen crossed himself and bowed his head. It was early morning, not quite daylight, as he knelt on the cold flagstones of the monastery church. Father Rafalet, the Father Abbot, at on a hardwood chair, leaning forward and waiting for the young priest's confession. With his lean, dark, Spanish face, the abbot appeared distant and unemotional, but Stephen knew better. They had met five years before, when Stephen had come to the monastery for a retreat before taking his final vows, and in that time he had come to see Father Rafalet as a kind man, and the finest priest he'd ever met.

"Father, I've broken my vow of chastity. Within the last few weeks I've twice had sexual relations with a woman, a friend of mine from the university. This is not our first time. She's the person I confessed to you about last year."

The Father Abbot nodded but remained silent. He

waited, gave the young man time to say whatever was troubling him.

"I asked her to come up to Mossy Creek," Stephen continued. "It was my decision. We had agreed not to see each other until spring: I wanted time away from her, the university, and everything, so I could experience what it meant to be a real priest. A parish priest: saying mass, dealing with parishioners, caring for others. I wanted that simple life to see if the priesthood was for me. To see if I had what it takes.

"But then I started to miss her. I missed her very much. Not to have sex with her, but just to see her, to have someone I could talk to.

"It's very lonely up at Saint John's. Father Driscoll and I aren't close. He's a priest from the old school, very self-contained, used to being alone. And we don't really have much in common. He was a chaplain in World War II and Korea, and I'm sure he thinks I'm not much of an American because I once told him I'd marched in an antiwar demonstration. I understand why we don't get along, but it doesn't help me any."

"A priest's life is lonely, Stephen," Father Rafalet said, his voice soft and understanding.

"Yes, I understand, Father. But I haven't done very well even making friends in the mountains. Oh, I'm invited out sometimes for dinner or a party, and I play sports with some of the local guys, but I don't have anyone really to talk to. It's very different from the university."

The Father Abbot nodded and asked, almost curiously, "Have you tried God, son? Have you prayed to him and asked for his help?"

"Yes, Father, but I don't think it has done much good." Stephen kept his head down, afraid to look at the older priest. There were tears in his eyes, but he knew the Father

Abbot too well to expect sympathy for his weakness. Even so, he was stunned by the anger in his confessor's voice.

"A priest is a disciple of Christ and shepherd of his flock," said Father Rafalet sharply. "He isn't a man who cowers from responsibility and duty. A priest is given by God extra graces to help him live an austere life. You would have been better, Stephen, to have prayed harder for God's help rather than seek the temporal comfort of some woman's arms."

For a moment the two men were silent in the corner of the high-naved church, two shadowy figures almost obscured by darkness.

"I'm sorry," Stephen offered.

"It's not me you have offended," Father Rafalet answered. "It was not really loneliness, was it, son, that led you astray?"

"No, Father."

"What, then?" Father Rafalet pressed, encouraging the young priest to understand his actions.

"I wanted to see her ... talk to her ... I wanted to make love to her."

"And do you realize in your heart that this is a terrible affront against Jesus Christ and your life as a priest?"

Stephen nodded.

"And do you accept your punishment and ask God's forgiveness?"

"Yes, Father."

Father Rafalet leaned back and sighed, then slowly crossed himself and said the Latin words of absolution, absolving the young man of his sins.

Stephen said the prayers required by his penance alone in the monastery chapel. He took his time, happy to have the chance again of praying with a cleansed soul. For the first time in months he felt truly at peace with himself and his God, and he marveled at the power of the sacrament of confession. For no matter how terrible the sin, no one was ever lost from the goodness of God if they just believed in Christ.

Stephen believed. His passion for Deborah had obscured how much the priesthood and his religion meant to him. But as he knelt in the quiet chapel and let the serenity of the stone-walled building comfort him, he realized it was here that he belonged, and nothing else mattered in life but saving his own soul.

He finished his penance, then walked out into the sunlight of the monastery's cloistered courtyard. Father Rafalet met him with smiles and asked cheerfully, "Have you had any breakfast, Stephen?"

"No, Father. One of the monks offered me some when I arrived, but I wanted to see you first. I had to make my peace with God before I told you everything that has been happening up in the mountains."

The Father Abbott saw then that Stephen was still tense, that the sacrament had not completely eased his mind, and he answered quickly, "Well, we'll have breakfast alone and you can tell me what else there is that's troubling you." He smiled again and led the young priest across the courtyard and into the Retreat House.

"So you think you have a stigmatic in your mountain parish, Stephen?" The Father Abbot asked the question ironically, but also seriously, for the scholarly monk was both a practicing skeptic and a firm believer in the mysteries and marvels of the Roman Catholic Church.

It had taken Father Kinsella one hour—through breakfast and a cold morning walk in the monastery gardens—to tell in detail about the bleeding envelope, Betty Sue Wadkins, Father Driscoll, and his terrifying experience in the university chapel.

"I don't know *what* we have on Blue Haze Ridge." Father Kinsella sighed. "After I talked to Deborah yesterday I was ready to drive back to Mossy Creek and tell Father Driscoll that Betty Sue Wadkins needed therapy, not theology. But then I stopped at the chapel and she appeared ... and, well, I drove straight here." He smiled at Father Abbot. "And I told a lie that I should have confessed: I called Father Driscoll long distance and told him I was having car trouble and couldn't get home."

The winter sun had just reached the beautiful Romanesque church and it shone off the wet red-tiled roofs. Stephen would have liked to go on walking among the trees. He felt clean and refreshed in the sharp air, but he sensed that the older priest had something to show him. They turned and walked back toward the buildings, Father Kinsella matching strides with the tall, ascetic abbot.

"Oh, I think your friend is right about Theresa Neumann, Stephen," Father Rafalet answered as they walked. "I don't believe she or her parish priest were purposely deceitful; it's just that they didn't understand her illness. We have to remember they were peasant people in a remote German town."

They reached a side door and Father Rafalet led the way into the cloister. Both of them immediately fell silent, observing the rule of the monastery until they reached the Father Abbot's office on the second floor.

Unlike the small, austere rooms of the monastery, Father Rafalet's office was spacious and elaborately decorated with handsome oak and walnut furniture made by the monks. Three of the high walls were lined with bookshelves, and the fourth was a long window that looked out over the monastery's fields and woods. That morning the trees were shrouded in low clouds, making Stephen feel as if the two of them were on top of the world. He wondered how many other priests had come to this room, hoping to have their lives saved.

"Sit there, Stephen." Father Rafalet gestured toward a set of walnut and leather chairs that faced the window, while he went to the bookshelves. Tucking up his black-and-white robes, he climbed the step-ladder and reached up to the top shelves for the volumes he wanted. They were not, Stephen noted, books used every day.

"Whatever we need to know about stigmata should be in these." Father Rafalet stacked the half-dozen books on the coffee table in front of Father Kinsella and sat down opposite. Slipping his hands into the folds of his robes, he took out a black case containing a pair of round, rimless glasses. They made him look sterner, and his dark eyes, set deep, now dominated his face.

It was a calculated look. Father Rafalet's slate eyes, magnified by the thick lenses, seized a person and held him to the pain of truth. His heart was understanding, Father Kinsella knew from experience, but the Father Abbot's mind was uncompromising. He didn't dabble in questions of theology. To him, they were the reasons for life and death.

"Father," the young priest said hesitantly, embarrassed at his own ignorance, "I know the Theresa Neumann story and that's about it. Mysticism wasn't a big thing when I went through the seminary."

The abbot grinned wryly. "No, your generation of priests, as I recall, all wanted to be *involved.*" He pulled a book from the pile and opened it carefully, the thick pages crackling as he turned them. Stephen leaned forward. The book was in Latin and he could make out the name of Saint Francis. The abbot continued, "As you may know—not from your seminary days, but from the good sisters who taught you in grammar school—Saint Francis of Assisi received the stigmata on Holy Cross Day, in September 1224, and is our first known stigmatic. But what I'm looking for is something

about the Dominican nun, Blessed Helen of Hungary ...
yes, here's a bit.

"Blessed Helen lived at the same time as Saint Francis."
He nodded toward the open book. "How good is your Latin,
Stephen?"

"I'm afraid not very, Father. I majored in Semitic
languages."

Father Rafalet's small smile returned. "Well, if Archbishop Lefebvre has his way, you fellows ordained during
Vatican II will all be returning to the seminaries for Latin
instruction. Anyway"—he took off his glasses and gestured
toward the open book—"these Dominican convents, like the
one Blessed Helen lived in, were rather remarkable places.
Only cardinals, bishops, reigning kings and queens, the
nuns' confessor, and, in emergencies, an approved doctor, 'a
grave man of reverend years,' could enter the convent
without desecrating it.

"These enclosed Dominican convents became centers of
the highest mysticism, and it's not surprising that there have
been many stigmatics among the Dominicans, the last as
recently as 1895."

"But we also know that all the nuns who supposedly had
stigmata weren't as saintly as Helen seems to have been,"
Stephen pointed out. "I read about two nuns in the sixteenth century who faked their stigmata. The Pope sen-
tenced them to life imprisonment."

The abbot nodded. "Even in the seventeenth century the
Church had a healthy skepticism about stigmata." He
opened another volume and quickly found the passage he
wanted. "This was written by a cardinal in 1655." He
translated the Latin as he spoke. "He says that persons
claiming to have stigmata 'ought to be sharply reproved as
victims of a too lively imagination—or, worse still, as foully
deceived by a diabolic illusion. Unless indeed they are
persons of most rigid life, lovers of retirement, contempla-

tives, shunning the world, in which case of course, they will be the last to speak of such charismata, heartily endeavouring to conceal the secrets of Heaven, deeming themselves utterly unworthy!' In other words, true stigmatics do not go out and hire a public relations consultant. Francis and Helen did everything they could to conceal their wounds, even from fellow monks and nuns."

Stephen nodded his head thoughtfully. "But judging by the people who've been recognized as true stigmatics, I'd feel a lot more certain if Betty Sue Wadkins was a cloistered nun who went to mass and received communion every day. But she isn't—she's a perfectly normal, pretty seventeen-year-old girl, and a Baptist. I doubt if she has ever been inside a Catholic Church. Where's the connection? Why should she be a stigmatic?"

"The majority of stigmatics are nuns and priests, I suppose. But not all. Moslem ascetics have stigmata as well, corresponding to the wounds received by Mohammed during his battles. Yogis and Brahmin ascetics have produced similar phenomena. It's not limited to Roman Catholics."

It was not the answer Father Kinsella wanted. "But whoever has them, it's still just hysteria, isn't it, Father? Men and women obsessed by the Crucifixion?"

The Father Abbot put his glasses back on and his face softened. He studied Father Kinsella, as if to make sure of the man before he said more. Then he went on softly, speaking like a man who had accepted his faith and put his doubts behind him. "Unquestionably some of these stigmatics have been disturbed people, women and men suffering from one form or another of hysteria, but we're fooling ourselves and being dishonest to our religion if we think all stigmatics can be explained away with a medical examination. Mysticism does not easily lend itself to practical science.

"Jesus Christ has blessed some of our saints with his five

wounds. The holiness of such people as Saint Francis of Assisi, Saint Catherine of Siena, and Saint John of God, all blessed with stigmata, cannot be disputed." The abbot gestured again toward the books. "The documentation, if you need it, is here."

The young priest leaned forward, eager for a definite answer. "Is there a way I can test this young woman and see if her stigmata are divine?"

The Father Abbot frowned. "Stephen, I want you to think carefully about whether to become involved with her. Take your time deciding."

"Why, Father?"

"Do you think you're strong enough to handle it?" He asked the question point blank, staring at the young man.

"Yes, I think so. But what do you mean, Father?"

"These are the trying weeks for a stigmatic, Stephen. We're in the midst of Lent; the girl's ecstasies will become more severe and physically exhausting as we approach Good Friday. As her spiritual advisor, you'll be drawn into the web of her suffering. Do you think you're strong enough to live with her through that? It is no failing on your part not to accept the involvement. It is not your responsibility. Father Driscoll is the pastor."

"But I am the one she has sought out. I promised her——"

"Your first responsibility is to your own soul. You must be wary of placing yourself in precarious situations." The Father Abbot gestured, as if to say not to worry, and quickly added, "But your decision needn't be made this morning. Do some reading about stigmata, Stephen, and find time to pray. God will show you the right way."

"Would you advise me to go to the Chancery for help?" Stephen asked.

The Father Abbot framed his answer carefully. "Stigmata have always been an explosive issue within the Church. I can't even imagine what sort of consequences to expect if this situation were to get picked up by the press and attract national attention. It could be devastating for your small parish. Especially since this girl isn't a Catholic. The ecumenical movement has gone quite far, but it hasn't embraced the Baptists."

"Do you have any suggestions, then, Father, about what I might do?"

"Yes, but I'm hesitant to make them. You're not one of my priests and I haven't the authority to tell you what to do, but perhaps a suggestion from an old friend .... I'm concerned that your pastor has moved so quickly in deciding that this young woman's stigmata is of divine origin. He'll have to be more cautious, and if he isn't, then I suggest you go directly to the Bishop.

"Meanwhile, an orderly documentation would be useful, especially if an Ecclesiastical Commission is eventually established. Calling in that doctor was a wise move.

"If you decide to continue your association with her, then you should keep detailed notes of her ecstasies, her prophecies and clairvoyances. Also get to know the young woman. A personal knowledge of her when she's not in her ecstatic state would help tell us how devoted to God she is."

The abbot paused. Intrigued as he was by the story of Betty Sue Wadkins, his first obligation was to be the young priest's spiritual advisor. "But Stephen, listen to me. Your chief responsibility is your own soul's salvation, and I must warn you: don't become involved in this without considering the risks."

"Risks?"

"We know in our studies of theology that the Devil has used stigmata for his own purposes. We tend today to disregard the Devil, to think of him as some sort of antique prankster, but I've seen his work inside this cloister, among our own priests and brothers.

"He's very much part of our modern world, trying always

to corrupt, especially those who are most holy. If this girl has been marked by God, you can be sure Satan is at her left hand. Saint Francis and Saint Catherine struggled for their lives with the Devil—why not Betty Sue Wadkins? A true example of stigmata—a living saint in our times—is too great a threat to Satan. He will strike back at her, and at you, and in ways you cannot imagine."

Father Rafalet caught the young priest's eyes with his own and then continued, almost whispering in his intensity. "As much as we need to love God, Stephen, we need to fear Satan. He is relentless, cunning, and capable of great deception. He wants our souls most of all. The souls of priests. To claim a priest as one of his own slaves is his greatest victory."

The young priest felt a chill run down his spine.

"But I have to do something, Reverend Father," he said haltingly. "I had more or less decided that Betty Sue was just a sick girl—until she appeared to me in the chapel. How can I go on until I find out what that meant? I can't avoid it, pretend it didn't happen."

Father Rafalet hesitated. He looked at the books, fingered the bindings a moment, then stared directly at Father Kinsella. "These last few days, this whole year, in fact, you've undergone a tremendous amount of tension. It might have affected you so you *thought* you saw the young woman on the cross.

"Your mind and soul have been suffering because of your relationship with this graduate student. The guilt you've experienced because of her could have produced this Crucifixion manifestation.

"Certainly it's not miraculous—not the way she looked. I'm inclined to think you had a temporary breakdown, that's all, brought on by your guilt and the unusual stress you've undergone."

"Am I going crazy?"

The Father Abbot smiled, his first warm look since they had sat down in the office. "I don't think so, certainly not any more than the rest of us. Take your time deciding what to do, Stephen. Pray and ask for God's help." He shook hands with the young priest. "And thank you also, Stephen, for coming to me. It's not often I have the opportunity to be a real priest these days, instead of an administrator."

"I'm the one who should be thankful, Father. You were my last hope."

There was fear in Stephen Kinsella's gray eyes. The abbot could see that the shock of what had occurred in the college campus chapel still tormented him. Or was it his past coming back to trouble him once more? The abbot gripped the young priest's elbow. "We all fail, Stephen, and fall from grace. That's just part of being human. Our challenge is to come back from sin and not despair. We must remember that Jesus loves us more than we love ourselves."

Father Kinsella knelt to kiss the priest's ring and then went to find the Retreat Master. The Father Abbot had agreed to call Father Driscoll and explain that he had asked the young priest to stay for a few days.

The room in the Retreat House was small and simply decorated, with white walls and a crucifix hanging over the head of the bed. Father Kinsella found himself looking anywhere but at the cross.

There was also a single bed with a firm mattress, not the straw kind the monks slept on. He would have preferred that additional hardship, a further penance, but he was grateful to sleep anywhere and he stripped off his clothes and slid into bed. He fell asleep immediately, but it was not a peaceful rest.

It was the nightmarish dream of his adolescent years in the junior seminary. He was in the empty dormitory on a Good Friday afternoon. The proctor, an older student, had told him to come to his room and when Stephen touched the proctor's door, the door just faded away and there was the senior student sitting on the edge of the bed, smiling and waiting for him. And next the proctor was unbuckling his trousers, pulling them off and reaching for Stephen. He tried to make him stop but he couldn't and then he went on struggling, but he didn't run away, and the dream went on and on, an endless moment of pleasure and resistance.

Stephen woke in the twilight of the late winter afternoon in the silent retreat house, bolting up in bed and knowing instantly from the silence that he had cried out in his nightmare. His legs were curled up tight and both his hands gripped his penis. He had already begun to come and the warm semen creamed over his bare skin.

8

Thursday, February 23

Feast of Saint Polycarp

At the end of February the weather turned unexpectedly to spring and the temperature reached the sixties. The heavy winter snow melted and filled the mountain streams that tumbled down the pine slopes so by the time these waters reached bottom land they were roaring whitecap rivers, so cold they numbed one's fingers at the touch.

The breeze that blew across the hills was warm and southerly, but it was a false spring. There would be more cold weather and winter snows. Still, the sudden warmth bolstered Father Kinsella's spirits as he climbed with Betty Sue through the trees behind her house, up toward the crest of Blue Haze Ridge.

The air this far up was sharp and thin, and within fifteen minutes the priest was short of breath. He was trying to keep up with Betty Sue but she outdistanced him easily, her long stride unaffected by the sores on her feet. She wore the special shoes Rufus had made and she was dressed in jeans and a dark blue sweater. Her blond hair, tied back with a bright ribbon, bounced loosely on her shoulders as she walked. She was wearing woolen mittens to cover her hand wounds, and she looked, Father Kinsella thought, like any girl out for a morning hike.

"Wait!" he called out at last, and leaned against a tree to catch his breath.

He had halted in a clearing, a narrow, grassy shelf on the ridge, and they stood for a moment looking back at the house, the Pit, Rabbit Hop road, and the hollow. The view of the hollow was spectacular; it looked like an ocean, a sea of evergreens tossed by the warm wind.

"I come up here lots," Betty Sue said. "It's real pretty, ain't it?" She turned and smiled, standing close to him.

On the mountainside she seemed so alive that he couldn't imagine her ever being ill. Her eyes flashed as she smiled and he kept staring at her, thinking how lovely she was. Her face did not have the soft shape of an adolescent's, but the defined cheekbones and strong chin of a woman. He thought fleetingly of how she had appeared to him in the college chapel, her face distorted with pain.

"You like it here, Betty Sue?" he asked, talking to keep his mind off that memory.

She nodded. "When the weather is right fine, me and Rufus, we climb all these hills." She waved expansively at the forest. "No one to make fun of me, y'know, call me names."

"Who makes fun of you?" he asked, angry at the idea.

"Oh, the kids mostly, because of these." She held up her mittened hands. "They say I'm queer 'cause of these sores." She glanced nervously at the priest. "Rufus tells me not to pay them no mind, but"—she shrugged, tears in her eyes—"it hurts, them names they call me. That's why I don't go to town much. I don't want people gawking at me. I don't need them anyhow. I got Rufus; he's my best friend." She looked sideways at Father Kinsella and dropped her eyes. "And now you'll be my friend, won't you, Stephen?"

She looked precious and adorable and impulsively he threw his arm around her shoulders and hugged her. "Of course, I'm your friend." Her hand touched his chest and he could feel her thigh press against his, her long legs matching his, and he backed off, embarrassed. "Sorry," he mumbled.

Then the priest saw Rufus. The hired hand was above them, hidden in the trees. He slid behind one when Father Kinsella looked up, but he took his time, as if he wanted to be noticed.

The priest was going to call out, to show he had nothing to hide, but Betty Sue said quickly, "Don't do nothing." She dropped her voice. "Please don't. He's funny that way."

"What way?" The priest was puzzled.

"He doesn't like it when I don't spend my time with him. He's afraid ..."

"Afraid of what?"

She shrugged. "I don't know. That I won't like him anymore. He's been mighty nice to me, Rufus has. I ain't got no friends but Rufus and I don't want to hurt him."

"That's okay, Betty Sue. I won't say anything. I understand."

"Are you ready?" Betty Sue was smiling again.

"Sure!" He tried to sound enthusiastic, but looking up he saw they weren't anywhere near the crest. "But remember, I'm not as young as you, Betty Sue."

"You're not *that* old." She studied him a moment. "You're not thirty, are you?"

"That's a Vatican secret, Betty Sue. The Pope won't let us tell our ages."

"Oh, Stephen, don't you be silly!"

He laughed and tried to duck past her but she grabbed his arm and held it. Now she was insistent. "How old are you?" she asked, determined to know. "Rufus says you're thirty, but I know you're not." It surprised him how quickly her personality changed from the bashful adolescent to the strong-willed young woman.

"I'm certainly not thirty," he said. It was only a half-lie. His birthday wasn't until May.

She grinned, pleased that she was right, and spinning around she stepped off, climbing again toward the top of Blue Haze Ridge.

They reached the summit and stepped onto the flat top. The wind whipped across the crest and howled into their faces. The trees were bare and they could see down the other side of the ridge, toward Mossy Creek itself. Father Kinsella made out Saint John of the Cross: the red brick elementary school, the rectory, and the round dome of the new church, looking like the crown of a mushroom.

He stepped close to Betty Sue so he wouldn't need to shout over the wind. "We'll have to go on a picnic here when it gets warmer."

The smile left her face and she shook her head. "Sometimes I don't think I'll even live till summer."

"There's no reason to think that. You're a strong young woman; you outwalked me to the top, didn't you?"

She sighed and kept looking across the valley. "I know, but it's just gettin' worse, that's all. The bleeding's been lots worse since fall. When I was small, y'know, it weren't so bad, but now! Lordy, it gets so I can hardly stand the pain, the bleeding, all those funny dreams. I think I'm goin' crazy sometimes."

"But there's some reason for your bleeding, Betty Sue."

"What?" She cocked her head and waited for his explanation.

"Well, I'm not sure yet," he finished lamely. At the university he had always had some sort of solution for the students, but with her he had no idea of what to do. It made him feel foolish and useless.

"It's just I ain't got much time," she said.

"No?" He wasn't sure what she meant.

"It starts tonight," she answered. "It's Thursday. I start bleedin'." She sounded almost desperate.

He stepped closer and took her by the shoulders, turning her toward him, but she wouldn't face him. "Betty Sue," he said. "I'll be with you." His voice was sincere and confidential and he knew it inspired trust. He used it as he used his good looks and his priestly robes: as currency, to buy his way and persuade people. But it was for their own good, he reasoned.

She looked up, smiling demurely, and nodded.

"You won't be alone," he whispered.

"It's always so scary when it starts."

"What's it like, Betty Sue?" he asked. It might be easier for her to talk about it away from her family and Rufus, he thought.

"It just comes over me," she said slowly, as if trying to remember. "I can't seem to stop it from takin' me. And then I'm in the Holy Land watching Jesus suffer and I'm sufferin', too. I feel the pain like Jesus does .... And it gets so bad sometimes I plumb pass out and when I wake up— My hands and feet are bleeding and there's blood all over the bed."

"Do you remember what has happened to you?"

She nodded. "It's like it happened to me in another life, or a long time ago. I'm there with Jesus and his mother and Mary Magdalene and all the disciples. I didn't recognize none of those people at first, but Rufus, he told me. He knows the Bible real good." She nodded firmly. That was something which impressed her. "At first he'd even give me questions to ask them, y'know, the next time it happened."

"And would you?"

"Sometimes. But it's always so hurried when I'm there in Jerusalem. There ain't hardly enough time——"

"Time for what?"

"Time to save Jesus."

"But Betty Sue, that's not possible," he said slowly, trying to think how he could explain this theological problem. "Christ died for our sins. He died to save our souls, yours and mine. Without the passion of Christ and the Crucifixion there would be no Christianity. It is the basis of our Christian faith."

Betty Sue shrugged. "I don't know about that stuff, Stephen. I just know when my visions come, and I'm there in Jerusalem, all I want to do is save Jesus from dying. I just want to get him out of there and I don't know why."

"And what does Rufus say?"

She smiled. "Oh, y'know, Rufus. He's always playin' around. He says, 'We'll save that bastard yet, Betty Sue!'. That Rufus is bad. But I don't pay him no mind."

The two priests went to see the parents that afternoon to tell them what they now believed. Mrs. Wadkins had made coffee and cut the men slices of apple pie and they sat at the kitchen table, their elbows on the oilcloth. Father Kinsella talked slowly, using simple language so the parents would understand.

"Doctor Lear couldn't find anything medically wrong with her. He is still waiting for some tests at the university lab, but he thinks your daughter is perfectly healthy, a fine young woman."

He stopped and looked at the parents. Her father leaned back in the wooden chair and glanced at his wife, sharing a silent communication, then stared down at his own leathery hands. "It's the snakes, like I told you. She got bit real bad that time."

"Mr. Wadkins, I don't think Betty Sue's sores are because of snake bites," said the young priest carefully.

The old man raised his eyebrows. He looked worried,

afraid of what more the priests might tell him, but before Father Kinsella could continue, the pastor interrupted impatiently.

"Your daughter is what is called a stigmatic," he said loudly, in his pulpit voice. "It is a blessed and glorious event. She has been blessed by Jesus Christ Almighty with his sacred wounds." The pastor's booming voice filled the small kitchen. His face was flushed and he sat straight up, his hands flat on the table as if he were about to deliver a sermon.

"What Father Driscoll means," Father Kinsella interposed quickly, "is that the wounds and visions Betty Sue is experiencing are similar to what is called—in all religions, Baptist, too—stigmata."

He began to explain the complex nature of stigmata, but her father interrupted.

"She ain't no Roman." Mr. Wadkins looked indignant.

"Yes, we know," Father Kinsella continued, still keeping his voice soft and calm. "But often religion doesn't matter. Betty Sue's stigmata could be caused by a mental illness, something we're not yet aware of—"

Father Driscoll cut him off, his thick Irish brogue dominating the room. "I know, good people, that this is all very strange to you and what Father Kinsella has told you about stigmata seems very unlikely. But we want you to know that we, too, are concerned about the well-being of your sweet precious child."

The young priest looked away, embarrassed by the pastor's ranting. But Father Driscoll kept on, whispering now, uttering the words lovingly in his brogue. "This is truly a wonderful thing that has happened to your child and this family. God has blessed you in a special way. Never before has he seen fit to honor a family in America. You have been touched by his hands and only goodness will shower on these mountains and your home."

Father Kinsella glanced at the pastor. Father Driscoll's eyes flared with the intensity of his delivery and the muscles of his thick neck bulged under the tight white Roman collar. Father Kinsella was sure he'd been drinking. But before he could speak, Father Driscoll's voice soared again into the tiny kitchen.

"You feel alone. You feel lost and sinful because of the strange sickness of your child, your little Betty Sue, and I tell you the hand of Jesus Christ, our Savior, is laid on this house!"

"Yes," whispered Mrs. Wadkins, nodding her head in agreement.

Shocked, Father Kinsella turned toward the woman. Her eyes were riveted on the older priest. She was leaning forward, waiting for the pastor's word.

Father Driscoll began again, speaking slowly, pulling them closer with his voice. "You feel alone here on this mountain ridge. Outcasts. Shunned by your own church and your own kin. And why? Because your poor child suffers and bleeds. A sickness so strange no doctor can cure her. They tell you Betty Sue is fittified, suffering from *spells*. They tell you that your dear sweet young child is crazy, and that you should send her away to the state institution. Lock her up! Forget she's yours; your own flesh and blood."

The pastor leaned back in the chair, his hands flat against the kitchen table, his head up. He seemed to tower over them as he shouted, "But your daughter is not crazy! You know in your hearts that this child of yours is as sweet and lovely as any child on Blue Haze Ridge. This last child of yours—your precious little girl, your baby—is as normal, healthy, and smart as any child in the whole wide world. You know that as well as you know God is in his Heaven, and you are right!"

Then silence, absolute silence, so quiet that Father Kinsella could hear the grandfather clock ticking from the next room. Father Driscoll began again, whispering once more, the words coming slowly, "But Betty Sue isn't like the other mountain children. She is not like your kin or anyone you have heard about, or seen on television, or read about in your Bible. Betty Sue is someone special, for God has blessed her as he has blessed other saints in the long, glorious history of Christianity.

"And don't ask why!" The pastor waved his arm across the table, as if anticipating their objections, but the Wadkinses, Father Kinsella saw, believed his every word. "Don't ask why," Father Driscoll whispered, "for we do not always understand God's way. We must only remember that he has a divine plan for each and every one of us, including Betty Sue.

"Your daughter's stigmata—these bleeding hands and feet—are part of God's plan. She is not a freak, but a child who joins a long list of blessed souls, all special children of God; some of our holiest saints who have been marked with God's sacred wounds." He paused again. "I believe your daughter has been chosen by God to take her place with these radiant stars of heaven."

The parents did not protest. Father Kinsella waited for them to shout the priests out of their mountain home, but instead they only bowed their heads, as if in submission, and the pastor continued to instruct them. "Now we shall all pray together. Pray that Our Lord give us the understanding to help this child, pray that he will give Betty Sue the supernatural grace and strength to carry her through this ordeal."

The two priests and her parents stood, pushed away the wooden chairs and knelt silently at the kitchen table, bowing their heads against the table top as the pastor of Saint John of the Cross led the Baptists in the Lord's Prayer.

Father Kinsella stood at the head of Betty Sue's bed and watched the young woman suffer. He had been there all night as she silently endured her pain. It was terrifying to see her re-enact the passion, and know he was helpless to stop the cycle. Her agony was predetermined, as it had been for Christ on Calvary.

Stephen wasn't alone. The pastor stood at the end of the bed. He wore his black cassock and a purple stole around his neck. In his hands he held the Bible and a crucifix.

The parents were against the bedroom wall. They stood passive and resigned, consoled, for the first time in five years, by the knowledge that there was a reason for their daughter's suffering.

Rufus stood across from Father Kinsella at the head of the bed. All night he had been wiping the perspiration from Betty Sue's forehead. Her face was flushed with fever and pain, and the sweat poured from her body.

Then Rufus glanced at Father Kinsella and nodded. The priest turned and pushed the record button on the tape recorder. His hands, he saw, were trembling. It was almost dawn, he was thinking, when Betty Sue sat up in bed and cried out. Her body went rigid and she stared across the room, her eyes open and wild. "No, no!" she shouted. "Don't hit him!" Her body shook and she fell back into the bed, hands flying to her face. At the foot of the bed, the pastor raised his cross and held it before him, as if to defend himself.

Rufus seized Betty Sue by the shoulders. "Lie down!" he ordered, and she obeyed. For a moment she lay peaceful, her arms crossed over her chest, then she turned on the bed so that she was lying on her stomach and screamed again. The cries pierced Stephen's ears and echoed in his head. It was inescapable, as if it were the agony of generations of sufferers. The scourging of Christ at the pillar had begun.

Again before Stephen's eyes, Betty Sue hurled herself off the bed, then thumped back onto the mattress. Her thin, pale arms thrashed from side to side as she kept twisting to escape the beating. Stephen moved toward her. He would hold her, he thought, take her in his arms and comfort her, but Rufus stopped him.

"Leave her be," he ordered shortly, "there's nothing you can do." Then he smiled, seeming apologetic, and explained. "She needs to suffer. It's her blessing."

Betty Sue hit the mattress and clutched the corners of the bed. Her body was soaked with sweat; the cotton nightgown clung to her body, outlining her limbs. A half-dozen raw welts ran across her body in parallel marks. They were lashing Christ.

Stephen felt as if he could hear the leather straps cut through the cold Jerusalem dawn and then the sharp crack, like a rifle shot, as the leather broke over Christ's back. Betty Sue jerked on the bed and screamed as the Roman centurion struck her and the skin on her shoulder ripped open. Stephen watched helplessly as the bloody welts formed on her soft skin, and blood ran from the blisters.

Father Kinsella counted twenty lashes before the scourging stopped and Betty Sue began to breathe evenly.

"We have to move her," Rufus directed. "Pick her up and turn her on her back."

The young priest hesitated. He did not know how to touch her without causing more pain.

"Go ahead!" Rufus ordered. He had placed fresh towels on the mattress. "She must be turned over and we haven't much time."

Stephen slid his arms under Betty Sue and lifted her. She was light in his arms, and he placed her gently on the fresh towels, resting her head on the pillow. As he did her lips brushed against his arm like a kiss.

She lay quietly for a moment, her face paler than the blond hair that streamed across the bloodstained pillow. How lovely she really was, he thought, a victim of this strange possession, and he touched her face as if to reassure himself that she was real.

But it was not over yet. Sweat ran down her cheeks, and beads of bloody perspiration broke on her forehead. Then the thorns blossomed on her head. Her forehead bulged, as if a crown of woven branches were bursting out from beneath the skin.

"My God!" Stephen exclaimed. It was as if the thorn branches were being hammered into her brow, breaking the skin in a dozen places. Blood dripped off her forehead and ran like tears. She lay before him in agony, her body bloody and beaten by the soldiers. He blessed himself, closed his eyes and prayed silently for her, and when he opened them again she was watching him, her brown eyes filled with love.

"Stephen, I have been worried about you." Her voice was calm.

"Worried about what, Betty Sue?" He held his breath.

"Stephen, kneel beside me," she said.

Father Kinsella dropped to his knees and bowed his head. She reached out and touched his head with her bloody palm.

"Stephen, God is pleased that you have given her up." Startled, Stephen tried to look up, but her hand was like a millstone on his head. "I know she made you happy, made you feel like a man when you made love to her, but it was a false pleasure, Stephen. You must promise you will not see this woman again. She is a blasphemy to Christ, Our King. Give me your word and I will cherish it as I cherish the sacred blood that pours from my sacred wounds."

Under the heavy pressure of her hand he whispered, "I promise." His knees were trembling and sweat ran down his neck.

"And so you will know what I tell you is true," she went on, her voice clear and strong in the room. "I will accept a penance for the offense you caused God and bear the suffering gladly because you have repented. Your good pastor who suffers so with his leg will be cured. I accept his suffering. God and his Holy Family are pleased with you, Stephen. Go and sin no more."

She removed her palm and Stephen felt lightheaded. Slowly he raised his eyes. Betty Sue had folded her hands across her chest. Her breathing was steady and deep, and the radiant look of her face had passed.

"She'll sleep now." Rufus sighed.

Father Kinsella nodded dazedly and moved away from the bed. He sat down across the room from Betty Sue and stared. He couldn't keep his eyes off her.

She lay as if dead, her thin body barely disturbing the smooth flow of blankets. Only her pale face and pierced hands were visible in the dark corner.

Out of the corner of his eyes, Stephen noticed the pastor. The old man, he knew, would have trouble walking. His arthritic leg would be stiff from the hours of standing.

Father Driscoll stepped away from the bed and hesitated. Then he took another step, moving carefully, letting all his weight down on his bad leg. He took another step, more quickly this time, then strode across the room dramatically and stopped before Father Kinsella.

"My leg, Stephen!" The old man's face beamed. "The pain is gone! Blessed be to God, she's taken away the pain!"

9

Monday, February 27

"You can't move at all?" he asked.

She shook her head. There were tears in her eyes. "I don't mind," she said.

Her right leg was above the quilt and she had pulled up her nightgown, baring the calf. The leg looked healthy: no swelling of the joints, no sores. Tentatively he ran his fingers along the smooth skin of her calf and tickled the sole of her foot. He glanced up at her and she shook her head. There was no feeling in the leg.

"It's all right, Stephen," she said with a smile. "I asked for this." But there was pain in her eyes and the breath went out of him as he saw her eyes well up with the tears she would not shed.

"But you're suffering," he protested.

She shrugged. "It's fine, Stephen. I want to suffer for him."

"Why, Betty Sue?"

"I don't know." She looked lost. "That's the really funny part, Stephen; I just don't know why. I don't recollect, y'know, how it all happened. Rufus, he told me afterwards."

The priest frowned. "Do you remember what you told me that day?"

She shook her head. Her young face was innocent. "When I make those prophecies, I don't recall them. Rufus tells me what I said."

"Did he tell you about what you said to me?"

She looked away, as if embarrassed, and answered slowly, picking her words. "He said I told you about a girl. Some girl at the university. He said I told you not to see her. Is that right, Stephen?" She looked back at him, her brown eyes full on his.

He nodded and answered, "I was involved with a woman at the university. A student. The Bishop found out about it and transferred me last fall to Mossy Creek. Since then I've seen her once or twice, here in the mountains and at the university. But finally we stopped seeing each other. I was hurting her and she was hurting me and we couldn't go on."

"Do you love her, Stephen?" She had slid down on the pillows and moved to the edge of the bed so that their faces were inches from each other.

"Yes, I guess I did love her. Our whole friendship was so strange I didn't realize what I felt, but love is what it was. I wanted her to just be"—he halted, searched for the right word—"I wanted her to be *happy*. I don't think I gave her much happiness, but that's what I wanted, and when we were together, she made me happy. At least, at the very beginning. Then other people found out and it got complicated and sordid."

He fell silent and she reached out and touched him. Her fingers caressed his cheek and he forced himself to look at her.

"And now I'm causing you pain."

"I don't mind, Stephen; I don't mind a'tall! If God wants me to suffer for you, then I'm happy." Her eyes were bright.

"But I'm the one who should be punished, Betty Sue. Not you! It's my sin. Why have I been spared my punishment?" He had raised his voice so at first he did not hear her soft reply.

"What?" he asked, stopping.

"I said, maybe he's got something planned for you." She had retreated into the deep comfort of the goosedown pillows and her face had the fresh hopefulness of a very young child, still unaccustomed to disappointment.

"Betty Sue, what do you mean?" And he knew, then, instinctively, that somehow this woman would affect his life and he was afraid. It was an irrational fear, the kind that begins in the back of one's mind and plows through the body like a stroke. But she smiled: the spontaneous smile of a child.

"Stephen, I don't know anything. Like I told you. I don't remember what I said."

"Why did you say that perhaps God has something planned for me?"

She looked off, as if she were daydreaming or had lost her thought. Then she answered slowly, "Rufus, he said. I told him I thought you were real nice and Rufus told me you wouldn't go away. I was afraid you might, you know, go back to the university and I wouldn't see you again. But Rufus said no. He said you had work to do here. He's real smart when it comes to knowing things. He said you'd come help me, didn't he? So I believe him, and I don't want you leaving me." She was near tears once more and he took her hand gently in his and murmured, "I won't leave you."

She studied him, as if she couldn't see enough of him, and asked, "Promise?"

He nodded.

Slowly she lifted his hands and kissed the tips of his

fingers. "Thank you, Stephen." She lay back and closed her eyes, but she kept hold of his hands, nestled them under her chin, in the hollow of her neck.

"Stephen," she asked after a moment, "do you think it might happen again?"

"What, Betty Sue?"

"Do you think you might fall in love?"

"I hope not."

She opened her eyes, frowning.

"It complicates my life, Betty Sue. I took vows—made sacred promises—that I would lead a celibate existence."

She kept frowning, not understanding. He tried again. "When I become involved with a woman and have relations with her, I commit a grave sin. And God punishes me because I am his priest. That's what happened with Deborah, but because of you—your ecstasy, and the stigmata—you took on the suffering for my offense. I can't ever get involved with another woman. I won't cause you more pain."

She shook her head and said, "You can't help it."

"How do you know?" Another moment of fear ran through him. She sounded so sure and knowing.

"Rufus said you'll make me suffer."

"I better talk to Rufus," he commented jokingly, relieved that that was her only reason.

"No, Stephen, don't." Her voice was panicky. "He told me not to tell you anything." She was whispering fast. "I don't want him mad at me."

He stood and leaned over the bed so he could see her face. "Betty Sue, what is it?"

She shook her head.

He slipped his hand under her chin and turned her face toward him. She resisted at first, then looked up.

"Are you afraid of him?" he asked.

She nodded slowly.

"Why?" he whispered. "Do you think he'll hurt you?"

She shook her head. "No, I'm afraid he'll hurt you."

"But why me?"

"He don't like you, Stephen. He never told me so, but I can tell the way he talks."

"I haven't done anything to him. I don't know the man."

"It don't matter none. He was like that before you came up to Blue Haze. He'd talk about you, how we had to get you to cure me, and, y'know, the way he'd talk, I could tell he didn't like you much. It was how he said your name, mostly, and that you was a Catholic. No one around here likes Catholics much."

Father Kinsella tried unsuccessfully to place Rufus among the students he might have met at the university. "Is he from the mountains?" he asked.

Betty Sue shook her head. "He came up here first when I was a little girl, but I don't know where from. He just came around and asked for work during tobacco pickin'."

Father Kinsella sat back. He would go see Rufus, he thought, and find out why the hired hand had such a strange influence on the girl.

"Don't!" she said. Her eyes were hard brown and almost angry. "Don't go seein' him, Stephen!"

"I didn't say I was."

"But you were thinking it, weren't you?"

"He might be able to answer a lot of questions about you, Betty Sue."

She kept shaking her head, not listening. "I don't want you gettin' hurt on account of me."

"He won't hurt me, Betty Sue."

"Yes, he will, Stephen."

"How do you know?" He smiled, touched by her concern.

"Because"—she reached out to touch his face—"because I love you."

The bedroom door burst open and slammed against the

thin wall, shaking the house. Father Kinsella looked around the room. They had been talking for so long in the corner that it had become dark in the meanwhile and he had not realized that they looked like lovers, talking in the last light of day, when the door flew open and Rufus stood in the doorway, out of breath and towering above hen,

"Betty Sue, you all right?" His fists were clenched.

"Yes, Rufus, I'm fine." Her voice was suddenly submissive.

He stood a moment glancing back and forth between them, silent and angry.

"Come in, Rufus," Father Kinsella offered, "we were just talking." His tone was conciliatory.

"Betty Sue, you need your rest." Rufus ignored the priest. "It's late and you haven't had your nap. And it's time for your medicine."

"I'm fine, Rufus. We've only been talkin'. I'm not tired a'tall." Her voice was shaking.

"Did you take your medicine?" Rufus asked, still ignoring the priest.

She shook her head.

"I'll go fetch it," he said, and left the room.

"What medicine is that?" Father Kinsella asked.

"Rufus, he gives me medicine for my pains," she answered. "Stephen, you better go. He'll just get worse with you hangin' round."

Father Kinsella had his hand on the bed and he could feel the mattress shake with her trembling. He couldn't leave her now, not alone with Rufus and without her parents at home. He decided to stall.

"Who prescribed this medicine, Betty Sue? Have you been seeing a doctor?"

"This ain't store bought, Stephen. Rufus makes it from roots and plants he finds in the holler."

The young man came rushing back into the room, carrying a small bottle of dark brown liquid in a jam jar.

"What's that, Rufus?" the priest asked. His voice was calm, but there was a hard edge to it.

"It's just home-brew medicine. Mountain medicine." Rufus carefully poured out a half-inch of the brown syrupy liquid.

"Hit taste good, Stephen. I don't mind it none." Betty Sue spoke quickly, sensing trouble between the two men.

"It might taste good, Betty Sue, but that doesn't mean it is any good for you." He spoke nervously. He couldn't let her drink that concoction, yet he felt there was a strange alliance between them, a secret pact that excluded him. "What's it made of?" he asked.

"Oh, just some mountain roots, that's all. I got some black cherry and yellow root, ginseng and camomile flowers, plus a little maidenhair fern, baneberry, and blue cohosh." He smiled and his teeth flashed in the soft light.

"Ginseng?" The priest frowned.

"*Panax quinquefolius,* Father," Rufus grinned. "That's its Latin name, as you should know."

"That's a drug! What are you doing, Rufus, giving her a drug?" He was furious now.

"I like it, Stephen," she interrupted. "Hit stops the pain."

The young priest stared at her angrily. He hated to hear her defend Rufus. "But you told me you wanted to suffer. That you were suffering gladly for my sins."

"Yes, I do, but——" She glanced at Rufus, then away. She looked confused. "Sometimes, Stephen, it gets hurtin' so, I just can't take it no more."

"Is that what you want, Father?" Rufus asked, his voice cold. "To have her suffer? Does it make you feel better having her suffer because of you? Is that your idea of being a good Christian?"

"What I want, Rufus, is some of the medicine. I want to take it to the university and have it examined in their laboratories."

"No, you don't." Rufus backed off, beyond the perimeter of the bedroom light.

"What's the matter?" Father Kinsella asked. "Why are you afraid to let me have it? What's in it besides wild roots?" Father Kinsella felt the tension in the room shift, and now he had the upper hand.

"You people will just take my secret, slap a label on it, and manufacture it yourselves," Rufus said, talking fast.

"That's not why I want the medicine and you know it."

"It's okay, Stephen," Betty Sue cried. She sat up in bed and grabbed his arm, pleading with him.

"No, it's not all right, Betty Sue. He's been giving you something unlawful. Something that's been causing you to suffer with those wounds and visions." It was becoming clear to him as he spoke. That was what caused the strange sores and trances. There was nothing supernatural about her ecstasies. They had only been drug inflicted. He shook his head at how he and Driscoll had been so gullible. Deborah was right: this could be some kind of mountain plot against the Catholics.

"What have you done to this girl, Rufus?" the priest asked. He stood up, prepared to take on the younger man.

Rufus moved away back against the wall as the young priest approached, cornering him.

"Stephen, please!" Betty Sue cried from her bed, but the priest kept circling, trapping Rufus inside the bedroom.

He was a coward, Father Kinsella realized, and the resentment he had always felt toward Rufus surfaced. He half hoped Rufus would try something. He had an almost uncontrollable urge to slap the kid's face, to wipe the sneering smile from his lips.

Because that was what he was doing: smiling. A thin,

curling grin, mocking and self-satisfied. Stephen knew that look. He had seen a similar grin on another young man years before and the dark memory tore through his mind.

The older student at the seminary had pulled him forward, smiling, whispering like a mother, hugging him. He wanted to get away, yet he didn't. He was afraid. Afraid of what the older boy would do to him. And also he liked the security of the boy's arms. And he had let him have his way then and whenever he wished.

In the far corner of the bedroom Rufus said, "Here, I'll show you this ain't nothing more than a good old mountain tonic." He raised the jam glass in a mock toast and drank half the dark liquor. "You want some?" he asked, grinning and holding out the glass.

"Are you afraid of my medicine, Kinsella? Is that it? Do you think it's too strong for you?"

The priest didn't have the courage to find out. As Rufus moved closer, Stephen caught the foul odor of the young man, that rank smell he had first experienced in the confessional, and Rufus, realizing Father Kinsella knew, began to laugh, and his loud voice carried across Blue Haze Ridge as Stephen retreated off the mountain.

10

Friday, March 3

He went with Father Driscoll to Blue Haze Ridge on Friday morning, but not to participate. He had spent the week trying to convince the pastor that Betty Sue had been victimized, that Rufus had staged her ecstasies with drugs, but the pastor wouldn't listen.

"And how do you explain my leg, Stephen?" he had asked. "It has been almost a week without pain or swelling."

"That could be nothing more than autosuggestion. I spoke to Doctor Lear again and he thinks that's a possibility, though he'd like to examine you himself."

Father Driscoll was waving his hand, dismissing the idea. "You won't let yourself believe this cure was miraculous, will you?" he said to the young priest. "I've had arthritis most of my life and suddenly it is cured without a trace of pain—at the intercession of this saintly woman—but you won't let yourself believe in the power of God. And you call yourself a priest."

"I could believe in her until what I saw on Monday. Rufus wouldn't let me examine the medicine."

"And so you think he's drugging her?"

"You said yourself, Father, you didn't trust him."

"I said I didn't like the influence he has over Betty Sue. He has assumed the role of her spiritual adviser, interpreting her ecstasies. That's a role for someone versed in the New Testament and the passion and death of Christ."

"Someone like yourself?" Father Kinsella asked.

"Yes, someone like myself who can direct the girl's spiritual growth."

Stephen did not have to ask any more questions. He knew what all this was worth to the old priest, what his new role meant to him. There was nothing he could do to change the coming events, so he went along to Blue Haze to watch, to be the only thing he knew he could be: a witness.

"The way of the cross has started," her father said, showing them into the house. "She's been in her trance for 'bout an hour."

Father Driscoll brushed past the parent and rushed into the bedroom. Rufus was standing close to Betty Sue, but when the priests arrived, he slipped off to one side.

Betty Sue was sitting up. She had raised herself to an awkward oblique position in the bed with her arms across her breasts. She did not look at all like the girl Father Kinsella knew. Her sweet freshness had disappeared and she had aged with her suffering. He remembered Saint Theresa's description of her own ecstasies—"the body is like dead." The pale figure of Betty Sue appeared close to that death.

Stephen braced himself. He would not be overwhelmed by this woman's suffering, nor her powerful presence when she slipped into ecstasy. He would not be a willing witness, wanting to find a divine stigmatic in the mountains. He was set to challenge with logic and theology everything that might occur before his eyes. To emphasize his detachment, he stood well away from the bed, against the back wall, as if distance would afford him some protection.

"Betty Sue, what do you see?" asked the pastor.

"I see Jesus," she softly replied. "I see Jesus among the crowd of people and soldiers." Her hand reached out, pointing toward Jesus in the invisible scene. She was staring intently, her eyes enthralled. Her silence kept them motionless in the bedroom. Father Kinsella could hear his own fast breathing.

Then she began to struggle. Her hands grabbed at the emptiness before her face and she strained forward as if trying to lift a heavy object. Her right shoulder bent down as if she were lifting something, then she slumped over on her side as if she had fallen.

"*Kumi, Kumi,*" Rufus called out from the far corner of the room as if giving orders.

Stephen jerked his head back. He knew the word, *Kumi.* It was the Aramaic for *arise.* Aramaic, the language used in the Holy Land at the time of Christ. A language that had not been spoken since biblical times.

Betty Sue raised herself off the bed, leaned forward in that same oblique position. Father Driscoll approached her and asked, "My child, what does Christ's Cross look like?"

"The Cross is not like what we imagine," she answered, concentrating on her words. "Jesus is not carrying a cross at all, but only the wood for it. It is two beams, one short piece tied to the longer."

"Will our Savior be nailed to those beams?"

She turned slowly towards the pastor, her eyes sorrowful but unseeing, and nodded yes. Then she looked away, stared off into the room and said, "Come, Veronica, do not be afraid."

Betty Sue had reached the sixth station of the Cross, Stephen realized, when a kindly woman named Veronica wiped the sweat from the face of Jesus and later found Christ's image imprinted on the cloth.

She began to smile. For a brief moment her face sparkled and she was lovely and young again. The color returned to her cheeks and her brown eyes gleamed. It was just for an instant, and Stephen wasn't sure he had seen the change because when he looked closely again, death hung in her eyes.

She would die, he thought: all the pain and suffering would take their toll on her. He glanced at his watch. They had already been an hour in the bedroom.

Betty Sue slumped a second time on her side and again Rufus ordered, *"Kumi! Kumi!"*

Slowly, painfully, she pulled herself up. *"Come, daughters,"* she whispered, *"weep not over me, but weep for yourselves and for your children."*

She was greeting the women of Jerusalem, Stephen realized, continuing the way of the cross, the inevitable journey that would take Betty Sue out of the walled city and to the place called in Hebrew Golgotha.

Again Christ fell and again Betty Sue cried out. She looked up, her eyes flinching as the soldiers bore down on her with their whips. She twisted to avoid the rawhide, but it came down on her face, bloodying her nose, breaking the fair skin of her cheeks.

"My people, what have I done to thee?" she gasped, raising her arms in lamentation, *"Answer me? I brought thee out of the land of Egypt, and thou hast led me to the gibbet of the Cross. Forty years I fed thee in the desert, and thou hast beaten me. What more could I have done for you?"*

She wept into her hands. Her parents had moved closer to the bed and now all of them surrounded her, standing like helpless guardians as she raised her arms to Heaven and looked off into the emptiness before her. Her lips were bruised and cracked and there were black-and-blue marks under her eyes. Her whole face was bleeding.

Rufus stepped out of the corner and handed her a white cloth. She brought it slowly to her face and wiped the perspiration away, then dropped it on the bed.

Then, unexpectedly, she sat straight up. Taking hold of her cotton nightgown, she ripped open the front, exposing herself.

"Cover this child," Father Driscoll cried out, shocked by her nakedness.

She was beautiful, Father Kinsella thought, with her full heavy breasts and slim long-waisted body. They were stripping Christ of His garments, and Betty Sue knelt with her head bowed, accepting this final humiliation. She waited for her crucifixion, her body scarred and mutilated from the terrible way of the cross.

"The woman's indecent!" Father Driscoll kept shouting, enraged at the blasphemy.

Betty Sue fell backward into the bed and Stephen stepped forward and pulled the sheet up, covering her nakedness and silencing the pastor. He thought she had lain back to rest, but when he stepped away she threw out her right arm and gasped.

They were nailing Christ to the Cross. He watched helpless and horrified as the iron pierced Betty Sue's right hand and the thin transparent shield covering her wound burst open and the blood gushed into her palm.

Her body thrashed on the wide bed as her left arm was violently pinned against the mattress. The sheet had slipped off her tormented body, again exposing her lashed breasts, but no one moved to cover her. The agony of the young woman paralyzed the priests. Another invisible spike was hammered into her palm and the blood bubbled forth as her fingers curled around the spike in pain.

They were manipulating Christ's body now, stretching it on the crude cross, and Betty Sue's long legs were jerked on the bed, her feet pressed together as one spike drove through both arches and nailed Christ's feet to the wood.

Father Kinsella could hear the ringing of metal as the soldiers rhythmically hammered the spike home, breaking bone and tearing muscle. The sharp metallic sound rang across the hilltop, over the heads of the multitude, as the Cross was lifted and dropped into place in the hole that had been dug for it.

Betty Sue screamed as Christ's body shook, jarred by the impact of the foot of the Cross striking the ground, but her cries were lost, smothered by the wailing of the women of Jerusalem.

Her body on the bed was twisted into the familiar pose of the crucified Christ. She appeared as Father Kinsella had seen her on the cross at the Newman Chapel: her body naked and distorted, hanging from the wooden beams, her breasts tight, and all the muscles of her arms strained from the weight of her suspended body.

Betty Sue gasped, *"Sachena."*

Stephen leaned closer, not believing the word he had heard.

"Sachena," she repeated. It was Aramaic for "I thirst."

"What is that?" Father Kinsella asked. But he already knew what Rufus had to be holding.

"Wine and vinegar," he answered, staring back at the priest who now blocked his way to the girl.

"Can't you give her water?"

Rufus shook his head. "This is the way it must be." He pushed his way forward and touched Betty Sue's parched lips with the bitter gall. She swallowed a small mouthful and choked, then turned her head to one side and vomited up the liquor.

"Leave her alone!" Stephen shouted, angry at himself for letting Rufus give her the drink. He reached for the white cloth Rufus had used to wipe away her perspiration and then he saw Betty Sue's face. It was outlined on the cloth, a perfect image of her sorrowful eyes and battered face. This was no autosuggestion or the effect of a drug-induced trance. There was a word for this, a word Father Kinsella had never thought to use in his life as a priest. He stared down at the face of Betty Sue imprinted on the white cloth, and knew that his intuition had been right that day in her bedroom: she *had* changed his life. And that was another miracle.

"*Abba schabok lahon,*" she whispered in Aramaic. She was asking God to forgive them.

Christ was dying on Calvary. Father Kinsella could see it in Betty Sue's face as she twisted feverishly. Her parents moved nearer, wanting to help their daughter. They had lived through this death of Christ hundreds of times and knew the final agony Betty Sue would endure. Only Rufus stayed away from the bed. He stood with his arms crossed and smiled down at the sight of the dying Christ.

It had begun to rain, an early spring mountain rain that beat hard on the tin roof. The thunder in the mountains rolled across Blue Haze Ridge and shook the tarpaper shack.

Betty Sue screamed and her fragile body, weak from suffering, arched itself from the soaking mattress. She pulled at the invisible spikes and tried to free herself from the Cross, but the gashes in her hands only split further and ripped the tender flesh of her palms.

She lay back, exhausted, on the bed, breathing deeply, her body trembling from the sudden cold in the bedroom. Father Kinsella reached to pull up the quilt and saw that under her soft young breast her heart had been lanced; blood mixed with water spilled from her side.

She was dying, he thought frantically. The passion and

death of Jesus Christ were too much for her. But when he put his hand to her mouth, he felt a warm puff of breath on his palm.

"Betty Sue," he whispered. "What happened to Jesus?"

"He died," she answered without emotion, and fell asleep. The pain had passed from her face. She looked young and beautiful again, a girl who was too exhausted to stay awake.

Father Kinsella glanced at his watch. It was three o'clock.

In his bedroom at the rectory, Stephen turned on the tape recorder and listened again to Betty Sue's whispered words. He had been awake all night, going over the tape of her way of the Cross and crucifixion. Now he moved the tape forward and listened as she made her revelation.

"Stephen," he heard her say, as she had that afternoon, "you have been troubled with a terrible sin from your youth. Do not worry any longer, for God understands and has forgiven you."

How could she have known? It was something he had only told Father Rafalet years before in the confessional and her knowledge terrified him. There was only one explanation and he accepted it.

Betty Sue had been touched by God and did possess the power of revelation and prophesy. Her stigmatic wounds and visionary ecstasies were divine, a blessing from God. She had been chosen by God for some special purpose, and though he did not know what it was, Stephen accepted her as a chosen one, knowing, as he had been taught by the Catholic Church, that it was not always possible to understand the mysterious ways in which God showed his Almighty Presence.

It was almost six A.M. but Stephen was not tired. He felt at peace, knowing that God was directing this miracle on Blue Haze Ridge.

He went down the back steps to the kitchen for a glass of milk before turning in. The darkness had softened in the predawn and he could see the silhouette of the church through the kitchen windows. Father Driscoll would be up soon to say mass. Lately, with all the time he was spending on Blue Haze, the pastor hadn't much rest. Still, Father Kinsella realized, even with the extra work, the pastor had never looked better.

Father Kinsella stood by the kitchen windows drinking his milk and watching for the March sun to reach the crest of Blue Haze Ridge, watching for it to turn the hillside golden with its morning light. The long night of listening to the tapes and keeping himself awake with black coffee had left him too restless to sleep. He would go for a walk, he thought: a quick walk around the block. That would take the edge off his nervousness.

He left the rectory by the back door, and circling the school and the nuns' convent, came back along Church Street and passed the front of Saint John's. Now the sun had reached the ridge and the sharp clear light swept across the slopes of Blue Haze. He was watching the way the light played across the hillside and did not notice that the front door of the church was open until he was almost by the entrance.

It was too early, he thought, for mass, but Father Driscoll might have awakened early. He went up the stone steps and into the church, thinking it would be a nice gesture to assist the pastor at mass, when he saw the black rooster on the floor of the vestibule. The bird's throat had been cut and the eyes, heart, and tongue ripped out. Steam rose from the warm remains. The cock had only just been killed.

Father Kinsella ran up the aisle toward the altar. Whoever it was would have gone for the tabernacle. The sun had hit the huge stained-glass windows and the church was brilliant with the play of biblical pageantry across the pews.

He jumped onto the platform and thought at first that the altar had not been disturbed. The silk frontal was in place, as was the linen altar cloth, but then he saw that he was wrong: the tabernacle had been broken into. He moved cautiously around the platform, afraid of what he might find.

The silver ciborium had been tipped over and the Eucharist wafers spilled onto the floor. He walked carefully so as not to step on them, and then he spotted the black cock's feather. It had been sharpened and dipped in the sacred altar wine, and a message traced with the sharpened tip on a yellowing parchment. He saw it was the same illiterate scribbling:

I WANT You, Stevie, Your Mind

He refused to stop and think. He needed to hurry. To clean the altar and the vestibule before mass, before the parishioners arrived and saw the sacrilege.

11

Wednesday, March 8

Feast of Saint John of God

The letter from Father Rafalet arrived at the rectory of Saint John of the Cross by registered mail late on Wednesday evening.

Dear Stephen:

I have decided to answer by mail rather than telephoning long distance because of the nature of the material.

I did a search of the literature on such worship to see if there is any historical explanation for what has happened at Saint John's. We have, surprisingly, a large library concerning acts of blasphemy. Such sorcery is as old as the Church itself.

The *Grimoire of Honorius,* a ritual for summoning the spirits of darkness, touches on what you told me. The ritual was used by magicians to strengthen their powers and protect themselves from demons.

A magician—usually an ordained priest—said a mass of the Holy Spirit in the middle of the night. Then came the part of the ritual that you witnessed: At sunrise a black cock was killed at the altar and its eyes, heart, and tongue ripped out. Then one of the black cock's feathers was sharpened and dipped into the consecrated wine and water and the magician/priest used it to write prophesies on a piece of parchment. The magician/priest also kept part of the consecrated host, wrapping it in clerical vestments.

Two days later, again at midnight, the magician/priest lit a candle of yellow wax, made in the form of a cross, and recited Psalm 78, "Give ear, O my people, to my law." Then he said the Mass for the dead, calling on God to free him from the fear of Hell and to make the demons obedient to him.

He extinguished the candle and at sunrise cut the throat of a young male lamb. At some later time the carcass was buried with prayers in which the magician/priest identified the slaughtered lamb with Christ.

This is all of the ritual that I have been able to locate at the monastery, but our librarian is checking further.

Meanwhile, I implore you to tell your Bishop. I have not said anything to His Excellency as I consider much of what you told me to be sealed by the sacrament of confession.

And to answer your question: Yes, I do think this sacrilege at Saint John's is directly related to the work you have been doing with the stigmatic woman in your parish.

You said the young woman's ecstasies are awesome and convincing. But it is not up to you, Stephen, to determine whether her stigmata are truly of divine origin. You can act in good faith toward her and let an

Ecclesiastical Commission decide. Such investigations take many months, if not years, and will require men much more learned on the subject than you or myself.

Act on your own good common sense, Stephen, and your faith in God. The truth will soon be known. I have asked the community at the monastery to remember you and Saint John's in their prayers.

Yours in Christ,
Father M. William Rafalet, O.C.S.O.

Stephen folded the letter and slipped it into his desk. The letter had arrived too late to help him. The night before, the church had been broken into once again and in the morning Father Driscoll found the skin of a slain lamb stretched across the altar. But it did not matter. Stephen now knew who was doing the sacrilegious deeds at Saint John's.

"Stephen," Betty Sue said, turning on her side and smiling at the priest, "tell me some more stories about people who had stigmata."

"But I've told you all of them."

"Well, tell me again," she insisted like a child.

"Which one? About Saint Francis of Assisi?"

"Oh, no—tell me about the nun who grew the lily."

"Blessed Helen?"

"Yes, Blessed Helen!" Her eyes lit up. "That's my favorite."

"Well, let's see, Blessed Helen died in 1250 and was, after Saint Francis, our second stigmatic saint," Father Kinsella began, slipping into a storytelling voice, speaking softly and slowly as if he had great secrets to share. "Blessed Helen had wounds like you on both hands, her feet, and on her breast.

"The first wound was in her right hand and it appeared in October, on the Feast of Saint Francis. She cried out—and the other nuns of the convent heard her and told how she called out, 'Lord, refrain, do not this thing, my Lord.' But when they rushed in to help her, the nuns couldn't see whom she was talking to.

"The second wound was made at noon on the Feast of the Holy Apostles Peter and Paul. And on this wound of her right hand there one day budded a stalk of gold, and from this golden stalk a fragrant lily grew."

"How, Stephen?"

"It was a miracle, Betty Sue. God made it happen, but Blessed Helen was very humble about God's special treatment of her, and she didn't want anyone to know.

"To keep it a secret, she would uproot the lily everytime it grew in her hand. But the other nuns knew anyway, and they found the flowers and kept them, even after Lady Helen died and went to Heaven.

"A lily also grew from her breast wound. It was a marvelous lily with a sweet perfume, and this flower, too, she tore out from its roots. But she couldn't keep it a secret. Sometimes, as she walked around the convent grounds, flowers would grow wherever she had walked. And often when she prayed in the chapel with the other nuns, fresh flower petals would drop from her bloody palms.

"When she died and was buried within the walls of the convent, lilies grew from her grave and even today they bloom throughout the year, winter snows and all. When strangers are permitted inside the cloistered walls they can always find Blessed Helen's grave because of the fragrance that fills that sunny corner of the convent." Father Kinsella stopped and smiled at Betty Sue.

"Oh, what a lovely story," she whispered, her brown eyes shiny with tears. "Tell the part again about the petals coming from the palms of her hands. That's the best part."

Stephen laughed, amused at her childlike desire to be entertained. "Not now, Betty Sue, we have to spend some time learning about the Catholic Church so you can be received into the faith."

"I know all about that stuff," she answered smugly. "Rufus already told me."

"Like what?" Stephen asked and leaned back in the chair, tipping it off the front two legs.

"Oh, like how to make the sign of the cross." She sat up, excited, and showed him.

Stephen laughed. "No, Betty Sue, you have it backwards," he said, and showed her how. She practiced it a few minutes and then the priest asked, "What else did Rufus tell you?"

"Oh, stories, y'know, about Jesus. Stories that I never heard before. Stories that ain't even in the Bible."

"Like what?"

"Well," she said, sitting back and concentrating, "Did you know Christ was a queer?"

"Rufus told you that?" Stephen kept the smile frozen on his face.

She nodded. "All those apostles—Peter and Paul, all those men. Rufus, he said they were all queer." She talked freely, like a child telling stories on her parents and having no idea of the significance.

"But some of his apostles, Betty Sue, were married."

"Oh, you can still be married and like men, Stephen. Everyone knows that." She blushed, embarrassed at all this talk.

"What else did Rufus have to say about Christ?" He kept himself controlled. She was not to blame. There was nothing vicious in her attitude toward Christ. To her it was all just historical pageantry, a movie in which people dressed in strange costumes and she played a role.

"Oh, he told me how Jesus wasn't a very good son. Here he was thirty years old and still living with his Ma and Pa, and they didn't have much money. He was kinda lazy and if it wasn't for his Pa, Jesus would have probably starved to death because he was just so dumb, y'know?" She shook her head. "That's strange, Stephen. The only person I know who's livin' at home and full grown is Minyard Parker and he ain't right in the head. Everyone knows about Minyard."

"Jesus lived hundreds of years ago, Betty Sue," said Stephen. "In those days sons and daughters stayed with their parents until they married." She had no concept of time, of all the years since the age of Christ because in her ecstasies she easily transported herself from the present to the biblical days. Both periods were intimately known to her. She had lost all idea of time and space—she was like a science-fiction character who could reach out in time and touch the hand of God.

"How come he didn't marry Mary Magdalene? She sure enough loved him. You can tell the way she looked at him. And when they killed him, Lordy, did she cry!"

"Do you know who Mary Magdalene was?"

"Sure. She was a whore. She gave herself to men for money."

"And what did Christ do?" Stephen asked, almost afraid of what she would say.

"He fucked her," Betty Sue answered matter-of-factly.

"He did? But you just said Christ was queer."

"He was," she answered quickly, flustered by all of the priest's questions, "but he also slept with whores like Mary Magdalene."

"How do you know? Do you know that from one of your trances? Did Mary Magdalene or Jesus tell you?"

She shook her head. "Uh uh. Rufus did."

Stephen was finally exasperated. "Betty Sue!" he said urgently. "It is a sin—a serious, mortal sin—to have sexual relations with a woman outside of marriage. You know your

Bible history. It's one of the Ten Commandments. A rule Moses got from God."

"It's not so terrible if he loved her, Stephen," she answered smugly. "I think it's natural and good and no sin at all." She stole a quick look at the priest.

"Betty Sue, two weeks ago when you were in your ecstasy you told me God was pleased I had stopped seeing my friend Deborah. I don't understand how you can tell me it's okay for Christ to sleep with Mary Magdalene and also tell me God and the Holy Ghost are pleased I have given up Deborah Laste."

"Oh, Stephen, you don't understand! I'm not myself when I'm in those trances." She sighed, trying to explain, trying to understand it herself. "It's like someone has taken me over. Whatever that person says, it ain't *me* talkin'."

A schizophrenic, Father Kinsella thought. She was a person with two personalities, one human and one supernatural. Except her human person was so incongruent with the divine. She did not have an intense love for divine things. She was a flirt, telling him all the time that she loved him. And she did love him, he knew, in the same innocent, emotional, and idealized way many young women were attracted to him.

That did not trouble him when he evaluated her saintliness. Nor her lack of piety. He found her spunkiness refreshing. Prayer was too often thought of as somber when it was meant to be a celebration of life rather than a denial of joy.

Still Rufus had filled her with lies, half-truths, and misconceptions about Christ's teaching. He had filled her with his hatred of the Catholic Church, the kind of anger one usually encountered in a failed seminarian or a defrocked priest. No one seemed to know Rufus's background, but it clearly included more than a passing acquaintance

with the Roman Catholic Church. Rufus had distorted the
details of Christ's life to Betty Sue, just as someone had
distorted the rituals of the Catholic mass on the altar of
Saint John's. But in order to distort, Rufus had had to know
the original story. And in order to commit sacrilege, whoever
slit the cock's throat on the church altar had to have been
familiar with the true celebration of the mass. Stephen
remembered his church history well enough to know that
the most bizarre and diabolical acts of sacrilege were usually
committed by perverted Roman Catholics. And in this case,
all the evidence led to Rufus.

"Betty Sue, tell me again how you met Rufus."

"Oh, I don't remember now," she answered impatiently.
She was always uncomfortable when he asked that. "I don't
remember *exactly!* He was always around. He was in the
mountains since I was twelve or thirteen."

"When did you become friends?" Father Kinsella pressed.
There was no way of knowing if Rufus had ever been in the
seminary, but he knew for sure that Rufus wasn't just
someone who had suddenly turned up on Blue Haze Ridge.

"Well, when I got sick he'd come 'round to see me, play
games, y'know, in the afternoon. Ma and Pa took me out of
school after the snakes bit me."

"What was that like? When the snakes bit you?"

She squirmed in the bed, then said vaguely, "I don't
remember. I told you 'fore I don't remember."

"I know it was terrible for you, Betty Sue, and I don't
want to upset you." He kept his voice low, unexcited. "I
won't ask you again about the snake bites, but I must tell
you I'm worried about Rufus."

She looked at him, raising her eyebrows and waiting for
him to continue.

"I don't think he's a good influence on you. Most of the
stories he has told you about Jesus and Mary Magdalene are
not true. Jesus was not queer. He did not have sexual

relationships with Mary Magdalene, or any woman. These are just lies spread by people who hate Christianity and the Catholic Church.

"I wish you'd tell him not to come around anymore."

She was shaking her head before he finished speaking. "I can't," she whispered, sounding lost.

"Then I'll tell him for you," Father Kinsella offered.

"No, don't!" She sat up in the bed, looked frantically at Father Kinsella. "Please don't say anything to him."

"I know he doesn't like me, Betty Sue, but I'm not afraid of him. I can handle Rufus."

"No you can't, Stephen," she said knowingly, "you can't beat him." Her voice sounded final.

12

Sunday, March 19

Palm Sunday

He gently undressed Betty Sue, taking his time with her nightgown. She helped him, lifting herself so he could slip it over her hips, then sitting up and raising her arms. He pulled the gown free of her body and tossed it away, then settled her again on the wide bed.

Her body was creamy white and free of wounds, and she was suddenly shy without clothes. She reached for him with both arms, lowering his face into the softness of her breasts. The heavy, sweet perfume of her stigmata filled his nostrils as he hungrily wrapped her into his arms.

She reached and slid him into her. He could feel her tightness as he broke into her body. She gasped and clung to him, dragging her nails across his body and breaking the skin.

Father Kinsella woke breathing rapidly. He tossed off the warm blankets and swung his legs over the side of the bed, then dropped his head into his hands. He stayed that way for a few minutes, clearing his head, before fumbling through the dark to see what time it was. Six A.M. Time to get up. He had masses to say. He stood and moved slowly toward the bathroom.

It was daylight when Father Kinsella finished showering and dressing and got downstairs to the kitchen. He leaned across the sink and stared out the windows at the morning sky. New snow had fallen during the night, but now the clouds had cleared off Blue Haze Ridge. Through the snow, the bare black trees stood out singly against a bright blue sky. It would be a lovely morning in the mountains.

He thought of Betty Sue asleep in her bed with those heavy homemade quilts tucked up around her. The pain and agony were over for a few days. This was the peaceful time of her week. She would sleep late today. He smiled, thinking of how lovely she must look snuggled up and asleep. He found himself missing her.

The front doorbell rang once, tentatively, as if the person weren't sure. Stephen frowned. They weren't usually bothered on Sunday mornings. He glanced at the kitchen clock. Father Driscoll would be almost finished with the early mass.

Stephen set his coffee cup down and walked along the dark hallway to the foyer. He could see a woman's figure through the cut-glass door, but he didn't realize it was Deborah until he pushed open the storm door.

She flashed a brave smile and asked, "May I come inside?" She looked cold.

He stepped aside and she walked into the warm house, being careful not to touch him as she passed.

"What's wrong?" he whispered, closing the door behind him.

"Can we talk in there?" she asked, pointing to the parlor. She kept her eyes down, like a nun.

He led the way into the front room and shut the double

French doors behind him. They would be safe in there, he knew, even when the pastor came back from mass.

"I couldn't hug you or anything, could I?" she asked, standing in the middle of the room, head bowed, her hands deep in her pockets.

"No," he said, "we'd better not." He wouldn't lie to her anymore. "You can sit," he added, like an offering.

She sat carefully on the edge of an upholstered chair, crossing her legs and slowly pulling off her leather gloves. She had not yet looked at him.

He sat across the room and the space created a gulf between them. He knew he should move closer, to make it easier for her, but instead he only asked, "Is there something wrong, Deborah?"

She nodded, tilting up her face and staring at the priest. "I'm pregnant, Stephen," she said.

He had not expected it. At first he had realized that pregnancy was always a threat, but over the months of seeing her he had forgotten it as a possibility. Women, he had come to believe, didn't get pregnant unless they wanted to. Now the news left him momentarily bewildered.

"Are you sure?" he managed to say.

"I'm sure." She loosened her coat, doing it quickly as if she was very warm, but she did not take it off. "I haven't seen the doctor," she went on, "but I have all the signs: I'm queasy in the morning; I always have to go to the bathroom; my breasts feel funny." She shrugged as if the whole situation were hopeless. "And besides, I'm almost two weeks overdue with my period."

"But when . . .?"

"I guess that afternoon here."

He stood up, as if for some purpose, but only walked to the door and turned around. She looked very small in the chair, dark and waifish, like someone who smoked too many cigarettes and lived on black coffee.

"You weren't using anything?" he asked.

"I guess not."

"Oh, come on, Deborah, be serious."

"Do you men have a bathroom for women handy?" she asked, grabbing her purse.

"There's one across the hall. Are you feeling okay?" He was afraid now she would get sick.

"Yes, I'm okay, but this room is stifling. Open a window or something." She slipped out of her coat and went across the hall quickly.

Stephen headed for the kitchen to make coffee. He wouldn't let himself think about the baby, not until they could sit down and talk it out. He wished they were somewhere else besides the rectory. The house was too confining, too close to his life as a priest. He pushed open the hallway door and strode into the kitchen. Father Driscoll was sitting at the table, dressed in a shirt and slacks and with the Sunday sports pages spread before him. The first mass was over.

"Morning, Stephen!" He sounded cheery.

Oh, Christ. He didn't need this.

"Good morning, Father." He walked around the table to the kitchen cabinets.

"No problems at the six o'clock," the pastor commented as he scanned the box scores.

"Uh huh."

"The altar boys showed up all right."

"Uh huh." Stephen lifted two porcelain cups and saucers from the shelf and set them on the counter.

"The nuns, you know, do a fine job with those youngsters, getting them out on winter mornings. Timmy Lynch, Patty's boy, was there this morning."

Stephen reached up again to the top shelf and took down the parish's good silver tray. At least he could show her they weren't two hick priests living primitive lives in the mountains.

"Fine boy, that Timmy. He comes from a good family. Did you know Timmy Lynch's grandmother was from my place in Sligo? Her name was Moran. Nora Moran." He folded the sports pages and picked up the comics. Then he glanced up and saw what Father Kinsella was doing.

"What's this, Stephen? Is someone out front?" He half turned in the chair and looked toward the kitchen door.

"Yes, Father." He kept his back to the pastor and busied himself with getting the silver creamer and sugar bowl.

"Why didn't you say? Here I'm half dressed." He was annoyed.

"They're in the parlor, Father. No one will see you back here."

"What is it, Stephen? It's a bit early for anyone to be calling." He studied the young priest. Father Kinsella, he knew, had his private confidences with parishioners, and he respected the young man's position, but still, the boy had been in trouble.

"Just a friendly chat." Stephen poured the coffee, trying to hurry out before the pastor got too inquisitive.

The pastor pushed the paper aside. "And who would it be, Father?"

"A friend from the university." Stephen looked straight at the pastor as if to show he wasn't concealing anything.

"Drove all that way this morning?"

"I think they stayed somewhere in the mountains."

"Oh, yes, well, that's possible." The old priest sipped his coffee, contemplating that. "And who would they be, Father?" the pastor asked directly.

"What's that, Father?" Stephen lifted the silver tray stacked with coffee cups, the creamer and sugar bowl.

Father Driscoll nodded toward the front door. "Who's nice enough to visit you here in the mountains?"

"One of my former students. She's having trouble with her PhD thesis and I've agreed to read it for her. She's writing about the concept of sanctifying grace in existential philosophy." Stephen put his back to the door and pushed it open. "She comes from a good family. Her father is from County Mayo and her mother was taught by the Daughters of Wisdom nuns." Then he was out of the room, leaving the pastor speechless at the kitchen table.

She was back in the parlor, sitting tensely in the same chair.

"I've made some coffee," he said.

"Thanks." Her voice sounded small. "Is someone else here? I heard voices."

"Father Driscoll is out in the kitchen."

"Oh, God! He's not going to come in here, is he?"

"Easy, Deborah, don't worry," he whispered. "He won't bother us. Besides, he has another mass to say in a few minutes." Stephen glanced at his watch. There were still fifteen minutes to go.

They drank in silence, neither one wanting to resume the conversation. He spent the time trying to determine how he felt. But he didn't feel anything—no pain, not even a dullness. It was all too much to comprehend. Finally he asked, "Deborah, I need to know something."

She raised her eyebrows, looked at him over the rim of the cup. She had both her hands wrapped around it, hugging the warmth of the porcelain.

"Was it an accident?"

"What do you think? That I plotted it?"

"No, I don't think so. There wouldn't be any reason for you to do that, but you're also too smart to get yourself pregnant."

"I know what you're thinking: Jewish girls don't get pregnant, right? Well, this one did. After you left the university I got off the pill. I wasn't thinking about getting involved with anyone right away. I just wanted to be alone for a while. It was nice, you know, like being a virgin.

"Then you telephoned and I drove up here. I really didn't think we'd have sex. I thought you were very firm about that and I was going to respect your decision. But when I saw you and we got back into the room ..." She shrugged. "It isn't the end of the line, Stephen. I can handle it myself. I even debated about telling you. Then I decided that wasn't fair. Fair to whom, I don't know." She sighed.

"I'm glad you told me," he said.

She smiled. "So what do you think, Father Kinsella?"

He shook his head. "Think! I can't think. I'm still too numb even to react." But the realization of what he had done began to affect him. It was like a slow suffocation. A feeling of helplessness.

"You don't expect me to keep it?" she asked.

He leaned forward, ran his hand through his hair, then rubbed his face.

"How can I agree to let you abort that child, Deborah? Whatever other terrible things I do, I'm not going to start taking human life."

"It's not yet a human life, Stephen." The look on her face hardened. "A simple D and C will handle it. They can do it in the doctor's office. No pain or operation. I can do it between classes." She tried to sound hard.

"Is there anything else we can do?" he asked.

"Yes—we can get married and live happily ever after."

"Deborah, shut up, will you!"

She kept quiet for a moment. Then she said, "I'm sorry, Stephen. I think my nerves are worse than I realize. Everything pisses me off these days. This is my problem and I'll handle it." She began to gather her things.

"Wait!" He came over and sat near her. "Do you want an abortion?"

"Stephen, what should I do? Have the child? I'm not Hester Prynne, you're not Dimmesdale, and this isn't Salem, Massachusetts. I haven't the time or wherewithal to raise a kid by myself. The mere thought of having a baby makes me shudder. Not now. Not this way."

"We could get married." He said it without thinking. It was one of those thoughts that lay deep in the subconscious and came out without intention.

She glanced at him, a hard, unforgiving look. "Don't talk like that," she said. "Don't say things you don't mean."

"But I do mean it!" It was a wild notion, incomprehensible, but his saying it gave the idea validity.

She leaned back in the chair and studied him.

"You mean leave the priesthood and marry me?"

"Yes," he answered. It was like playing a dangerous game of chance. "I could get a teaching job. I have the degrees. We'd have to move. They won't take me back at the university, but you've almost finished your class work."

"That isn't why I came up here," she said, fighting her happiness until she could believe in it. "I wasn't thinking of blackmailing you with a child."

"I realize that."

"Is it possible? I thought you were a priest for life."

"It's possible." He sighed, already weary at the thought of the complex process of laicization, the letters and struggles with the Bishop. "It takes time, but, yes, I can get out of the order."

"There are other problems," she said. Yes, she thought, she would say it all, get it out front from the first. "I don't want my child raised a Catholic. I'm not saying it has to be raised Jewish—God, I'm not going to lay that trip on any child—but not Catholic." She was shaking her head. This she had to be firm about.

He saw clearly then how hopeless it was. They couldn't shake off their pasts, their childhood beliefs and family. His religion, that nightmare world of guilt and repression, could never co-exist with her world of logic and reality, a world without the magic of faith. He realized that immediately, but Deborah was still caught up in the fantasy.

"I could leave the city by June and write the thesis next year, after the baby is born." She smiled at the thought of having a baby. She knew then with sudden clarity that she did want a child, and the realization made her immensely sure of herself, as if he had just told her she was unequivocally beautiful.

"Well, we'll have to decide a lot more before that," he said, trying to slow down the rollercoaster of possibilities he had triggered with his loose talk of marriage.

"I just meant I could leave the city as early as June," she explained, her feelings hurt because he did not want to engage in the fun of speculation. Then she saw the worry in his face. He looked lost, like a man without options.

"You really don't want to get married, do you, Stephen?" She said it nicely, feeling sorry for him.

"I don't know, Deborah. Everything is happening so fast." But he did know. He just couldn't bring himself to tell her the truth. He was protecting himself from her scorn, and she knew it. She stood, picking up her bag and her suede coat.

"Deborah, don't leave," he said, sorry he had hurt her again.

She paused and looked down at him. Standing, she felt a brief sense of superiority, a kind of triumph over him.

"Why," she asked. "Do you want me to give you absolution? To tell you that it's all right, that I didn't want to get married in the first place and there's no child growing in my belly?" Their affair, she saw, had been nothing more than battles between them, each one fighting to win. She wondered if they had ever been happy.

"What about the baby?" he asked, disregarding her sarcasm.

"That's my decision. Haven't you heard, the Supreme

Court has given us control over our own bodies."

"Deborah, I have a certain responsibility toward that child."

"Don't worry. I won't tell the Right to Life people about you."

They were both standing, moving towards the glass parlor doors. She wouldn't look at him. Her eyes were down, noticing the hardwood floor, the thick polish, generations of it, layer after layer.

"Deborah, I know I can't stop you, but I'll do whatever you ask to help you keep the baby. I have some money. It's family money and I can help support you both."

She started shaking her head. "I don't want to talk about it."

She had her hand on the old-fashioned cut-glass door knob. Her mind was whirling, unable to concentrate and she found herself thinking about the rectory, the details of the handcarved woodwork.

"Stephen, I don't know whether I'm going to go ahead or not. I still have time to think about it. But if I do, I don't want any of your money. I have more than you anyway. Let my trust fund pay for the baby.

"But if I have it, you must promise me you won't make claims on the child. I don't want it in writing or anything, just your word. I'll probably leave school in June, but I don't know where I'll go. Maybe back to New York. But I'm not going to tell you where I go or whether it's a boy or a girl. It shouldn't matter anyway and it's better the less you know.

"Now would you do me a favor and walk me to my car? I'm feeling a little unsteady this morning."

"Let me drive you into the city. I can take a bus back tonight. Please, I want to do something." He was pleading.

"No, I don't want you to. I'm okay. I just need some fresh

air. Why is this house so hot? Haven't Catholics heard about the energy crisis?"

She turned the glass knob and opened the parlor door but he moved his arm across, blocking the door, and pulled her into his arms.

She moved swiftly to him, slid comfortably to his body, even the bulk of her winter coat did not interfere. He slid his arms beneath the coat and around her body, hugging her to him. She pressed her head into the hollow of his neck and he bent his head and kissed her slowly on the cheek. He held her as if for the last time, as if trying to absorb all her tenderness and warmth, to feel one final time the shape of her body hard against his.

She began to tremble and he closed his eyes and held her closer. She struggled to free herself but he couldn't yet bring himself to lose her, to let her go, and that was how Father Driscoll found them. Stephen had not heard the footsteps, nor did he know they had been discovered until Deborah put her fists against his shoulders and pushed herself away.

"Is this how you receive guests in the rectory, Father Kinsella?" the pastor asked.

The two separated and stood awkwardly apart like sinners.

"Father, I'd like to—"

"And what's your name, miss?" the pastor asked, disregarding his assistant.

"Father, this is Deborah Laste," Stephen spoke out. He had to be forceful or the pastor would humiliate them both.

"You, I presume, are Father Kinsella's old friend from the university," Father Driscoll went on, still not addressing his assistant. "Well, I want you out of this rectory."

"I'm leaving anyway, Father," Deborah answered wearily.

"Father Driscoll, there's no reason to be disrespectful with

Deborah." Stephen moved toward the pastor, but the priest stopped his assistant with a cold stare.

"I think it would be wise if you did leave, young lady, and I suggest you don't return to Saint John's."

"Father, Deborah is my friend. I won't have you running her out of here."

"Stephen, it doesn't matter," Deborah murmured, dismissing the incident. She moved forward, trying to leave.

"Father Kinsella, this young woman understands perfectly well that she's not wanted. I'm sure she won't overstay her welcome." And now he was looking hard at the young priest. "I think it's time you and I had a long talk, Stephen. I'll see you after mass."

"I'm driving Deborah back to the city, Father. I won't be here after mass."

The pastor stared at his assistant, disbelieving what he had heard. His orders were final in the parish.

"Don't bother coming back, Stephen," he said. "I don't want you in my church, teaching the children. I will call the Bishop and tell him I want you transferred from St. John's."

He left them there, striding out through the front door and leaving it open. The blast of cold wind came back and hit them.

"Okay," said Stephen, "let's go. Just give me a few minutes to change and pack."

"Stephen, wait!" She touched his arm and searched his face. "You're going to get into more trouble. Stay the winter and get transferred in the spring. If you foul up now, after the Bishop took you out of the university, just think of what godawful place they might send you."

"He can't talk to you like that, as if you were some goddam slut." All his annoyances with the pastor, the months of being under Driscoll's control, came rushing into focus. He had not realized he had been carrying around such hostility. "What he said to you, what he was implying with that knowing look, that's the final straw. He's been impossible ever since we found Betty Sue."

He started up the stairs to get his things.

"Stephen," she called after him, "where are you going to stay?"

He stopped and looked down at her. "May I stay with you for a few days? Until I can work things out?"

She sighed. "You know what that means."

He nodded. "I don't care anymore, Deborah. I just don't care about any of them." And he turned and took the stairs two at a time, in a hurry to get his clothes and leave Saint John's, to get away from Mossy Creek, Matt Driscoll, Mother Church and everything she stood for.

That night they made love for hours in her dark apartment. Always before he had been in a rush, feeling guilty at being there and worried that somehow they'd be discovered, but now it no longer mattered.

He knew there were still problems. He would have to find a job, and explain to his family. It would break his mother's heart, he knew, to tell her he was leaving the church and marrying, especially marrying a Jew.

But he was leading his own life now. All his life he had done what he thought they wanted, never challenging them, always accepting their decisions. Now he had a sense of flying through life, free-falling through the sky, and he made love to Deborah with a heady sense of freedom, making her come again and again until neither of them could move. Then they lay quietly in each other's arms exhausted from their pleasures. He was stretched out on his back, staring up into the dark room and she had fallen asleep, her arm across his chest, her left leg over his.

He heard the rustling by her desk, as if someone was moving papers in the dark. He thought it was Percy the cat climbing across the desk, but then she came through the dark, emerged as if from fog to stand ghostly at the bottom of the bed. She was wearing her cotton nightgown and she was bleeding.

"Oh, Stephen," she moaned. Tears streamed down her cheeks and she wore the same incredible look of suffering. The thin gown was loose on her body, except for where the cloth clung to the open lance wound at her heart.

He dislodged himself from Deborah, who only turned over and hugged the warmth of the pillow.

"Stephen, why did you leave me?" She was speaking softly, but there was force and disappointment in her voice. She waited for his answer, standing at the end of the mattress, blood dripping from her palms.

"Betty Sue," he whispered, too frightened to comprehend her shadowy figure in the room. "Betty Sue, I don't understand."

"Don't try to," she said. "Just believe in me and the truth I know. Follow me, Stephen." She was smiling. The terrible pain had slipped from her face. Her brown eyes gleamed. Her whole face shone like a star and she radiated warmth and goodness.

"Betty Sue, I'm sorry."

She nodded understanding, endlessly patient, he knew, with his weakness.

"Leave her, Stephen, leave her," she instructed. "You know you must."

"But I've left Saint John's."

"Father Driscoll will forgive you. Return to me, Stephen. It is almost Good Friday, and I am afraid. Don't let me go to the Cross alone."

When Deborah woke Stephen was gone. She could feel his absence. She woke in the sunlight with Percy in a tight ball beside her in the bed. The cat blinked his eyes but did not stir.

"Stephen?" she called out. Saying his name was reassuring, a way of making him seem real. But there was no answer from the bathroom.

She got out of bed quickly, on edge now. He must have left some kind of note, she thought, but there was none on her desk, nothing taped to the mirror. He hadn't unpacked the night before and his bag was gone from where he had dropped it. Its disappearance was· like a blow, the final irrevocable proof that she would not see him again. That all his talk and good intentions, his words of love and their passion did not matter, that in the light of day he still was what he always was: a Catholic priest, and she had no claim on him. He belonged to the Church forever. And then she saw the trail of blood on the hardwood floor.

13

Monday, March 20
Monday of Holy Week

The Bishop let the young priest talk. He had learned long ago that the way to reach the truth was to give people time to explain and eventually they'd quit lying and tell him what he wanted to know.

He sat impassively behind his desk, fingers laced together across his wide stomach, and rocked slowly back and forth while Father Kinsella tried to justify—without telling the truth—why he wanted to leave Saint John of the Cross and be allowed to enter a Trappist monastery.

"I'm not sure it is the right place for me, Your Excellency, but I do think it's my last chance to remain a priest."

The Bishop did not answer, only raised his eyebrows, as if what the priest had said was intriguing.

"It didn't work out for me at the university and it's not working out at Saint John's. Father Driscoll and I just have too many problems. I don't think another parish is the answer. What I'd like to do is stay at the monastery for a while and see if perhaps that's the answer." He stopped abruptly and stared across the desk at the Bishop.

The troubled eyes of the young priest told the Bishop that this was a much more serious problem than he had thought. Father Kinsella wasn't just another young priest chafing under the thumb of a strict pastor.

The Bishop answered slowly, talking away from the topic, giving himself space in which to assess the seriousness of this problem. He began almost lightheartedly. "You've lost some weight, son."

"Yes, Your Excellency, some, I guess."

"You need to take better care of yourself, Stephen. Winters can be tough in the mountains." The stout man shifted positions and leaned forward, planting his elbows on the desk. He was wearing a black silk cassock with the red sash drawn tight around his body. Despite his chubbiness he looked regal in his clerical garb.

"I haven't been getting much sleep, Your Excellency." Father Kinsella had been up since dawn—since he fled Deborah's apartment—wandering the streets of the city, waiting for the Chancery to open.

"Does Father Driscoll know you're here?"

"He knows I'm in the city." Father Kinsella gestured awkwardly, not looking at the Bishop. "We had an argument yesterday morning and he sort of kicked me out." The priest sounded embarrassed, as if he had misbehaved.

"About what?" the Bishop asked casually.

"About my worthiness, really." A small, self-conscious smile slipped across Father Kinsella's face. "He doesn't think I'm much of a priest."

"Are you?" The Bishop swayed back again in his chair, the leather squeaking in the silent office.

Father Kinsella shook his head and looked away as he responded. "No, Your Excellency. Lately I don't think I have been."

"Is it that girl?"

Father Kinsella nodded.

"She visited you in Mossy Creek, right?" the Bishop asked, filling in the story himself.

Father Kinsella nodded again. That was it, he thought: let them believe it was because of Deborah.

"And Father Driscoll caught the two of you?" the Bishop asked, pressing further, as if this were the confessional.

Father Kinsella kept nodding.

"Where? Your bedroom?" An edge of anger had slipped into the Bishop's voice.

"No, nothing like that. I was just . . . kissing her goodbye. She had come to see me and was leaving, that's all. We were standing in the parlor when he walked by."

"That wasn't very smart of you, Stephen." The Bishop allowed himself a brief, cold smile. "You should know by now how not to get caught." The Bishop shook his head. When he had learned about Kinsella's behavior with the girl at the university, he had quietly telephoned the school's president and had Stephen removed from the campus ministry. Then he had given Stephen his choice of new assignment and the young priest had taken the remote mountain parish. To avoid the occasion of sin, he had told the Bishop. But now the occasion of sin had followed him. The boy didn't seem to be handling himself very well, the Bishop thought.

"So you think by going off to the Trappists you can keep the seeds of temptation away from you, is that it?"

"I'm not sure, Your Excellency. But perhaps if I can devote myself totally to living a simple life without distractions, God might give me the strength to handle these temptations. I know that when I'm at the monastery I feel at peace, closer to God and the Church. I feel secure. I don't want to lose my own soul or be a disgrace to other priests by staying out in this world." He stopped and let his position rest with those words. It was up to the Bishop to decide.

The Bishop took his time, pushed a few pieces of paper on

his desk, then picked up a pen and held it loosely in his fingers, spinning it as he answered. "You want to be locked up, is that it? Like a criminal? A child molester? Someone unfit for society? Do you think you can live your life entirely free of temptation, as if you were in some sort of germfree state?" He had not raised his voice, but there was a hard edge to it.

"I don't seem to be able to live like a priest anywhere else. Inside the monastery, I have the support of a community. All the monks working together."

"You can't hide there, son," the Bishop said. He stared solemnly across at Stephen, seeing not a priest who wanted a transfer of assignments, but rather a young man in trouble with his soul. "You can lock yourself away from that woman, Stephen, but you can't lock out your own weaknesses. Do you think the thick stone walls of a monastery will separate you from your own flesh?" The Bishop shook his head and tapped the desk top softly. "You must make your stand here, Stephen. You must confess to God and ask for his help. You'll never overcome the desires of the flesh without accepting that you need God's graces. That's your real failing, Stephen." He pointed his finger at the stunned priest. "Your cardinal sin is pride, not lust. You think that you yourself can handle the temptations of the Devil."

The Bishop leaned over the desk, still speaking softly, but with all the force and conviction of his years as a priest. "None of us can do it on our own, Stephen. We cannot succeed without our Lord. And you, a priest, should know that most of all."

The Bishop sat back, placed his palms flat against the desk, ready now to announce his decision, and Stephen spoke quickly, realizing the Bishop was not going to grant his request. "Your Excellency, it's more than just her and breaking my vows. It's more than living in Mossy Creek. I actually like my assignment. I like working in the parish; it's more than that."

The Bishop paused and tilted back his head. He frowned and waited, but the priest did not continue. The young man looked puzzled, dazed, as if he had forgotten what he was going to say.

"What is it, Stephen?" the Bishop asked sharply. He was already late in his morning schedule.

"I wanted to tell you, Your Excellency, what it was that I feared, but I can't—" His body was trembling. He was cold, freezing cold. His whole body shook. He saw the Bishop raise his hand and look alarmed, then reach and press his intercom, calling for help.

Stephen kept trying to talk, to say why he was so afraid, but he couldn't make himself heard, and then there were urgent voices and a rush of instructions, but none of it mattered. His head was spinning and he waited for the crash, waited for the peace and quiet.

"Stephen?" Her voice was so far away that he heard it as if through layers of gauze. Yet her hand was on his shoulder; he could feel her gently prodding, stirring him from his safe sleep. He kept resisting, trying to stay concealed in his unconsciousness, but she wouldn't let him. "Stephen," she insisted and there was a touch of reproach in her voice. "Wake up, please."

He opened his eyes in the dark room and she smiled.

"It will be Friday soon, Stephen. Are you coming back to Blue Haze to be with me?"

Stephen turned his head on the pillow. He was in a room he had never seen before, a large bedroom with a high ceiling. Heavy curtains were drawn across the windows and the room was dark.

"It was just a fever, Stephen. A mountain fever. Now you're all right again. Don't you want to come to me?" She smiled and leaned closer, whispering, "Now go to sleep." He felt her lips on his eyelids, kissing each one closed as he slipped back into a heavy sleep.

When he woke again the room was bright and sunny and
he was not alone. Monsignor Callaghan, the Bishop's ad-
ministrative assistant, towered at the edge of the bed, a tall
man wearing the red sash that denoted his position.

"Well, it's himself finally waking up." The Monsignor
smiled warmly, then moved around the bed and touched the
young priest's forehead. "The fever's gone," he declared.

"I passed out?"

Monsignor Callaghan nodded. "You did indeed; yesterday, right in the Bishop's office. The doctor gave you a shot
and you've been out since then. Nothing serious. Just the
twenty-four-hour flu combined with exhaustion. The Bishop
sent me over to see how you're getting along."

"Where am I?" Stephen attempted to sit up, but the
simple exertion left him dizzy and out of breath.

"At the Bishop's residence. You weren't ill enough for a
hospital and there's plenty of room here. Besides, His
Excellency wanted to keep an eye on you, I think." He
winked at Stephen, then added confidentially, "There's no
hurry in getting back to Saint John's. I telephoned Father
Driscoll and explained. He was very understanding, and
said that half of the elementary school children were out
sick. I guess it's going through the mountain region."

"Have I had any visitors, Monsignor, or telephone calls?"
Father Kinsella asked abruptly.

"Not that I know of, but I've been in and out of the
Chancery. You could check with Kim, the Bishop's house-
man. He'll know."

"I just had the impression that someone was here. . . ."

"You've been doped up with drugs, son." The Monsignor
glanced at his watch and added, "I'll leave you to rest now.
His Excellency will be stopping by when he comes home for
lunch."

"Thank you, Monsignor, for your concern."

The older priest waved, as if it were no matter. "Pull the

cord if you want anything. Kim is in the kitchen and he'll hear. Oh, you did have a telephone call at the office—a woman. At the time I didn't know you were in the city, so I told the secretary to give her the Mossy Creek telephone number."

"Did she say who she was?"

The older priest shook his head. "Just that she was a former student of yours at the university." He waved from the doorway and left, closing the door behind him.

Father Kinsella tossed off the blankets and sat up. He was weak and dizzy, but he got to his feet and walked uneasily across the room to the bathroom. It was on his way back to bed that he saw the lily. It was on a small table directly under a wall crucifix. A single white lily, its fragrant petals still wet with dew and the dark roots dripping with blood, as if the flower had been ripped from human flesh.

14

Thursday, March 23

Holy Thursday

Father Driscoll said both masses on Holy Thursday, and after the sisters had led the school children off to school, he returned to the sanctuary and prayed alone in the empty church.

Every day since the bleeding envelope had arrived at Saint John's he had prayed for guidance. He knew there was a reason God had picked the mountain girl, given her the sacred markings of his own Crucifixion, but Father Driscoll did not know how God wanted him to use this miracle. Yet from the moment the envelope had bled in his fingers and blistered his palms, the pastor had understood that God was trying to reach him, trying to tell him that he, too, had been selected by Christ for special sacrifice.

Still, this morning he could not pray. He was anxious and worried. Worried about Stephen Kinsella and what the young priest might have told the Bishop.

Callaghan had not mentioned Betty Sue when he telephoned, but the pastor did not trust Kinsella. The boy would tell the Chancery, he knew, and then the Bishop would be all over him. That was the way the Bishop ran his archdiocese. A tough administrator. The best-run diocese in the south, everyone said. He'd have his boys up to Mossy Creek immediately. Callaghan and his cronies. The Irish Mafia.

Father Driscoll's hands began to sweat and he fidgeted in the pew. "Give me a sign, O Lord," he said out loud, and his voice in the silent church startled him. He glanced up at the new crucifix suspended over the altar and thought then of the one that had fallen, and of Stephen's insistence that they publicize the trouble at Saint John's.

But there had been no trouble, the pastor thought; the parish had been blessed by God and given a stigmatic saint. Then Father Driscoll smiled as he gazed up at the hanging cross, for he saw clearly what he had to do to serve God faithfully and save Betty Sue. He had prayed and waited and as he knew would happen, God had given him a sign.

Stacey Graham strode into the newsroom of the television station feeling great. She had just been the guest speaker at the Lions Club luncheon and she knew she had been terrific. The men had given her a standing ovation, and she loved the attention, knew that she deserved it.

She was, in her mind, the best newswoman the station had ever had, and this was only the beginning of her career. She was a rising star and all she needed was some national exposure, a chance to get a few minutes of air time on the network. If she could only be seen up against Barbara Walters, then the network would realize how good she really was. Just thinking about that possibility made her excited.

What she needed to get on network news was some kind of catastrophe. A plane crash or a major forest fire in the mountains. An event that would focus national attention on the city. And she needed it now, while she was still young and fresh in the business.

She slipped into her desk chair, dropped her bag on a stack of incoming mail and immediately checked the yellow telephone messages to see if any news item had come in to her. Then she looked to see if Phil had called. He was to let her know if the weekend was okay, if his wife was taking the kids out of town, but there were only four long-distance calls from a Father Matt Driscoll of Mossy Creek, wherever that was.

The priest wanted her to telephone him—collect if necessary—and it was urgent. On the last message the switchboard operator had drawn a fat monk with a halo around his bald head. Stacey smiled. The priest must have been harassing them out front.

Well, she'd get this one out of the way fast. She had an inkling of what the priest wanted. A saint's holiday in his parish, or perhaps a high school dance. Something he thought she'd like for the six o'clock news. *Sure, Father, that's a biggy!*

The woman who answered the phone with a cool "Saint John's rectory" was reluctant to disturb Father Driscoll.

Forget it, Stacey thought impatiently. She had only twenty minutes before the afternoon news conference and she also wanted to call Phil's office and find out what was happening. But she disliked being put off by a snippy nobody so she said sweetly, "Well, my name is Stacey Graham, and I'm with Channel Three News and your Father Driscoll telephoned my office four times today. He says it's urgent."

There was a pause and then the woman answered, "Just a minute, please."

Stacey smiled at her small victory. Father Driscoll was on

the phone in moments, his Irish brogue booming into her ear with thanks for returning his call and a rush of words explaining what he wanted.

Stacey had to interrupt him twice and tell him to repeat himself, and for a few minutes she only half listened to his long, involved story about finding a girl in the mountains with strange body sores. She kept uttering an occasional "Uh huh" and trying to guess what the hell this priest was talking about, when suddenly the details of his narrative slipped into place.

Her mouth opened as she listened hard and a quick cold shiver of excitement ran through her. She grabbed a yellow pad and started taking notes, making the priest go back and tell his story once more, only this time she had questions. The kind of questions Warren Miller would ask her when she laid this bombshell on his desk.

When she finished she had five pages of scribbled notes and she told Father Driscoll she'd telephone him later that afternoon, after she had talked to the news director. She hung up and leaned back in her chair grinning. This was the real thing. A Catholic priest, the pastor of a church. A respected member of a mountain community. This was not some crazy guy telephoning about haunted houses and warlocks, and if it was only half as bizarre as the priest's explanation, she had herself one hell of an item. They could tape it in the afternoon and feed it to New York in time for the evening news.

She shuffled her notes together and headed for the front office.

"You're not going to believe this, Warren, but I just got a great story." She flopped down across the desk from the news director and told him about Betty Sue Wadkins.

He listened without any reaction, and answered matter-of-factly when she finished, "You better check this Driscoll out with the Chancery. Call Monsignor Callaghan over there. He's the Bishop's right-hand man."

"Driscoll said not to do that. He said if the Chancery finds out they won't permit him to appear on television, and we need Driscoll to get to the girl."

Warren leaned back and laced his hands together behind his head. "What's Driscoll's angle? Why is he putting this girl on the air? Doesn't he realize he's going to turn Mossy Creek into some kind of Lourdes? The miracle city! Come on, Stacey. You're buying this whole ball of wax."

"Warren, it's not that kind of story!" She slammed her fist against the desk top. "There's a girl in those mountains who bleeds like Jesus Christ every Friday and we've got a chance to get some exclusive film. It's bizarre, I know; it's the occult; but goddammit, it's a great piece of news."

Warren tipped his chair forward and his elbows hit with a thump on the desk top. "It's not news, Stacey, it's a freak show. Some sick woman who bleeds through her skin and a priest who's gone off the deep end. He's probably on the telephone right now talking to God.

"If I put Driscoll and that girl on the air, the Bishop is going to be on the phone asking why the station is attacking the Catholic Church." He shook his head. "Call him and tell him no. Tell him we're afraid the Episcopalians are going to want equal time."

Stacey sat tense and upright. She wanted to throw the yellow pad at him, but she made herself sit back and calm down. A few years ago, when she first started working, she would have stormed teary and rejected out of the office. She took everything too personally. As Phil kept telling her: for a girl with so much going for her, she had the emotional maturity of a fourteen-year-old. Well, she'd show them. This story wasn't going to be shelved.

"Let me investigate this further, Warren," she said coolly.

"I'll call the Chancery and snoop around. And the priest gave me the name of the university doctor who examined her. I'll call him."

"Drop it, Stacey! We don't have the time." He glanced at the wall clock, irritated now at her persistence.

"Give me a half-hour. That's all. Just let me make some telephone calls." She was on the edge of the chair, waiting for his okay. She kept herself from smiling, from trying to sway him with her looks. She'd tried that before and knew that it only amused him.

"Stacey, we have a goddam program to get on the air in less than three hours and you haven't written tonight's copy. When are you going to look at the tapes, for chrissake!"

"I can handle it, Warren. I can do it all within an hour. Look, we're wasting time arguing." She was on her feet.

He stared up at her, making his point with a stern, no-more-nonsense look. She knew she had pressed him to the limit and if she didn't make it pay off, she had lost a lot of points.

"I want you back in half an hour. You either have proof of this girl or we forget it. This isn't a newspaper, and we don't have all fuckin' day."

"Jim Lear here." He was breathless, as if he had rushed for the telephone call.

"Hello, Doctor Lear? This is Stacey Graham, from the evening news."

"Oh yes, Miss Graham." Now he was diffident.

"I just spoke with Father Matt Driscoll at Saint John's Catholic Church in Mossy Creek. He said you knew him."

"Yes. I know Father Driscoll." He sounded puzzled.

"He called me this afternoon—just about an hour ago— and told me a rather incredible story about a mountain girl"—Stacey glanced down at her notes spread out on her desk—"a woman by the name of Betty Sue Wadkins who he says suffers from stigmatic wounds and actually experiences the suffering of Christ's Crucifixion.

"Father Driscoll mentioned that you examined this young woman a few weeks ago and I'm telephoning to verify the existence of such a person and her condition."

"Yes, I did see her," the doctor began, unsure of what he should say. "She has wounds on her hands and feet, but I am not a Roman Catholic and I really wouldn't know about stigmata." He was edgy, trying not to be definitive.

"Father Driscoll said you couldn't explain her wounds in terms of medicine. Is that true, Doctor?"

"I'm not sure if that is exactly what I said, but you have to realize I only gave this young woman a cursory examination in her bedroom as a favor to Steve."

"Steve?"

"Father Stephen Kinsella. He's the assistant pastor at Saint John's and a friend of mine. I think, Miss Graham, you should talk to Father Kinsella about this."

"And why's that, Doctor?" She wrote down Father Stephen Kinsella's name.

"Well . . . is this off the record?"

"Yes, Doctor, it's off the record." She smiled.

"Well, according to Steve, Father Driscoll thinks he has a saint up there in Mossy Creek. The girl lives up on the ridge, a real mountain type, and she does have those five wounds, like Driscoll says. There's a doctor here at the Medical Center, a psychiatrist, who says she would probably be classified as a severe hysterical neurotic with conversion symptoms. He'd like to examine the girl, but the pastor won't let anyone near her."

"Doctor, what's your opinion? Is this girl stigmatic?"

"Frankly, I don't know what she is, but according to her parents, she's had these wounds since she was twelve. And they won't heal. A thin transparent shield covers the wounds when they aren't bleeding. What's so strange medically is that the wounds don't fester. In fact, they give off a faint sweet smell, like a perfume."

"And they do bleed?"

"That's what I'm told, every Thursday and Friday, when she goes into a trance. There's something else that's odd about all this," Jim Lear continued. "The last time I spoke with Steve he mentioned the young girl had cured the pastor's arthritis. Not only cured it but assumed the pastor's pain herself. Now that sounds like a classic example of autosuggestion. Weird, isn't it?"

"Weird?" Stacey Graham smiled. "I think it's just terrific." She glanced up at the newsroom clock and saw she was due in Warren's office. "Thank you for your time and this information, Doctor."

"That's okay, but no mention of my name, okay?"

"I promise," she replied, happy to oblige. Everyone, she thought, was afraid of fame except her. She stood, gathered her notes and strode into Warren's office. This time she had him.

"I thought you had cut yourself somehow. I thought you were hurt." Deborah talked as Stephen paced her apartment. "And then I couldn't find you. No one knew anything about you. I even telephoned Jim Lear and asked him, but he didn't know. I thought you might have gone to him because he was a doctor."

"But why?"

"Why?" She pointed across the room toward the bed. "Because when I woke you were gone and there was blood all over the floor and the bottom of the mattress." She was sitting in the only stuffed chair in the apartment, wearing jeans and a heavy wool sweater. "I thought you might have tried to kill yourself or something. I didn't know what to think.

"So I went to the emergency ward of the university hospital. The nurses must have thought I was tripping, frantically rushing into the hospital and asking if they had seen a bleeding priest. Then I started driving around campus, searching for you. I did that for a couple of hours, until it got to be a respectable hour. And then I telephoned the Chancery. Someone there gave me your telephone number in Mossy Creek. That threw me. I knew you wouldn't go back, especially if you were injured." She said all this very slowly, as if she were recounting a terrible experience. "Finally I came home, thinking you might be here, but you weren't and I started to clean up and that's when I noticed the footprints."

He stopped in the middle of the apartment, caught by her story.

"The footprints were in the blood. One clear one of a bare foot, too small to be yours and a couple of partials. I really got scared then. I didn't know what to think and I began to imagine these horrible things. You know, like someone got into the apartment and you had to kill him or something and take away the body." She gestured vaguely, embarrassed.

"I kept thinking you'd telephone, but by yesterday when you hadn't, I called Mossy Creek and talked to that woman, Mrs. Bringle, and she was very secretive. She wanted me to speak with Driscoll, but I couldn't handle that. So I telephoned the Chancery again and they said you were staying at the residence, that you were sick with the flu."

"It wasn't my blood," he said flatly.

"Whose, then?" she asked.

He went and sat on the floor next to the chair and tried to explain, as best he could, what had happened early

Monday morning. "I had almost talked myself into believing it was just another crazy vision of mine. I did have the flu and I guess I was delirious. I saw the blood dripping from her hands, but I thought I had fabricated all of that until what you've just said." His hands were shaking and she squeezed his fingers, trying to keep them steady.

"I believe you, Stephen. I believe you this time." She was as frightened as he was: he could see the fear in her eyes.

It was getting dark, the early winter evening, and they stayed huddled together, like two people alone in the world. Stephen had his head resting against her knees and she had leaned forward, put her arms around his neck. There was no light on in the apartment and when it became too dark to see, Deborah sat up and turned on the floor lamp, lighting with a soft bulb their small corner of the room. She didn't say anything to Stephen, but she was afraid of the dark now.

Percy moved off the bed where he had been sleeping and came silently across the room, hopping effortlessly into her lap and resuming his nap. She stroked the cat's back as she asked Stephen, "What I don't understand is how she does it. How is it possible?"

"It's called bilocation—being in two places at once. It's an ability many stigmatics have, just as many of them are clairvoyant. Do you know the story of Padre Pio? He was an Italian priest, a stigmatic, who died in 1968. During World War II an Italian regiment in North Africa was being shelled by the Allies and one soldier had taken cover by himself behind a large rock. A priest suddenly appeared to the soldier and began to pull at his sleeve, telling him to get out from behind the rock. The soldier wouldn't go, and finally the priest yanked him away—just before a shell exploded where the soldier had been standing. Then the priest disappeared.

"Later when the soldier told the story to his buddy, the friend showed him a picture of Padre Pio, which he carried with him. The soldier said that was the priest who had saved his life.

"When Padre Pio was asked how he could bilocate—that wasn't the only time—he said he was really in two places at once and he did it by a prolongation of his personality."

Deborah shook her head, still in doubt. "I wish all this made more sense. If I had seen Betty Sue myself it might be easier."

Stephen stood up. "If it wasn't for the blood, Deborah, and your seeing it, I'd have a hard time accepting it myself. Don't feel so alone. If you're looking for some rational explanation, think of what the psychologists in your own department have discovered in parapsychology—those cases of clairvoyance and telepathy that are just being documented."

"Those are different. They take place in laboratories and everything is controlled. She appeared to you in this apartment, bleeding. It scares me. I feel I'm being watched."

"It's not you who's being watched, Deborah; it's me." He was putting on his parka, getting ready to leave.

She thought, all he does is leave me.

"I don't want to be alone, Stephen," she said.

"She won't bother you, Deborah. As long as we're apart she'll leave you alone."

"Couldn't we go someplace? Couldn't we go out of town?"

"That wouldn't do any good. She finds me wherever I am. Have you read "The Hound of Heaven," by Francis Thompson?"

She shook her head.

"It's about a man being endlessly pursued by God. It begins, 'I fled Him, down the nights and/down the days;/ I fled Him, down the arches of the years;/I fled Him, down the labyrinthine ways/Of my own mind.'

"Do you know what God wanted from Thompson? His love. That's all, just his love. Betty Sue is like that. She's after me in the same way."

"What are you going to do?" she asked.

"I'm going to the Chancery and stay another night at the Bishop's. I'll leave for Mossy Creek tomorrow, but I think, all things considered, the residence is the safest place in the city tonight." He tried to smile, but he couldn't shake the apprehension he felt. He knew he wouldn't sleep that night. He'd lie awake watching the dark corners of the bedroom, watching and waiting for her to appear.

"She won't let me go, Deborah," he whispered, as if admitting defeat.

"You're going to her?" Deborah asked.

He nodded reluctantly. "I asked the Bishop to transfer me to a Trappist monastery but he said no. He said I was just running away from the problem—only he thinks you're the problem."

"You haven't said anything about Betty Sue?"

"He'd think I was crazy. Contrary to what you may think, priests, especially the higher-ups, are leery of talk of saints and miracles."

"And what do you believe, Stephen? Do you think she's a saint?" She watched him carefully, waiting for his answer.

He nodded. "Yes, Deborah, I do. If I could explain her away rationally, believe me, I would. If it weren't for her, I'd already be free of the Church. If I didn't believe in Betty Sue, I wouldn't have to give you up.

"But I'm not free. I realize now there is a divine hand in everything that has happened. Christ is using her, Deborah. She is his messenger to me. He is using Betty Sue to keep me a priest." His eyes were burning with emotion. "I love you, Deborah. I wish you could understand how much. I wish it could be different."

"I wish I could too, Stephen. It would make life a lot easier." She shook her head. "But I just don't."

"I'll pray for you, Deborah."

"You do that," she tossed back. Her tolerance had reached its limits. He was lost forever to her. He was a blind believer. A cradle Catholic who accepted his religion without one iota of intellectual consideration, and with no sense of irony. He was even worse, she thought: he was a born-again Christian.

She got out of the chair in one quick motion and went to her desk. "I'm going to the library. I don't want to hang around this apartment."

"I'll walk over with you," he said quickly, trying to be kind.

"If you want," she answered curtly. She slipped into her raincoat and picked up her books, declining his offer to carry them. She didn't want any more of his courtesies.

On the walk across the campus she told him what she thought of him, of his blind belief in Betty Sue, and his willingness to slip comfortably into the arms of Holy Mother Church.

"You take the easy way out, Stephen, You take the way of least resistance. It's easy to wear blinders and not try and reason out what has happened. You just accept Betty Sue as a saintly stigmatic and let the Catholic Church—all that history and tradition—support your belief like some sort of psychological scaffolding."

They had reached the entrance of the library and he stopped her before she could leave him.

"I'm not hiding from the truth." Stephen shook his head. "You found the blood on the floor. You saw her footprint. Who's hiding from the truth, Deborah?"

He waited for an answer, but she only stared coldly at him and then she turned and left.

She worked late at the library. She kept herself at the books, reading and taking notes because she did not want to go home and be alone in the apartment. Three times she had gotten up and telephoned friends in hopes of finding someone at home. If she could just curl up on someone's couch for one night, she'd be all right. One more day, she thought, and she'd be over her fear of Betty Sue Wadkins.

But by eleven o'clock she had not found anyone and she saw then the long rows of empty tables; the library was closing and she realized she was alone on the third floor. In a frenzy she grabbed her things and hurried downstairs.

She should have gone home then while the sidewalks were busy with people going back to their dorms, but instead she went to the Union for coffee and to search for a friend to stay with.

Again she couldn't find anyone and reluctantly she walked outside, thinking: I'll take a Valium and knock myself out for the night. That reassured her, realizing the sleeping pill would keep the nightmares away.

She circled the campus coming home, keeping away from the lagoon. It had begun raining harder, a chilling rain, and she bent her head against its force. Once she was behind the classroom buildings, where the sidewalks were empty, she began to run, but the rain and her heavy books made it difficult. She was out of breath from the effort when she heard footsteps behind her on the sidewalk.

She spun around to see who was following her and three fraternity men wearing TKE jackets sped past, racing ahead and out of sight. Trembling, she cut between the dormitories—taking the shortcut—and headed for her street. She was almost home, she told herself. Thinking of Percy waiting, curled up on her bed, made her feel better and she began to run once more.

It was well lit behind the dormitories, but the rain and fog had dropped the visibility to just a few feet, so when he stepped onto the sidewalk and blocked her path, she ran straight into him.

She tried to scream but the cry caught in her throat as he smiled and whispered her name. His cold smile and the rank odor of his breath were all she would ever know of him as his hand cracked into the side of her head, breaking her cheekbone like an eggshell.

15

Friday, March 24

Good Friday

Stacey Graham stood in the wind on Blue Haze Ridge and tried to get her shoulder-length auburn hair under control. The rain and thick fog had done its work, and if she went on the air now, she told her cameraman, her hair would come out looking like spaghetti.

Finally she put her wool ski cap on and combed the loose ends behind her ears. "It's inappropriate, I know, for a religious clip," she told him, "but what the hell am I going to do?" Then she positioned herself so the Wadkins house was behind her on the hillside as she faced the video camera.

"Start wide, Ted," she directed, "and take in the whole yard. I want that old truck, the bathtub, and the house. I want everyone to know what kind of place this is. Then come in tight on me. I'll need about fifty seconds for the teaser before I move to my right and start the interview." She smiled over at the pastor. "You stay put, Father, and be looking up at the house as I approach. When I say your name turn and look at me, but no smiles, okay? We want to keep the tone religious." She wet her lips and took two deep breaths. "Ready when you are, Ted."

She watched for the red light, then began, her voice clear and confident, implying that she knew what she was talking about.

"Stigmata. It's a word many of us have probably never heard before, but it goes back to the time before Christ. The word is the plural of the Greek stigma, meaning mark, and in ancient history it referred to the marks branded on cattle, on all the slaves in the orient, and on fugitive slaves in Greece and Rome.

"But today on Blue Haze Ridge, two miles from the mountain community of Mossy Creek, stigmata means Betty Sue Wadkins, a seventeen-year-old girl who has experienced since the age of twelve the suffering and excruciating pain of Christ's passion and death.

"Today, in an exclusive Good Friday television special, we are bringing you the actual ecstasy and supernatural seizure of this young girl." Stacey paused, then moving slowly to her right, began again, "With us on this windswept slope of Blue Haze Ridge is the pastor of Saint John of the Cross Catholic Church, Father Matthew Driscoll, who discovered Betty Sue and the significance of her strange affliction. Father Driscoll, could you tell us how you found Betty Sue Wadkins?"

When Jim Lear couldn't reach anyone at Blue Haze Ridge, he telephoned the Chancery on the hope that they might know where Father Kinsella was. The telephone operator told him to wait and then Steve himself came on, his voice sounding puzzled at the telephone call.

"Steve?" The doctor was surprised, hearing his friend's

voice. "It's Jim. I just telephoned Mossy Creek looking for you and there was no answer."

"I had to come down to the city for a couple of days. I'm starting back to Mossy Creek now. What's the matter? You sound exhausted."

"Oh, Christ, Steve, it's terrible. I'm at the hospital. When I came on duty this morning, I spotted her name on Emergency. I've been trying all morning to reach you."

"What is it, Jim?"

"It's Deborah. Deborah Laste. They brought her in last night."

"Oh, my God!"

"Whoever the bastard was, Steve, he did a job on her. They had to operate."

"O God!"

The doctor kept talking, listing the injuries as if they were some sort of litany.

"Jim, when did it happen?" Father Kinsella interrupted.

"Sometime after eleven o'clock. The campus police found her in the bushes behind McNutley Hall. She was unconscious and had lost a lot of blood. They had her on the operating table for seven hours. Steve, I don't think she's going to make it."

"Jim, stay there, please. I'm on my way over and I need to see her."

"She's in a coma."

"I don't care. I have to see her. Please wait; I'm on my way."

"Father, what then are the aspects of Betty Sue's stigmata?"

"She has the full stigmatization, Miss Graham. That is, the five wounds, ecstasy and visions, clairvoyance, and the ability to speak in a foreign language. Not a language of today, not French or German or even Latin, but a *biblical language.* The language of Aramaic. The language Jesus Christ himself spoke in the Holy Land."

"And you say she is already in this trance?"

"That's right. She began on Thursday evening and it will continue until Christ dies on the Cross this afternoon. She suffers the complete passion of Christ, from the time he went into the Garden of Gethsemane with Peter and the two sons of Zebedee, James and John. This morning at dawn she experienced the scourging at the pillar, the crowning of thorns, and the way of the cross. And very soon—from exactly twelve o'clock to three o'clock this afternoon—she'll endure with Jesus his final agony and death."

"And who is with her now, Father, inside her home?" Stacey Graham half turned and nodded towards the tarpaper shack behind them.

"Her parents, Mr. and Mrs. Lamar Wadkins, and Rufus Tainter, a close friend of the family. With the exception of myself and my assistant, Father Stephen Kinsella, no one else has seen Betty Sue during one of her divine ecstasies."

"And it will be possible for us to film these final hours of her ecstasy?"

"Yes, her parents have given their permission."

"Father Driscoll, many of our viewers may wonder why you and Betty Sue's parents are allowing our cameras inside her bedroom during this obviously traumatic period. Why have you consented to open up, as it were, her private and sacred moments to a television audience?"

"Mr. and Mrs. Wadkins realize their daughter has been blessed by God Almighty in a very special way. And they want to share their joy by showing to the world through television that God is still demonstrating his divine presence in the lives of ordinary people, showing through Betty Sue that miracles are possible in this modern age, and happen to the simplest of people." He gestured toward the tarpaper house. "These people do not have much in the way of material possessions, but they possess much in the way of divine grace and goodness."

"But isn't it true, Father, that the Wadkins family are not members of your church? That Betty Sue is a Baptist, as are her parents?" She had held back that one bit of information until she had the priest on television and pinned under the lights of the video camera.

It did surprise him: his black eyebrows closed together above his eyes. "Yes, it is true the Wadkinses are Baptists," he answered carefully, selecting his words. "But Mr. and Mrs. Wadkins recently asked me to begin giving them religious instruction in the Catholic faith and I expect that soon they'll be received into my parish.

"Betty Sue has not as yet begun any instruction, but the child every week talks to Jesus Christ himself, and she is closer, I should think, to God and the Holy Family than any of us, Catholic or Protestant." He smiled down at Stacey Graham.

Nicely done, padre, she thought, and returned his smile. Then looking directly at the camera, she went on, "We have been talking with Father Matthew Driscoll, pastor of Saint John's Catholic Church of Mossy Creek. In a few minutes we'll be going inside the home of Mr. and Mrs. Lamar Wadkins and be with their seventeen-year-old daughter Betty Sue while she travels through space and time and lives once again the passion and death of Jesus Christ on Calvary. But first, we'll pause briefly for these important messages."

Doctor Lear was waiting for Father Kinsella at the entrance of the university hospital.

"She's in the Intensive Care Unit," he said, leading the way down the wide hallway. "The bastard really worked her over. It looks as if he wanted to break every one of her bones."

"Do they know who did it?"

Jim Lear pushed the doors of Intensive Care and answered in a whisper. "The cops were here earlier to see her but she's still in a coma. I don't think they have anything to go on, but I know they want to talk with you."

"Me?" The priest stopped.

"When they found her she was semiconscious and according to the campus police she kept mumbling your name. That's one reason I was so frantic in trying to reach you."

Jim Lear stopped in front of one of the rooms and touched Father Kinsella's arm. "This isn't going to be a pretty sight. They've got her wired up. The sonofabitch kicked in her pelvis. And both legs and arms are smashed. They've got tubes connected to every orifice." He saw the shock register on the priest's face, and added softly, "She was pregnant, Steve; did you know?" He touched his friend's arm, as if to say: that is the worst I have to tell you. It's all over now.

Betty Sue sat up in the bed, her eyes wide open and sightless as she stared blindly into the bright video lights.

"She is with Christ now as he approaches Calvary," Father Driscoll whispered into the microphone. He stood with Stacey at the end of the bed, in full view of Betty Sue. Her parents and Rufus were out of the way. The pastor had taken over.

"You mean she is actually in the Holy Land?" Stacey asked.

"Yes, she is with Christ. She is suffering his agony." Father Driscoll sounded proud.

Betty Sue fell forward on the bed and began to moan.

"Christ has fallen for the third time," the priest explained.

Betty Sue raised her head and Stacey gasped at the sight of fresh blood on the young woman's face. Betty Sue's nose was bleeding from both nostrils and the skin across her cheeks was lashed.

"The soldiers are whipping Christ to make him stand," Father Driscoll continued. "Now listen to his lament." He moved the microphone closer to Betty Sue's bruised and bleeding lips.

"My people, what have I done to thee? Answer me. I brought thee out of the land of Egypt, and thou hast led me to the gibbet of the Cross." Betty Sue sank back onto the bed and the cameraman moved closer for a head shot.

"Turn off your camera," Father Driscoll ordered, realizing too late what would happen next.

But Stacey Graham couldn't react. She was mesmerized by the sight of Betty Sue and her bloody trance. It was beyond anything she could have hoped for. She couldn't believe her good luck. It had just dropped into her lap like a godsend, she was thinking, when Betty Sue sat bolt upright and ripped open the front of her nightgown, exposing her battered breasts.

Stacey spun around to her cameraman and disregarding the audio shouted, "Are you getting this, Ted? Goddammit, don't fuck up this seg!"

There was a nurse with Deborah. She stood aside silently and gave Father Kinsella room to approach the bed. The priest moved forward slowly. He could not even tell it was Deborah. Her whole body was wrapped with bandages and suspended in traction. Only her lips and one eye were exposed.

"Have her parents been told?" Stephen whispered.

"Yes. I understand they're flying down this afternoon. Do you know them?"

He shook his head. "I've met a younger sister, that's all. Jim, is it okay if I stay awhile with her?"

"There's nothing you can do, Steve. It's no telling how long she'll be in a coma."

"I'd like to stay and pray for her."

Jim Lear touched the priest's arm. "Sure, Steve. Sit over there away from the bed. There'll be nurses coming in here all afternoon."

Stephen sat on the edge of the hospital chair. The nurses had left the room and he was momentarily alone with Deborah. He fumbled in the pockets of his trousers and found his rosary beads and silently began to say the Sorrowful Mysteries.

"Ted," she whispered frantically, "get a tight shot of those palms." Stacey stood petrified as Betty Sue's slender fingers curled in torture around the driven stakes and blood gushed into her palms. She could not think of anything to say, but she also realized that the agony of this young woman was more poignant than any comments. She knew when to shut up. Now Betty Sue was gasping for breath and mumbling incoherently. Stacey glanced at the priest. "What is it, Father?"

"Aramaic. The language used by the people of the Holy Land. Betty Sue is saying, 'I thirst.' As we know from the Gospels, this is what Christ said on the Cross."

The priest moved around the bed and touched Betty Sue's parched lips with a wet sponge. She turned her face from the liquid.

"This is a mixture of wine and vinegar," the pastor continued. "The Roman soldiers gave that bitter drink to Christ. Saint Matthew tells us, 'They gave him vinegar to drink mingled with gall: and when he had tasted thereof, he would not drink.' "

"*Abba schabok lahon,*" Betty Sue cried out.

Stacey Graham could no longer concentrate on what the priest was saying. All she was aware of now was the suffering of this young woman. She is going to die, Stacey thought. Betty Sue was going to die and somehow she was responsible. "Wait!" Stacey asked and raised her hand as if to stop the passion of Christ, but Betty Sue only screamed in pain and arched her body from the bloody sheets, trying to pull herself free of the Cross.

"Oh, my God, stop. Please, someone, stop this!" She watched horrified as the soft flesh of Betty Sue's palms tore away as she strained at the invisible spikes.

"Abba be ada afkid ruchi," Betty Sue cried and fell exhausted into the bed. The lance wound under her breast burst open and blood mixed with water spilled from her side.

Father Driscoll turned to Stacey and told her that Christ had died. That it was three o'clock and the passion and death of Jesus Christ was over, but Stacey couldn't respond. She turned away and rushed from the bedroom, fled the house to vomit her breakfast over the wooden railing of the front porch.

"Stephen," Deborah muttered. Her voice in the silent room was so weak he was not sure at first that she had spoken, but he stood and approached the bed. "Stephen . . ."

"Yes, Deborah, I'm here." He leaned over her.

"Why, Stephen?"

"What, Deborah?"

"Why did he . . ." she only managed.

He was inches above her, tears streaming down his face, when the doctors and nurses came rushing back into the room and pushed him aside.

"It's the telemetry monitor," Jim Lear explained, arriving in the room. "It just sounded the alarm. Her heart, Steve. Her heart couldn't take it any longer."

Father Kinsella didn't wait for her parents. He realized he should be there when they arrived and help console them—it was one of his priestly duties—but how could he be with them and hide the truth of his relationship with Deborah?

So he left her. He left her broken body under the hospital sheet and went to walk in the cold day. He walked the campus, circled the lagoon as students hurried past him through the long afternoon. He would have liked to go to her apartment and be among her things, to let himself be hurt by memories, but her family, he realized, would return there and how could he explain his presence?

He left the campus and went across the street to a college bar. He expected it to be quiet and deserted on Good Friday, but it was jammed with students. They stood in the aisles intensely watching the television screen at the rear of the room as he elbowed his way toward the bar.

There was a wild shout, and then, just as abruptly, silence. It must be a basketball game, he thought, as he pushed through. He slipped by one young woman as she exclaimed, "I can't believe this. It's so real! Do you think they're faking it?" Next to her someone answered, "It must be for real; that's a Catholic priest."

Father Kinsella looked toward the screen and saw Betty Sue's anguished face as she exclaimed, *"My people, what have I done to thee?"*

Her face was bleeding from the whipping and the crown of thorns; blood dripped from her nostrils, and he heard Father Driscoll explaining that Christ had fallen for the third time. The camera pressed closer and Betty Sue's bloody face filled the screen. She was whispering, *"Answer me. I brought thee out of the land of Egypt, and thou hast led me to the gibbet of the Cross."*

Several of the coeds in the bar turned and hid their faces in the shoulders of men standing near them, but Father Kinsella could not turn away. The crowded bar let out a roar as Betty Sue sat up and ripped open the front of her nightgown, and the voice of Father Driscoll explaining the religious significance was lost in wild cheers.

Then Stacey Graham was on the screen, sitting sedately in a studio and saying, "We'll be returning shortly to the mountains and follow Betty Sue through her final stations of the cross as she travels with Christ to Calvary on this Good Friday afternoon." Her voice was somber. "Please stay with us."

Father Kinsella let himself be pushed away as the crowd rushed the bar to order beers. He was stunned by what he had seen and what the pastor had done. He had not been with Betty Sue when she needed him. In twenty-four hours he had failed both the women in his life, and he fled the bar, feeling like Judas Iscariot.

16

Saturday, March 25

Holy Saturday

Three miles outside of Mossy Creek, where the superhighway started north and local traffic had to exit onto a two-
lane mountain road, Monsignor Tim Callaghan ran into a
traffic jam. A solid line of cars, RVs, and campers crept up
the ridge road, moving slowly, inching their way toward
town under the supervision of four state troopers.

Monsignor Callaghan rolled down his side window as he
came abreast of a trooper and asked innocently, "An accident, Sergeant?"

The highway patrolman stared back blankly at the priest.
He looked bored and slightly hostile, his face hidden beneath his stiff, wide-brim hat. "Keep it movin'," he said.

Monsignor Callaghan slipped his hand into his sports
jacket and produced his special police badge. At the flash of
silver, the patrolman straightened up.

"No trouble," he answered, his voice soft and agreeable,
but with the same hard twang as the mountain people. "It's,

y'know, that stigmatic girl." He said "stigmatic" slowly, as if
it were a foreign word, and then he nodded toward the line
of traffic. "Thar goin' to see for themselves." He grinned,
showing missing teeth at the back of his mouth.

"You know anything about her?" the priest asked casually, thinking: well, I might as well begin working.

"Nope. I ain't even seen the TV. I work weekends. But I
hear tell they're gonna show it again tonight and I'll catch
it, I reckon. The wife says it don't seem human."

"Do you know anything about the people up there on
that ridge?"

The trooper grinned again. "Nothin' I care to tell foreigners."

Monsignor Callaghan smiled back and rolling up the
window he inched the Chancery car forward. Well, he
thought, the Bishop had told him it wouldn't be easy.

Two years before, at the Bishop's order, he had gone
incognito into North Carolina to see a woman on the north
side of Asheville who claimed her statue of the Blessed
Virgin was bleeding.

Her story had been reported in the Asheville paper and
picked up on the local television station. For a week she
made money by charging the curious to view her Blessed
Virgin. Callaghan had paid twenty-five cents himself and
stood in line with the crowd that filed past the blue-and-
white figure.

The statue was in the living room—roped off so it couldn't
be touched—and there was blood at its base and more blood
on the floor around it, but as he told the Bishop, the Virgin
wasn't bleeding. A week later, after no one had seen the
statue actually shed blood, interest faded.

Later he heard the woman had telephoned the local priest
and told him the Blessed Virgin had come to live in her
attic. The priest told the woman to call the police and have
the Blessed Virgin evicted, which, Monsignor Callaghan

thought, wasn't the worst way to handle the problem. Yet he had a nagging suspicion that the Stigmatic of Blue Haze Ridge, as the newspapers were calling her, wouldn't go away as quickly. Even the Bishop had suggested as much when they had met that morning.

"The press is onto this in a big way and you know how those bastards can be. They've been telephoning me since seven o'clock last night. ABC even picked up the story for the evening national news. Did you see it?" The Bishop grunted. "They showed a two-minute clip and I thought Barbara Walters would never shut up.

"I tried to phone Matt Driscoll last night," he went on. "He's either taken the phone off the hook or it's out of order." He fingered the brown files on his desk and then shoved them across to Callaghan. "Here are the personnel files on Driscoll and Kinsella. You might find them helpful. You know Kinsella's history, don't you?" Monsignor Callaghan nodded.

The year before the Kinsella affair had been one of the juicier bits of gossip at the Chancery. The official explanation of his sudden transfer to Mossy Creek was mental fatigue, but as the priests joked among themselves, "Some way to get mental fatigue."

"Kinsella, as you know, has been in town all week. But I can't find him today. Kim thinks he went back to Mossy Creek yesterday afternoon. He didn't stay at the Residence last night. Find him and put the fear of God into him if you have to, but get that boy to tell you what the hell is going on in those mountains."

The Bishop leaned forward and began to check off on his chubby fingers what he wanted Father Callaghan to do in the mountains.

"See this Wadkins girl. Go out to her place and just be part of the crowd. Don't let them know you're a priest. This might be just some kind of con game—a way to milk the religious fanatics—but, by God, I can't figure out why Driscoll was taken in.

"Tell Matt I want to see him tomorrow afternoon. Bring him back yourself if you can. And tell him no more statements about this Wadkins character! Now that's an order. I've had enough of Stacey Graham raving about miracles in the mountains."

Monsignor Callaghan edged forward in his chair, waiting to be dismissed.

"Now, Tim, I know you can handle this with discretion; I have all the faith in the world in you. You have my complete authority on this, but I'd appreciate it if you'd telephone me the first chance you get if you're not coming back this evening. With Easter tomorrow, we don't have much time to work out a strategy. I had Larry draft a short announcement to read at the masses if that's necessary. There's no mention of Mossy Creek, but we warn the faithful about being misled by false gods, that sort of thing. We'll use it only if there's more hue and cry this afternoon. They're running that damn film again, did you hear? I wish Driscoll had sprung this during football season. They'd be less likely to get all this air time."

"Have you seen the film, Your Excellency?"

The Bishop nodded and added, in a confidential tone: "It was actually very impressive. If that's the right word. Matt surprised me. He narrated the ecstasy with more sophistication than I would have thought him capable of. Very powerful . . ."

The Bishop's voice trailed off and he seemed preoccupied, but he snapped back, saying, "Now I don't know the first thing about stigmata, and where do you think Old Matt Driscoll found out everything he had to say? He sounded like a Jesuit with all his talk about Saint Francis and Saint Veronica Giuliani. We can probably thank Kinsella for that."

The Bishop paused, then closed the discussion. "Drive carefully, Tim, and go with God."

Just beyond Mossy Creek, the steady line of traffic left the main road and turned into the woods. Monsignor Callaghan followed the cars. It was difficult to see where he was, for the trees grew thick right up to the edge of the road. They were all kinds: hickory, oak and maple, spruce and ash, evergreen and pine. The woods looked medieval, he thought, and that for some reason made him nervous, as if he were being led astray.

The priest had driven for less than two miles when the traffic halted once more. This time there were no hesitations or false starts. Everyone stopped. Ahead and at the top of a rise, he could see drivers abandoning their cars and starting up the hill on foot.

He parked his car, took off his sports coat, and put on an old army surplus jacket. It was warmer and would blend better with the crowd. He locked the car and fell into step with the others. When he reached the top of the ridge he saw that he was not near the house. The line continued, stretching down the road where more cars and trucks were parked. He kept walking, wet from the fog, following the others as they moved into the hollow.

There were more parked cars at the end of the road: a mobile unit from the television station, the state police, and cars with press identification in their front windows.

The people kept going, off the road and into a pine woods where a wet dirt path led through the trees. They were going uphill, past an old quarry filled with wrecked cars, and still no one had spoken or given directions. He was exhausted, but he sensed he was near the house when they came out of the woods and into an open field.

A crowd of several hundred were spread thinly in a semicircle below the house, surrounding it like a half moon.

It was a silent gathering that stood patiently watching the tarpaper shack while behind them others clustered around small fires, more for warmth, he guessed, than companionship.

He continued up the hillside, moving closer, working his way through the throng. People stood aside as he pressed forward. They glanced at him as he came up and then deferred, sensing something different about him. He wasn't one of them. They could tell it in his face, the smoothness of his cheeks, and in his voice, the gentle way he excused himself as he moved forward. He got as far as the makeshift fence: a single strand of barbed wire stretched across the yard.

Beyond the wire, but standing away from the house, was the television crew. He recognized Stacey Graham. She was wearing a yellow rain hat and a safari jacket, and her tight jeans were stuffed into her knee-high leather boots. He stepped back into the crowd so she wouldn't spot him. He didn't need to end up on television debating Stacey about this girl's stigmata.

Three highway patrolmen stood next to the house, leaning against the wooden porch. They were dressed for the weather, wearing full-length yellow slickers and rain pants. They were the only bright spot on the dreary landscape. What a place, he thought, taking in the hillside.

The fog changed to rain and he could feel drops on his neck and running down his face. The police had climbed onto the porch, and Stacey Graham and the TV crew moved toward the same protection. Only the silent crowd stood passively in the rain. They must know something, he guessed. Perhaps an announcement had already been made, some word had spread among them before he had arrived. He'd wait a few minutes longer, he thought, and then leave.

There was a slight stirring in the crowd and behind him

he could feel the press of people. He glanced up at the front porch and saw that several more men had come out of the house.

He half expected Father Driscoll to be among them, but the men were all from the mountains: tall and gaunt, as thin as fence posts. A few had rifles tipped up against their shoulders. What were they fearing? he wondered.

The television camera lights came on and another murmur ran through the crowd. Stacey Graham was interviewing one of the men. The lights were only on for a few minutes and then there was more huddling and finally one of them stepped to the edge of the porch and spoke to the crowd through a bullhorn.

They could see Betty Sue, he told them, if they would just form a line at the porch. Betty Sue, he said, would give them each a small gift, "for coming so far and standing so long in the rain." And he told them it would cost one dollar to see her. Children were free.

Monsignor Callaghan smiled. So that was it, he thought. Someone with a sharp imagination had figured out a new way to make a fast buck. He felt immensely better. Now he had something specific to tell the Bishop.

The line was moving quickly, faster than he would have thought. At least they knew how to rush a crowd through the house. Out behind, he could see people gathering in tight knots when they came from the house; they talked intensely among themselves. The television crew had cornered a few and the cameras were lit. Stacey Graham was interviewing again. The priest took a dollar from his wallet and mounted the wooden steps.

One of the tall mountain men was taking the money. "I'm Betty Sue's kin," he told them, and smiled. "We're mighty thankful for this here donation. It will help feed and take care of little Betty Sue." He pulled a wad of single bills from his overalls and made change for a woman ahead of Monsignor Callaghan. "Now Betty Sue's in the back thar and you go right along. Iffen you want to say how-do, awright, but don't trouble her much. She's feelin' poorly."

Monsignor Callaghan handed the man his dollar and went inside, ducking his head under the door. He was too tall and the small room made him feel uncomfortable and out of place. It was crowded with people, relatives they looked like, and their presence surprised him. A few nodded hello, but most of them sat and silently watched.

"This way!" a young man called to them. He stood at the rear of the room at an open doorway. He wore the same mountain overalls, but he was not like the others. He was fair and handsome. "Go this way," he directed as Father Callaghan's group came across the room.

From down the hallway he could hear a young woman greeting people and thanking them for coming. One asked, "Let me see them sores." There were oohs and ahs and a woman said, "Does your Ma clean up after you, Betty Sue?"

She answered them politely, explaining in detail how she lived and what her mother and father did for her. "They're blessed people," she told the women and they nodded, agreeing. And then she said, "And here's a little something for you-all."

Her voice and manner surprised Monsignor Callaghan. He hadn't expected anyone so nice. He moved closer as the group ahead of him left, saying their good-byes and moving out into the yard.

Monsignor Callaghan stepped into the doorway, filling the frame, and she glanced up and smiled.

"Hello," she said, "thank you for comin' to see me." She was sitting in an upholstered chair wearing a blue housecoat. A quilt had been tucked around her legs, but her feet were bare, displaying the sores. She handed the Monsignor a holy card and when their fingers touched, she drew back, frowning, and asked, "You're a priest?"

"That's right, Betty Sue." He smiled. Her guess did not surprise him. Clairvoyance wasn't that unusual among hysterics.

"You've come sneakin' around here because you don't believe in me." She spoke kindly, as if she understood his doubts.

"I have my doubts, yes." He could not bring himself to be blunt with her. She had just been used, exploited by the men out front and by one of his fellow priests.

She held up her palms and showed him the wounds. "I didn't ask for these, Father," she said, as if to explain herself.

"I'm sure you didn't, Betty Sue, but people are being misled by your illness. If you want, child, I'll see that you get medical help."

She shook her head. "I accept God's role for me. I want only to bear witness, to be his humble servant, his obedient slave. I gladly make this offering of my body in obedience to his word. May it cleanse and renew me, and lead me to my eternal reward."

The priest pulled away, recognizing the words she was using, the paraphrasing of the words of the mass, the offering of oneself at the Eucharist. He bristled at the blatant sacrilege.

"All right, young woman, that's enough! If you want to make a little money conning the Baptists in these hills, fine, but when you start involving the Catholic Church, trying to corrupt good people, then you're asking for trouble."

He towered above her, his massive body blocking the doorway.

She smiled. "I'll pray for you, Father."

"Thanks. I don't need any of your prayers." He stepped out of the doorway. He had had enough of all this. She had closed her eyes and was looking down, looking young and innocent, like one of those kids in airports who kept trying to sell him flowers. "And so you will know what I tell you is true," she spoke up, "I must warn you to be careful. Your life is in danger."

Monsignor Callaghan smiled wryly. He knew this game. It was a practiced art of fortune tellers and palm readers: when telling the future, keep it vague.

"I'll do that, little lady; I'll just do that." He turned and tramped off down the hall and pushing open the kitchen door stepped into the rain.

Stacey Graham met him at the doorway. The video camera lights were on and she was ready with her microphone, but she hadn't expected a priest, much less someone from the Chancery. And what was Monsignor Callaghan doing in civilian clothes, she thought, as she stepped quickly forward and pinned him with the bright lights and her microphone.

"Good afternoon, Monsignor, and what brings you to Blue Haze Ridge and a visit with Betty Sue?" Stacey stepped aside so the cameraman could close in and fill the frame with the priest's square, bulldog face.

For just a moment on the film clip that was carried nationally by ABC on "Good Morning America," the priest appeared startled, but then he smiled and remarked nonchalantly, "Well, Stacey, it was my day off and I thought I might visit some friends in the mountains; then I got caught in the line of traffic and was sidetracked here." He smiled almost apologetically.

"You're not here investigating Betty Sue Wadkins? You are, as we know, one of the Bishop's chief aides, and a priest from your diocese, Father Matthew Driscoll, did discover and introduce this stigmatic young woman to the world." She knew the priest was lying.

"Oh, no," Monsignor Callaghan answered quickly, shaking his head, "the Bishop did not send me, or anyone else for that matter."

"Will you be seeing Father Driscoll?"

"As you know, Stacey, we have to go through Mossy Creek to reach the highway and I expect to stop in and just say hello. It will be around suppertime and I'm hoping I'll be asked to stay for dinner." He smiled and started off, saying, "Nice seeing you again."

"Monsignor, one last question if you don't mind." She followed him with her microphone and he had nowhere to hide: there were only open fields around them. He stopped at the corner of the house. It wouldn't look good on television, he realized, if it appeared as if he were running away.

"Monsignor, did you have the opportunity to speak with Betty Sue?"

"Yes, we exchanged a few remarks." Perhaps this was the way to handle it, he thought: nip the whole operation in the bud. Deflate the mystery, be open and obliging.

"And what is your opinion, Monsignor? Do we have a stigmatic saint here on Blue Haze Ridge?" She smiled warmly at the priest.

"Hardly a saint, Stacey. The process of canonization is long and complex in the Catholic Church. We wouldn't know about her sainthood for another hundred years or so." He shook his head and smiled, as if to suggest he was amused by this talk of sainthood. "Besides," he added lightly, "her sainthood is in God's providence; we just handle the paperwork!"

"I gather from your remarks, Monsignor, that you're not sympathetic to Betty Sue, and that unlike your fellow priest, Father Driscoll, you are not convinced this woman is a stigmatic saint." She was speaking slowly, letting her voice weigh on each word—as if she were interviewing him on "Meet the Press"—but she could hardly contain her own glee. This was terrific stuff. The Bishop's man was opening up, letting himself be interviewed, and disagreeing with the local priest.

"Well, I don't believe Father Driscoll has said this woman is a saint," he answered carefully. "Father Driscoll is, of course, familiar with the canon law concerning canonization."

"But Father Driscoll did say on television yesterday that Betty Sue was blessed with divine stigmata." Stacey knew she had him squirming. So far he was coming across cool and confident on film, but she had spotted the tension, the tightening of his neck muscles. He was beginning to breathe deeply and take his time answering. He was hiding something, she knew.

"The young woman does have sores on her hands and feet"—he refused to say *wounds!*—"but I wouldn't call them divine. And I must say I was amused to find a dollar being charged to see her. I should have gone to Six Flags instead; they have more thrills." He chuckled, but she did not respond. Graham was going the whole way with Betty Sue Wadkins. Well, not if he could help it. He'd blow her right off the evening news. He'd bad-mouth the whole charade.

"Then, Monsignor, if I understand you correctly, you're disagreeing with Father Driscoll. It is your opinion Betty Sue Wadkins is not a stigmatic saint."

"That's right." He smiled, a broad, good-natured smile. "My PhD degree was in psychology, Stacey, and though I wouldn't want to make a final judgment from such a short visit, I do think Betty Sue is suffering from what is sometimes called conversion hysteria. A rather severe emotional illness, but not divine."

"Then she's not blessed with the sacred wounds of Jesus Christ?"

"No, Stacey, she is not a recipient of any miraculous act. I will talk to Father Driscoll and see if some sort of psychiatric help might be obtained for her." He was talking quickly, confidently, making a final solution appear imminent.

"Monsignor, one last question. I understand some people in the mountains say that Betty Sue was attacked by the Devil—in the form of snakes—when she was twelve years old." Stacey Graham's face was turned away from the camera and she winked at the priest. *Let him try and get by this one,* she thought.

Monsignor Callaghan met her challenge. She wasn't going to tag him with that old chestnut.

"In my years in the priesthood I've had a lot of encounters with the Devil and I can assure you, Stacey, that this young woman is not under any demonic influence. She is a sweet young girl who needs understanding and prayers, as I might add, we all do. Now good afternoon, Ms. Graham, and God bless you." He waved and walked off quickly. This time she wouldn't stop him.

He went through the small pine woods again and came onto the road. The crowd was talkative now, comparing impressions of Betty Sue, and the priest walked along silently, listening to them. It was not normal, they said, shaking their heads. "It was not normal a'tall!" He knew he would not convince these people that what they had seen wasn't supernatural. They wanted to believe in strange powers, in a visual sign that God was still part of their world.

It wasn't until he crested the hill that he realized someone was matching stride with him, and keeping up. Monsignor Callaghan was not one to play cat and mouse. He stopped in the middle of the road and confronted the pursuer.

It was the young blond kid who had directed them into the girl's room.

"Anything I can do for you, son?"

"Betty Sue sent me," he said softly, standing away from the priest.

"Yes?" Monsignor Callaghan asked quickly. He was now impatient with another delay. He wanted to get off the ridge and out of the mountains.

"She said for you to go back to the city and not trouble Father Driscoll." He spoke as if he was delivering a message and the words had no meaning to him.

"You tell the young lady I'm not finished with my business in Mossy Creek."

"She says she can't save you otherwise." The young man looked directly at the priest, and Monsignor Callaghan found that just staring back, making eye contact, unnerved him.

"You tell her, boy, that I'm capable of taking care of myself." Their audacity was outrageous. He wasn't going to have some hillbilly tell him what to do. He half expected the young man to start threatening him, but the boy only grinned, bowed facetiously, and was off, running down Rabbit Hop road, his heavy boots thumping on the wet asphalt.

The priest watched him, feeling unaccountably anxious. He had the peculiar sense he hadn't done the right thing, hadn't handled the boy well. It was an unsettling, vague feeling and he couldn't put his finger on what disturbed him, but somehow he felt that Matt Driscoll and Saint John of the Cross parish would suffer for it.

"Hello, Matt," Monsignor Callaghan said, when Father Driscoll opened the kitchen door.

"Evening, Tim." He did not seem surprised by the priest's visit. "Care for some slim pickins? It's not exactly Chancery style, but we do our best."

"Thanks, Matt, but I'm trying to cut down." He patted his stomach. "Anything to drink?"

"Over the sink and behind the Tide. I've been off the stuff lately, but I think the young fella might be indulging." Father Driscoll sat at the table and began to make a sandwich, building it carefully, like a work of art. He took his time and waited Tim Callaghan out.

The priest had gone to the refrigerator for ice, making himself immediately at home, as if this were his own place. That pissed Father Driscoll off, but he let it pass. Tim Callaghan and he went back a long way. Why start complaining now about an old friend's habits? And besides, they had other issues to settle. The pastor knew what was coming, why Callaghan had driven up into the mountains, and to delay that confrontation, he asked, "Have you seen Kinsella?"

"Yes. He's been talking to the boss about leaving Saint John's."

"Good."

"He wants to join the Trappists."

"Oh, Christ!"

"The boss says it's a copout."

"The Bishop said that?"

"Well, not in so many words. Hasn't he come back?"

Father Driscoll shook his head. "I don't want him. You fellas keep him with you. Give him some sort of paper-pushing job at the Chancery. Keep him out of trouble, away from girls. I caught him with that girl friend of his. They were hugging and kissing in the rectory. Right in the front parlor after mass, can you believe it? I wouldn't have been surprised if he took her to his room when I left the rectory. The boy's a loser, Tim, get rid of him."

Monsignor Callaghan came to the table and sat down, swirling his scotch and water. The ice clicked in the silent room. He sipped the drink and watched Father Driscoll spread butter on a piece of white bread. Then he sighed and began, tired already of the discussion that confronted him.

"What's going on up here, Matt? First Kinsella and his college girl friend, then you with Betty Sue Wadkins and a nationwide telecast. Why didn't you let the boss know? He's furious about this television thing."

The pastor finished making the sandwich, but didn't eat it.

"You know what would have happened, Tim. If I had told the Bishop, he wouldn't have let me on television. I wouldn't have been able to whisper the girl's name."

"That's right! And that's why I'm here. He wants to see you right away. You're to say the Easter masses and then drive down. He wants the full story, and I'm telling you, Matt, it better be good. You've gone too far this time. He's ready to jerk you out of this parish, and you know what that means. You'll be shoved off into some convent. You'll spend the rest of your priesthood hearing the confessions of a bunch of nuns." Tim Callaghan swallowed half his drink.

"I'm not going down to see him, Tim."

"Matt, you don't have a choice. The Bishop told me: bring Driscoll. He wants to see you now, and the only reason he's waiting until tomorrow afternoon is because of Easter Sunday."

Father Driscoll shook his head and started eating. Between bites, he answered Callaghan.

"Tim, I already know what the boss will do. He's going to get all over me about Betty Sue. He'll tell me I'm making the church look ridiculous."

"She's not a saint, Matt." Monsignor Callaghan spoke quietly.

"And how could you know?" the pastor shot back. "Did you see her ecstasy yesterday?"

"No, but I've just been out there. I paid my buck like all the other suckers and talked to the girl. I got my Holy Card with Saint John of the Cross stamped all over it. I saw her, Matt, and she's a nice simpleminded girl, but she's no saint.

"They've played you for a goddam fool and compromised the Church, not only here in the mountains but throughout the country. I wouldn't be surprised if we heard from Rome on this one. And to tell you the truth, Matt, I wouldn't have thought it, not from you. You've been a priest too long. You're too smart to fall for some mountain hokum cooked up by a bunch of good ol' boys."

"She's not a fraud, Tim." Father Driscoll's conviction was so positive that Callaghan paused and studied the pastor across the table, weighing his reply.

"You know, Matt, the Church has only had a handful of stigmatic saints."

"Sixty-two. That's not a handful."

"But none of them have been in the modern age. You're talking about the sixteenth century."

"Padre Pio died in 1968, and the first phase of his beatification has already begun."

"Padre Pio was a Capuchin priest, not a mountain girl. And a Baptist to boot!"

"Betty Sue's parents have already begun their religious instruction, Tim, and I'm planning on receiving Betty Sue into the Church within the next few weeks."

"You're not going to be at Saint John's, Matt. I'm telling you as a friend how the boss operates. He'll pull you out of this parish and send you on a long retreat."

"I'm not leaving Mossy Creek. I'm not driving down to see the Bishop. I'm staying in the mountains, in my parish, until this child is received into the Church. Then the Bishop can do what he wants."

Father Driscoll had finished his meal and he glanced at the clock and stood, clearing the table as he did. "You'll have to excuse me, Tim. I'm due out at Blue Haze Ridge."

"You're going to disobey the Bishop, are you?"

"It won't be the first time, will it, Tim?" He smiled wryly again.

This wasn't the same Matt Driscoll he knew, Monsignor Callaghan realized. There was a sureness and confidence that always had been lacking before. He had settled something in his mind and he wasn't going to be intimidated by a lot of tough talk.

"Why are you so damn sure, Matt?" he asked, but the tone of his voice had changed. He wasn't implying threats.

"My leg," answered the pastor. "She cured my leg." He moved around the table, putting away the food and taking the dishes to the sink. "I've had arthritis in this leg for almost twenty years, and during the winter months up here I sometimes can barely stand the pain. But she cured it during one of her ecstasies. We have a tape of it. That's one reason I believe she's a saint. And because of the note."

"What note?"

"Kinsella didn't tell you fellas? Well, I'm going to give it to you, Tim, and I want you to deliver it to the Bishop. Then he'll understand what we have up here." He motioned for Monsignor Callaghan to follow him into the rectory chapel and, unlocking the tabernacle, he pulled out the ciborium.

"It's in here."

"What?"

"The note." He took off the tight lid and picked out the white envelope. It was sealed with plastic.

"Let me see." Callaghan reached for the envelope, but the pastor stopped him.

"No, don't open it, Tim. That's a warning. Take it to the Bishop and open it only when you are alone. It's miraculous, and it must be handled as if it were the Holy Eucharist itself. What you'll see will shock you, but it's real. It's a sign. A sign from God to tell us to believe in this young woman. When the Bishop sees this, he'll understand what I'm trying to achieve." The pastor's eyes gleamed.

Tim Callaghan took the envelope and slipped it casually

into the breast pocket of his jacket. And then he said abruptly, "If you have evidence of this girl's holiness, Matt, you could have avoided a lot of unnecessary trouble by just telling the Bishop first and not pulling this grand stand stunt. Going on television. Who do you think you are, Billy Graham?"

The priests had left the chapel and were standing in the foyer. Monsignor Callaghan was ready to leave.

"No, I'm simply a Catholic priest. A real Catholic priest, Tim, who still believes in the sacraments and the supernatural nature of our religion."

"And who doesn't, Matt? Who doesn't?"

"How can you ask me that? Sometimes I think all you people in the Chancery have given up the Church, what with your directives to have guitars in mass and deacons giving out Holy Communion. No one listens to what I have to say about theology, and I've been a priest for thirty-five years.

"It's you people who made all those reforms, who threw out the Latin mass and gave us new priests like this Stephen Kinsella. That boy doesn't even know what sin is. He has no conscience, no notion of his obligations as a priest. He thinks it is some sort of job that he works at from nine to five. And then he can forget about religion and go off on his own, carry on with this woman." Father Driscoll kept shaking his head. He couldn't stop talking. He had kept all this frustration inside of him over the years and it was his turn to talk. They had to listen to him now.

"I know what you fellas think about me at the Chancery. That I'm an old fool, a drunk. Sure I drink. But you would, too, if you had to live up here among these primitives, and suffer through the cold winters, year after year. I haven't a single friend in this town, Tim. No one who I can talk to and share my feelings with.

"You people send me these young kids fresh out of the

seminary. They're children. They have no idea of what life is like, how difficult it can be for a person. And they never have time to sit and talk to me, sit down and learn something. I've been around, Tim, I know a few things. I can teach these boys.

"No, you don't know any of this. You've got a dozen friends, a hundred things to do in the city. Every night there is some function. You're never alone. You don't have to wander around this drafty old barn of a place, suffering with arthritis so much that you have to drink just to be able to stand the pain.

"At times I've wanted to kill myself, Tim. That's the truth. I've contemplated it. All these years I've been here alone, all twelve of them, I have been suffering and I didn't know why. But there was a reason. God had a plan for me. He was getting me ready to accept his challenge."

The fierce fire had come back into the pastor's eyes and he leaned forward. "God was getting me ready spiritually, preparing me for Betty Sue Wadkins. I had been selected by him to teach this child and care for her." The old priest stopped, exhausted.

"By making a spectacle of her, Matt? By putting her on television from coast to coast? Is that what God wanted?"

"Yes, by putting her on television. By making people see God is still among us, still working his miracles and proving the existence of Jesus Christ."

"Matt, stop a moment and think of what you've really done. If this girl has the divine stigmata you haven't advanced her sainthood by exploiting her. You've just got a sideshow going on out there."

"Is Lourdes a sideshow, Tim?" he answered, silencing the priest. "Sure we'll get some crazies. That's to be expected, but millions of others will see the truth of Betty Sue and come to the Church. They have already. The telegrams have been arriving all day. Hundreds of them. Telegrams from

Catholics who had lost their faith until yesterday afternoon when they went the way of the cross with Betty Sue. *That's* what I've done, Tim. I've brought more people back to the faith with one telecast than all the priests and Bishops do in a lifetime."

Callaghan realized it was no use spending more time trying to reason with him.

"All right, Matt. I'll tell the boss what you said." He tapped his breast pocket. "I'll give him this letter."

"He'll understand, Tim. Show him the letter and he'll understand. You both will."

Father Driscoll opened the front door, then turned to shake the Monsignor's hand. "Thanks for coming. I appreciate that it was you. I thought he'd send one of those young hotshots."

"I'll do what I can with him. But he's not going to let you continue. He'll remove you with force if necessary. Take my advice, Matt, and back off. Come down tomorrow afternoon and give the man a chance to investigate. He's approachable, Matt."

"She doesn't need to be investigated. There's more goodness in that young woman than there is in the whole Chancery."

"Matt, you don't know. Only God knows what the soul of a person is really like."

"You can't believe in her, can you, Tim?"

Monsignor Callaghan shook his head. "She's got a good con: a sweet, innocent, victimized, and beautiful young woman. But she's a fraud."

Father Driscoll kept smiling, and then he asked, "Tell me, Tim, did she know you were a priest?"

Monsignor Callaghan's eyes widened, surprised at the question, and answered slowly, "Yes, she did know, but how did ... ?"

Father Driscoll nodded, kept smiling, the same understanding smile. "She knows, Tim. She knows. And when you see the note, you'll understand why I no longer care what the Bishop says. Her authority comes from higher than him. It comes from Christ himself. Now give the note to the Bishop. But be careful with it. It hasn't left the tabernacle since we first saw her on Blue Haze Ridge."

There was little downtown traffic and Monsignor Callaghan went quickly through Mossy Creek. It was still raining, but his big car handled the wet road easily.

He wanted to drive fast. All the events and talk of the afternoon had exhausted him and he just wanted to clear his mind. He opened the side window a few inches and let the wind whip into the car. In a few minutes he was beyond the town limits, moving toward the superhighway and home. He began to relax.

Reaching into his jacket pocket for a cigar, he touched the sealed white envelope. He pulled it out and turned it in his fingers, glancing at the crude printing on the envelope. What was so special about this? he wondered as he negotiated the tight turns. Why had Driscoll made such a fuss about not opening it until he was with the Bishop?

He took his foot off the gas and pulled off the road. He kept the car running as he broke open the seal of the plastic and picked out the white envelope.

A sharp quick electric shock ran up his arm. What the hell, he thought, and reaching into the envelope, he pulled out the letter.

In the dashboard light he read the one-line message and saw the dime-sized bloodstain. He turned the letter over, looking for something more, but there wasn't anything else. Was that all? He frowned. Discarding the envelope, he slipped the letter back into his shirt pocket and eased the car back onto the mountain road.

There was no traffic and he touched the high beams. It was a dark night with patches of fog, but the road wasn't icy and he pressed down on the pedal, hurrying. He wanted to get home.

It was now hot and stuffy in the car, but when he reached over to turn off the heat he saw it wasn't on. He opened the window wider and let the cold wind whip across his face, yet still he was uncomfortably hot. His chest felt clammy. A cold, he thought, goddammit. That's what he'd get for tramping around Blue Haze Ridge, standing out in the rain.

Monsignor Callaghan wiped his face and neck and felt the dry skin. He slipped his hand beneath his jacket to touch his chest and came away with blood on his fingers. It burned the soft flesh of his palm and he could feel it spreading across his chest and stomach and seeping down to his groin. He tried to pull away from the fierce pain, but the seat belt held him captive.

His car was out of control. It swung wildly from one edge of the road to the other and when he slammed the brake the heavy vehicle skidded and fishtailed and failed to take a curve. Monsignor Callaghan hung onto the wheel as the car tore through a low guard rail and sailed into the dark hollow.

It sailed silently, hung in the night like a spent bullet, then dropped into the trees where it broke branches and tree trunks and tumbled down the valley, bouncing off rocks and boulders until the gas tank exploded like a bomb.

It lit the night with an orange ball of flame and then burned silently. In Mossy Creek, Father Driscoll heard the explosion and wondered momentarily what it was. Then he got into the church station wagon and drove slowly on the wet roads up to Blue Haze Ridge.

Rufus knocked softly on her bedroom door and stepped inside. She was sitting up, the illustrated Bible open on her lap, and leaning forward, studying the picture of the Cruci-fixion in the soft light.

"His car crashed, Betty Sue," he reported.

She nodded slowly as if she had expected the news. Then, hesitating as if trying to remember how it went again, she blessed herself, but did it backwards, and using her left hand.

17

Sunday, March 26

Easter Sunday

It was after ten o'clock when Father Driscoll returned to the rectory from Blue Haze Ridge. He had spent the evening teaching Catholic doctrine to Betty Sue's parents, and now he was too tired even to sleep. He lay in bed saying his rosary and listening to the sounds of the old building: the banging pipes, rattling windows, the creaking walls, and once sure of these noises, he fell asleep for an hour, but then woke again, this time for good.

It had been like this all week, since Father Kinsella had left, and he realized he couldn't last long, living like this. His body was taking too much abuse. He would die, he knew, keel over with a heart attack. That thought did not frighten him. He had only one prayer: that he'd live long enough to accept Betty Sue into the Catholic Church. A convert for Christ. His saint. Then he'd be ready for his reward.

Yet now when he woke again it was quiet in the rectory,

there were not even the familiar sounds of the house. The wind had died. No howling or rattling of loose windows. No sound from outside, not even street traffic. Silence, and then the laughter.

A young woman's laughter: high and nervous and oddly melancholy. It filled the small bedroom as if it were coming from just outside the window, and as suddenly as it had burst into the quiet night, it stopped. It could have been carried to him on the wind, he thought, but there was no wind.

He tossed off the blanket and moved quickly from the bed, moving with more agility than he ever remembered, and he thought of Betty Sue and her miracle. A second-class miracle, the Church would call it, but she had cured him of a lifetime of pain.

Again the laughter. It could have been within fifty feet of the rectory or miles away. The mountains were that way: they distorted sound.

He stepped into his slippers and pulled on his flannel housecoat as he went out of his room and down the hallway to the kitchen. He did not turn on any lights. If someone was outside, he wanted the advantage of darkness.

More laughter, and next the woman began to sing. He stopped to listen. Her voice was lovely and she was singing, he realized, the words from the *Gloria in Excelsis Deo* of the Latin Mass: *Laudamus te, benedicimus te, glorificamus te.* We praise you, we bless you, we glorify you.

Through the kitchen windows he spotted a dim light reflecting in the stained-glass window of the church next door. He held his breath and waited, watching the huge red-and-blue glass window.

The light flashed again: faint and flickering like a candle's. There was someone inside Saint John's and it didn't surprise him. He had known someone would attack the church, especially now because of Betty Sue.

He wrapped his robe tightly around him, and taking the church keys off the backdoor hook, he went out into the yard. He would not call the police. This he wanted to deal with himself. He was the pastor and it was his responsibility to protect God's House.

He entered the church through the sacristy door. There were no lights, but the cabinet doors to the cabinet where the vestments hung were thrown open and the albs and amices and chasubles were scattered on the floor. He was picking up the silk and linen garments when he heard voices from the sanctuary and he moved to the curtain and peeped out at the altar.

The sanctuary had been changed. A black cloth hung as a backdrop behind the altar. Black drapery also covered the altar stone, and on it were a black cross, candles, and a small wooden box. And standing in the priest's place was Rufus Tainter.

Rufus had combed out his blond hair and let it fall in smooth curls to his shoulders. He looked older and more handsome, dressed in Father Kinsella's maniple, stole, and chasuble, wearing all the black vestments of the Mass of the Dead—except they were turned inside out and worn backwards. He called out into the empty church, "Our Father, which wert in heaven, hallowed be thy name; thy will be done on heaven as it is on earth. Give us this day our daily bread; Lead us into temptation, and deliver us not from evil."

He was reversing the words of the Lord's Prayer, Father Driscoll realized, saying the Satanist version. In the liturgy of the high mass he had reached the Consecration, the changing of wine into blood, but he was doing that backwards also, filling the chalice first with water, then with wine.

He set the chalice aside and opened the small wooden box on the altar. From it he carefully lifted out three human skulls, crying out as he did to these sons of Adam, "First you, Gaspard, who bring riches to relieve our poverty, give us the wisdom of the future and the precious gift of your counsel." He lifted the second skull. "You, Melchior, proud old man of the long beard, you who offer incense to humility." He picked up the third skull and gently wiped the dust off it and into the chalice. "You, Balthazar, who are the closest to us, you who love the Queen of the Sabbat. Unloose the all-powerful passion of my senses, wed me to blind ecstasy that I shall be inspired, if not by grace, at least by desire."

He took the chalice and held it up, crying, "Great astrologers, your dust prophesies. The flame of your hearts have gathered the wisdom found beyond the tomb."

The church organ began to play, softly and slowly, and its sweet music filled the sanctuary. Father Driscoll could not move. His fingers gripped the thick sacristy curtains, held him up. The fierce pain had returned to his leg and he gasped for breath. What he was witnessing was too blasphemous for him to comprehend.

A young woman was singing. A song of celebration from the new guitar masses:

> Gonna sing, my Lord, for all that I'm worth;
> Gonna sing, my Lord, for all that I'm worth, Lord, Lord.
> Gonna sing, my Lord, for all that I'm worth;
> Gonna sing, my Lord, Lord, Lord, till I see your face.

Father Driscoll saw her approach the altar, walking out of the darkness of the vestibule, but he was unable to move. She carried two small black candles and the oily smoke clouded the church and smelled of fresh tar. She was moving gracefully to the organ music, dancing naked, her tall, slim body gliding through the shadows.

Rufus came forward and took her hand as she stepped onto the altar platform, her bare feet silent in the thick carpet. She moved to the marble altar and he helped her up onto the black shrouded stone. She held the candles in each hand as she lay back and stretched out on the altar.

Rufus walked around her, the chasuble flowing as he moved quickly, swinging incense from the thurible and singing in Latin the most sacred words of the Mass: *Hoc est enim corpus meum; Hic est enim calix sanguinis mei*—For this is my body; this is the chalice of my blood.

Placing the chalice of consecrated hosts on her chest, he bent forward and kissed her between the legs, crying out, "Lamb of God, you take away the pleasures of the world: be gone! Lamb of God, you take away the pleasures of the world: leave us be! Lamb of God, you take away the pleasures of the world: grant us peace from your domination." Then with his thumb and forefinger, he plucked a host from the chalice and holding it high with both hands, he cried, "This is the Lamb of God who takes away the pleasures of the world," and reaching down he shoved the white wafer into her vagina.

Then taking the chalice of wine, he poured it over her, washing her genitals with his hands as he whispered, "Life listen; Death speak!" and climbing onto the marble altar stone, he mounted the girl.

Father Driscoll stumbled forward, trying to cry out, trying to stop them, but the words would not form, he could not make himself heard. What he had witnessed was a blasphemy almost beyond his comprehension, shocking proof that he had been wrong, that he had failed God in his ministry, and the force of the massive cardiac arrest sent him reeling into the sanctuary, ripping the curtains as he tumbled forward, dead before he hit the floor.

Father Kinsella reached Saint John's at three o'clock in the morning. He had driven wildly for hours, racing across the state and up into the mountains. The church was lit when he arrived, and he could hear organ music blaring an unmelodic tone, as though the organist were insane, but it halted abruptly when he ran into the empty church.

Father Kinsella stopped at the vestibule doors, paralyzed by what he saw. Slowly his eyes panned the church, taking in the massive destruction.

All the maple pews had been overturned and stacked, as though a bulldozer had circled the altar and shoved the pews into piles. The marble baptismal stand and pillar were smashed, and the ceramic stations of the cross ripped from the walls. Even the huge handmade hickory crucifix had been cut down and leaned against the other side of the altar.

Stephen walked cautiously forward and circled the altar. He stopped when he saw Father Driscoll. The priest's naked body was nailed to the Cross. The sharp spikes that had been used to fix the Christ figure to the wood were now driven into the open palms of the dead priest and the blunt end of the black metal altar cross jabbed into his heart. The pastor's eyes and mouth were wide open, as if he had just witnessed a revelation. His blood made a thick pool around him, soaking the deep carpet and turning it crimson.

Father Kinsella wanted to be sick, but he owed the pastor more than that. Swallowing his bile, he knelt at the foot of the huge Cross and prayed for the man's soul. It was all he could do for him now: *"Saints of God, come to his aid! Come to meet him, angels of the Lord! Receive his soul and present him to God the Most High. Give him eternal rest, O Lord, and may your light shine on him forever."*

When he had finished the prayers for the dead he knelt a moment longer beside Father Driscoll, then returned to the sacristy and opened the Ambry. He took out the holy oils for the rite of anointing and the sacred vessels used in communion. He filled the thurible with incense, and taking it, holy water, and a purple silk stole of Lent, he went to save Betty Sue. Those sacred vessels and vestments, he knew, were his only salvation against Rufus Tainter.

It was almost dawn on Easter Sunday when he reached Blue Haze Ridge. The sun was up but the house was still in shadows. And it was cold, the sharp cold of late March. It was a day without promise.

In the empty yard below the house a few wood fires smoldered, but the people were gone; there were none of the crowds that he had seen on television. He ran through the trees and up to the house, his boots shaking the building as he leaped onto the porch and pounded the front door.

Betty Sue answered. She had come from her bed with just a quilt wrapped around her for warmth.

"Stephen?" She frowned as she pushed open the screen door, "What's the matter?"

"Are your parents asleep, Betty Sue?" he asked softly, stepping inside.

"They've gone off to sunrise services, Stephen."

"Sunrise services?"

She nodded. "They go every year. It's a mighty big event here in the mountains."

"But your parents asked to become Catholics."

"That don't matter, Stephen; we're all Christians, ain't we?" She smiled and added, pouting this time, "Why weren't you here Friday? Lordy, I thought I would die! But yesterday"—her eyes brightened—"all those people came to see me. They saw me on TV. I've never seen so many lovely people, and they came from as far away as Georgia. I never thought they'd like me, y'know, because of these sores, but they all wanted to see them. And Miss Graham! She was real nice. Did you see me on the TV, Stephen?"

"Betty Sue, where's Rufus?" the priest asked.

She shrugged. "I guess he's down at his place." She began

to shiver then, standing on tiptoes, her bare feet cold on the wood floor.

"Betty Sue, you better get back into bed." Stephen took her by the arm and led her through the house to her bedroom. He helped her in and tucked the blankets tightly around her, and then he sat next to her on the bed. He was going to tell her what had happened to Father Driscoll and the church, and why he was looking for Rufus, but decided to wait until her parents returned home.

"Stephen, I've missed you," she said softly, smiling up at him. The sunlight had reached the windows and touched her face, turning her hair golden in the morning light. He could smell her body next to him, the sweet perfumed scent of her wounds mixed with the sensual odor of her body. "I'm glad you're here." She took his hand and cupped it between hers.

He turned his head slightly to look at her, and she briefly met his eyes, then lowered her gaze. He could see only part of her face, her eyelashes, the soft curve of her cheek, and the fair skin where the nightgown had slipped away from the nape of her neck.

"Would you stay awhile with me, Stephen? I'm all alone . . ."

"Yes, Betty Sue, I won't leave you." His voice was tight.

She lifted his hand and kissed his fingers one at a time and then, as if accidentally, she brushed the back of his hand against her breast. The top of her nightgown had come open and he could see where the soft slopes of her breasts swept to startled nipples. She was breathing rapidly.

"Betty Sue," he managed to say.

She gazed up at him, held him with her sad and lonely eyes as she slowly, carefully, took his hand and placed it on her breast. His eyes flashed as he touched her.

Her breasts were fuller, heavier than Deborah's; their softness filled his hand. He paused, waited, and she immediately pressed her body against him and lifted her face to be kissed.

He touched her lips gently, but she slipped her tongue into his mouth and wrapped her arms around his body, pulling him down beside her.

"Stephen," she sighed, pulling him to her, "I've waited so long." She ran her fingers through his long hair, and then, without his help, she pulled off her nightgown, tossed it aside, and came back into his arms.

He lay passive, his body shivering with excitement. "Darling, what's the matter? Don't you want me?"

He was thinking of Deborah, of Father Driscoll, of how he had compromised their lives because of his actions. He could not let the same thing happen to Betty Sue. But she would not stop. She began to unbutton his shirt, to kiss his chest. And he wanted her. From the first moment he had seen her in her passion, he had wanted to make love, to hold her and comfort her in her pain.

"Please, darling," she murmured, "come to me." She had opened his shirt; now she unzipped his jeans and slipped her hand inside, seizing his erection, and then she slid down and took it in her mouth.

"No," he begged. "No, Betty Sue." He eased her away.

"But I want to make you happy," she protested.

He did love her, he realized. He loved her in a way he had not loved Deborah. Loved her because she needed him and he would not leave her.

"Hurry," she said, seeing his changed expression and she moved in the bed to give him room.

He slipped out of his jeans and boots and stretched out beside her. Her eyes were bright and excited, waiting for him, and she eased him down on top of her. She reached for his penis and brushed it against the lips of her vulva.

"Oh, darling . . ." She shuddered as the pain of pleasure shook her. He kept rubbing the top of his erection against the thickening clitoris, letting the shock waves rip up her spine.

Without waiting for her to be ready, needing to dominate her, he forced his penis through the tight rings of her wet vagina. She grabbed hold of him and raked her nails across his back.

He kept after her, driving his erection again and again into her. She cried in his arms and told him not to come. He thought it was because she wanted the pleasure of him hard inside her, but she was struggling now, telling him to stop, to let her go. But he could not stop. He would not. He had lost control and would not heed her.

Betty Sue was crying that he mustn't come, that she didn't want his semen in her. She pushed at him, tried to get away, to escape, but it was too late for them both and he ejaculated.

He lay exhausted on her. She was crying, whimpering in his arms. He could feel her tears and her strange remorse puzzled him. He raised up and saw that there were no tears on her cheeks, but rather warm, flowing blood. She had begun to bleed again. The crown of thorns had burst out across her forehead, the skin peeling away as the thorns pierced her skin.

He pulled out of her and she cried, trying to explain. "He made me do it, Stephen. He wanted you to make love to me. I'm sorry. I tried to stop." Her nose began to bleed. The blood spurted from both nostrils as she tried to sit up. "I can't help myself, Stephen. Please, you must help me."

The priest was standing, horrified at the sight of her. Blood poured from her eyes and ran in streaks down her cheeks. It ran from her ears and mouth and gushed from her vagina. Her whole body was a battlefield of wounds and bruises.

She tried to speak, to say something more, but blood filled her mouth and she gagged.

He remembered then the story of a Spanish nun he had read about in one of Father Rafalet's books. Magdalena de la Cruz had lived in the 1490s and had all the signs of a divine stigmata. Yet one day when she was seriously ill she confessed that when she was twelve the Devil had solicited her and for thirty years she was under his influence, at a time when she had been considered a saint and made abbess of a monastery. The Devil had fooled everyone, as he had fooled Father Driscoll and himself.

Stephen grabbed his clothes. He had to get off Blue Haze Ridge, he knew, before Rufus arrived, before he knew of this fornication. He dressed frantically, then glanced back at Betty Sue to see that the hemorrhaging was out of control, worse than he had ever seen it. She would die this time, he realized, unless he could pull her from the satanic trance.

He could not leave her. Taking the stole from his jacket, he kissed it and slipped the vestment over his shoulders. He took out the blessed olive oil and the holy water and returned to the bed. He would give her the last rites, the final sacrament of extreme unction, a blessing that had throughout the history of the Church saved lives and brought people back from the verge of death.

"My brothers and sisters," he began. *"To prepare for this holy anointing, let us call to mind our sins."*

"It's no good, Kinsella, you can't save her." Rufus stood in the doorway, leaning against the frame. "All that mumbo jumbo doesn't mean anything to her."

"You brought us to salvation by your paschal mystery: Lord, have mercy."

"Quit fuckin' around and let the cunt die! She did her job; she's of no use to me."

"Why did you use her?" Stephen shouted across the bed.

"Because I failed with that other guy."

Stephen stared.

"That student at the seminary. The one you let blow you.

Once you got away to that monastery and under Rafalet's influence, you were too strong for me. So I waited for another chance. I knew you'd fuck up.

"I found this Rufus Tainter; he couldn't resist me either, so I took over." The young blond boy smiled. "We came up here to the mountains and got Betty Sue. It took awhile to get her ready for you, but I had time, Stephen. I have all the time in the world and I knew you'd come."

"What do you want, Rufus?"

The boy smiled. "I want you, Stephen. I want your body and soul." He nodded toward the bleeding girl. "And you see, I'll kill for you. I'd rather have one priest than a hundred sluts like her." He stared hard at the priest, his blue eyes flaming. "I almost had you once and I have you now forever."

"Why did you kill Deborah? It was you, wasn't it?"

Rufus nodded. "She was making you ask yourself too many questions about Betty Sue."

"And Father Driscoll?"

"He wanted to make this slut into a saint. I hadn't planned on people finding God because of her."

Betty Sue's body jerked on the bed and she began to vomit.

"See, Stephen, I told you your magic wouldn't save her."

Father Kinsella leaned over Betty Sue and anointed her forehead with the blessed oil, saying quickly, fiercely, with all the power of his belief, of his desire to be a good priest: *"Through this holy anointing may the Lord in his love and mercy help you with the grace of the Holy Spirit. May the Lord who frees you from sin save you and raise you up. Amen."*

Betty Sue continued to bleed. She had no reserve of grace, Stephen realized. Her soul was filled with the cancer of Rufus's corruption. She did belong to him.

"Free her, Rufus—or whatever your real name is."

"Why?"

"I'll come quietly then. There's no reason for her to die. She's innocent."

"You'll come anyway, Kinsella."

"No, I won't. Not without a fight. Free her first. Let her live."

Rufus's eyes shifted across the priest's face as he weighed the proposition. On the bed Betty Sue was no longer bleeding. Only water ran from her wounds.

"If she dies, Rufus, you won't have me. I'll kill myself before I'll let you touch me."

Rufus Tainter studied him. "You're not the same punk kid, are you?" He nodded, as if conceding a point. "Okay, stand away."

He raised his hands over the lifeless body.

"Aquerra Goity, Aquerra Beyty, Aquerra Goity, Aquerra Beyty—the Goat above, the Goat below; the Goat above, the Goat below. I conjure you, Astaroth and Asmodeus, to free the life of this child, which I offer in return for what I ask: the body and soul of this false priest Stephen."

Rufus went to the corner of the room and took the Saint John's thurible and dumped out the incense. "Your sweet-smelling gums and spices are no use," he said to Stephen, and began to refill the gold censer. "We burn rue and myrtle, some dried nightshade, henbane and thornapple." The foul, bitter scent filled the bedroom. "Nice, isn't it?" Rufus grinned and circled the bed, shaking the censer at Betty Sue and muttering, "Lucifer has died, Lucifer is risen, Lucifer will come again. Lord Lucifer, come in glory. *Sanguis eius super nos et filios nostros*—his blood be upon us and upon our children."

Rufus lowered the thurible. "She's free, Kinsella."

The priest stood by the bed and watched Betty Sue's wounds heal for the last time. The sores faded from her hands, side, and feet. The crown of thorns disappeared from her head. She began to breathe slowly, as if she were asleep.

He lifted the quilt and covered her. He wished he could bathe her but that could wait until her mother returned. She was all right now. The pain and suffering of her stigmata was over. She was free. He said a silent prayer for her final salvation.

"Okay, Stephen." Rufus's voice was impatient.

The priest walked around the bed and the two men stood facing each other.

Rufus was grinning. "I've had to wait a long time for this. Wait until you did something unforgivable, like fuck Betty Sue." He shook his head. "Tacky, Stephen."

Father Kinsella stood motionless. He was taller and stronger than Rufus, but he let Rufus reach up and touch his face.

"Kneel down, Stephen," he ordered. "You priests like kneeling to your god, don't you." He unbuckled his belt. "Hurry up, asshole, and blow me."

Stephen felt his knees weaken. He could not resist the other man's will. Rufus was right. He had done the unforgivable. He was lost and condemned. He had sinned too often and had fallen forever from grace. He dropped to his knees.

"Take it, Kinsella," Rufus ordered.

Stephen looked up. Rufus towered above him, an immense force blocking his view. Stephen stared up into those blue eyes, filled with all the evil of the world, and felt his strength melt as Rufus's power swelled and filled the room, and slowly he began to bow his head.

As he closed his eyes he thought of Deborah, of her life lost because of him. And Father Driscoll, who had wanted only to believe that God had given him a sign. He thought of Betty Sue. Of all the years she had suffered needlessly, a victim of Rufus's plot. All these people had been tormented because of him, because of his struggle to live as a good priest. Rufus's triumph made a joke of their suffering, of their belief in him, of his own faith in God. He could not let it happen.

Slowly he raised his head, his rage filling him, bringing back his strength. And the rage he felt toward Rufus for what he had done was a just rage. Their eyes met once more and then Stephen struck out, hitting him in the groin, and Rufus doubled over in pain.

Stephen was on his feet. He slipped the purple stole from his neck and wrapped the silk band around Rufus's neck, jerking it tight and squeezing the life from him.

It was murder, as cold-blooded as Father Kinsella could make it. Rufus gagged and gasped, then hung from the taut vestment of the Catholic Church. When the body was found, Father Kinsella knew, he would be questioned, but he was innocent. This killing had been, in an Old Testament way, an offering to God. A sacrifice and proof that God did live and triumph over evil.

And for the lost soul of this Rufus Tainter that Lucifer had possessed, Stephen Kinsella whispered the Latin words of the sacrament of extreme unction—*"Per istam Sanctam Unctionem et suam piissimam misericordiam adiuvet te Dominus gratia Spiritus Sancti, ut a peccatis liberatum te salvet atque propitius allevet"*—then let the demon drop from his hands.

Epilogue

Friday, June 2

Feast of the Sacred Heart of Jesus

Frater Matthew stopped for a moment on the late Friday afternoon and taking off his straw hat, wiped the sweat from his eyes, then gazed across Saint Michael's field at the other novices of the monastery. They were in constant motion: bending, stretching, sweeping the long sickles through the first cut of green alfalfa, always moving forward across the high farm land behind Mount Olive Knob.

Stopping, he felt again the pain of hard work in his arms and legs and across his shoulders. Every muscle hurt. Since coming to the monastery, he had spent long days and nights in work and prayer, and though his mind had adjusted to the routine and welcomed the enforced discipline, his body still was soft from his years of idleness.

He looked at his hands. The blisters in both palms had broken open and were bleeding. He thought again, as he did every day of his new life, of Betty Sue, and then quickly he blocked that memory from his mind and pushed himself to work, swinging the heavy sickle and silently praying, *"All for Jesus! All for Jesus!"*

He worked hard through the hot afternoon, pushing himself into a numb exhaustion so that he did not have the strength to remember. It was what he had been doing every day since arriving at the gate and begging Father Rafalet to take him into the cloister.

At five o'clock the undermaster clapped his hands, signaling the end of work, and Matthew turned from the green field of alfalfa and headed toward the monastery with the other novices. He took out his rosary beads and for Deborah he began to pray, *"Hail Mary, full of grace, the Lord is with thee . . ."*

He could catch glimpses of the monastery below him and through the trees: the huge gray stone buildings with red tile roofs, the wooden barns and barnyards, the gardens of summer flowers, all tidy and perfect under the clear azure sky. It made him feel secure and peaceful, knowing he was part of it, a member of the community and safely away from the world.

Inside the novitiate, he changed out of his work clothes in his small, bare cubicle. He put on his white oblate's robe, the scapular and cowl, and left the dormitory, went along the hallway toward the abbey church, walking with his eyes down, listening to the shuffling sandals of the monks as the whole community made its way to the church for evening prayers.

It was the Feast of the Sacred Heart of Jesus and the church rang with the voices of the choir. He stepped into his pew, his close-cropped head bowed under the cowl. He knew that from the visitor's balcony, he was indistinguishable from the others. He took pleasure in the sureness of his anonymity.

When vespers were over he did not leave with the others, but stayed on his knees to make his special daily devotions. He loved the stillness of the church, lit only by candles, vigil lights, and the soft afternoon sun that slanted through the thin high windows and made oblong patterns on the pews and stone floor.

Throughout the long nave there were occasional sharp, distinct sounds as a kneeler was dropped, or a door closed. Then silence. The silence was almost palpable.

He began to pray for Deborah, reading from the Old Testament. That would amuse her, he thought. From the Book of Job, he read: *Is not man's life on earth a drudgery? He is a slave who longs for the shade, a hireling who waits for his wages. So I have been assigned months of misery, and troubled nights have been told off for me.*

He looked towards the high altar, a shadowy shrine in the darkening church. The nave was empty except for another hooded monk who moved down the north aisle, pausing at each station of the cross.

Frater Matthew bowed his head again and prayed for Betty Sue, *"Strengthen the hands that are feeble, make firm the knees that are weak, say to those whose hearts are frightened: Be strong, fear not! Here is your God. He comes with vindication; with divine recompense he comes to save you."*

He finished the reading from the book of Isaiah and looked again towards the altar. The sun had dropped below the windows and the church was almost dark. He would have to leave soon for the refectory and the evening meal, but he had one last prayer to say for Father Driscoll.

When he entered the monastery, he had requested Matthew as his new name and the father abbot had granted him this special wish. He carried the name like a cross, a daily reminder of this good priest's tragic death.

He closed the book of Old Testament readings and looked up again. The other monk had crossed the nave and was starting the last stations of the cross. Stephen squinted in the dark but he could not see who it was.

Frater Matthew placed the psalm book in the pew and stood. It was late and he would need to hurry. Since coming to the monastery, he had diligently kept to the schedule and met all his obligations. Here inside the thick stone walls, following the ancient rules of the cloistered life, he knew he would survive. He had faith in himself and his ability not to give up. He trusted himself and that was a source of comfort.

He made the sign of the cross and stood, then walked up the aisle, genuflecting before the Blessed Sacrament, and turned toward the dormitory exit.

He had overcome more than most men, he reflected: The homosexuality of his adolescence, his love affair with Deborah, then Betty Sue and Rufus—the direct assault by the Devil. It had made him stronger, he realized, conquering such sins of the flesh.

The other monk was bowing before the last station of the cross, and Frater Matthew glanced at him as he went by. He had never seen the man before. He attempted to step around him, but the monk blocked his way, speaking out loud, breaking the rule of silence.

"There's no reason to rush, Frater Matthew. We don't have to be at their beck and call."

"But I think it's wise for us older priests to set an example," Stephen answered automatically, for that was what he did believe: he was more knowledgeable than the younger novices. And then he knew. Their eyes met as the other monk nodded agreement, and Stephen saw those same familiar blue eyes: eyes the color of early morning sky, so clear Stephen thought he could see through them and into the distance, could see the assault that was beginning all over again, the struggle that would follow him down all the days and nights of his life.